Blue Sailing

by

F. S. Winstanley

Volume 2
of the story of George Eefamy

July 2006

Published by
F S Winstanley
7a Blakeley Brow, Raby Mere, Wirral. CH63 0PS
Tel/Fax 0151-334 7085

Printed by Gorman, Shorrock & Davies

Again I have had very welcome help and encouragement in my attempts to bring this book out. Julia Oxley, Mr and Mrs Ralph Lake and Paul Steinson were warm and receptive of my offering. My lifelong friend Jim Taberner (to whom this volume is dedicated) offered friendly advice and support. My wife Lorna has been with me from the start and Doreen and Rob Mosedale have helped me through every stage of the transition between a kilo of foolscap handwritten pages to the form and presentation you now see – without their help I would have been in real trouble.

F S Winstanley

CHAPTERS

Foreword

This is the second book covering the life of young George Eefamy. The first book 'Number Eighteen' ended with his decision to escape from a tyrannical Victorian household. In this book George stows away on a three masted ship and sails to Denmark, the Shetland Isles, France and then to Italy and it is in the Mediterranean Sea that he first experiences blue water sailing. This was a term used by sailors to differentiate themselves from sailors who merely plied their trade in coastal waters. Blue sailing is traversing an area of sea where no land is in sight.

Mr Penaluna, George's captain, has a very Cornish name. The author's great grandmother was from Truro area, and her maiden name was Penaluna.

CHAPTER 1

Turmoil at Number Eighteen

The day after George's ordeal, very early in the morning at No 18, Rose awoke, even earlier than usual. She looked into George's room and saw that it was empty, his bed had not been slept in. On the bed was a note addressed to 'Rose'.

Dear Rose

I have decided to leave home and since you are the only friend I have in this house I am letting you know. No doubt you will have to show this to others but they do not care about me. By the time you are reading it, I will be well on my way and no one will be able to catch me.

I hope you will be very happy, and that now I am out of the way, things will settle down for you.

Love, George xxx

Rose knocked on Mrs Eefamy's door and then walked in. Rose suddenly realised the enormity of the message she carried, she burst into a flood of tears and held out the letter to Mrs Eefamy. Clarissa lit a gas mantle and read the letter. She had seen the extent and severity of George's injuries and had hardly slept all night, but she had not expected this. "Where has he gone to Rose, do you know?"

"He did say yesterday that no one would ever do this to him again and he was going to sea."

"To sea?"

"Yes M'am that's what he said."

"Why didn't you tell me yesterday?"

"Well M'am things was in such a kerfuffle yesterday I clean forgot about it, and I didn't think he was serious."

"You were quite right to wake me early Rose, I'll get up now and we'll see what can be done – wake Mrs Collins and Rooney and make some tea and toast – tell them I say to be downstairs in ten minutes."

Rose was now a new Rose, invigorated by the new power invested in her by her employer. She knocked loudly on Rooney's door, opened it and shouted, "The Mistress says she wants us all downstairs in ten minutes sharp." Rooney groaned acceptance of this instruction and took a nip of brandy to accelerate her progress. Rose then approached Mrs Collins' room – it was still only four thirty am, six hours before Mrs Collins' preferred time for rising. But Rose knew she had Mrs Eefamy's full backing. Armed with this, and her hatred for Mrs Collins, she stormed into the bedroom and heard snoring of a complexity and loudness which caused Rose to hesitate for a moment. She stopped in her tracks partly in amazement and partly to enjoy the sheer variety and virtuosity of Mrs Collins' snorings. She approached Mrs Collins' bedside – her dentures were smiling at Rose, as they enjoyed their off duty period in a glass of water. Rose shook Mrs Collins more vigorously than was really necessary and the great lady rose from her delicate slumbers and tried to look affronted and dignified, but she failed because, without her teeth, her face, was so deflated, that by comparison, the skin of a prune would be judged taut and supple. Her hair was awry and any attempt to look serious with all these disadvantages was bound to fail. She glared at Rose and said, "What time is it?"

"I don't know, but Mrs Eefamy says she wants us all downstairs in ten minutes."

"I suppose it's about that wretched boy."

"Yes it is – he's left 'ome – 'cos of you and Rooney and Mrs Eefamy knows all about it."

Rose slammed the door shut as she left, out of anger, but also to preclude any possibility of Mrs Collins dropping off to sleep again.

They all arrived in the kitchen punctually, and took up sides of the table. Mrs Eefamy and Rose on one side and the two guilty parties on the other. Mrs Eefamy began, but was immediately interrupted when Mrs Collins pointed at Rose and said, "That girl woke me rudely and without a word of apology," at that instant Clarissa broke into the tirade and said, "This is no time for anyone to assert their supposed superiority over anyone else, we are all in this together and apart from Rose we have all contributed to this dreadful situation." She handed the letter round so everyone could read it.

"Mr Tonbridge, the Schoolmaster, will need to know where he is – they are friends and he will be round here in

3

a day or two to enquire. Furthermore Mr Haggle will shortly want to know why George is no longer going to the Wednesday Bible Classes – I shall not shirk telling him exactly what I saw last evening by way of injuries, and word will quickly be spread to Mr Hemsley."

At the mention of this holy name Mrs Collins complexion changed from white to pale grey – she knew her days as a Church Elder were over.

Clarissa continued, "I believe I heard Dr Montrose say that he intended to inform the Police, so no doubt they will be making enquiries, perhaps talking to neighbours and to Mr Tonbridge too, so all in all this is a right kettle of fish, and all about nothing." She continued: "I have to go into the factory today, but I shall be home by twelve o'clock – I would like us all to think hard about what to do next, and on my way to work I will alert Tom to this problem and see what he thinks he can do to find George." This was a very different Clarissa from the timid girl of six years ago, and both her mother and Rooney knew who was making all the decisions now at No 18 Wellington Terrace.

Clarissa left for work and once there her first call was to see Tom in the stables. "Tom, I am dreadfully ashamed that anything so terrible as that could happen in my home, you were right to interrupt the beating, so please don't think for a minute that I regard your actions as uncalled for."

"Well I never seen anything like little George's back M'am."

4

"No, and neither have I, but more to the point he has taken his clothes and some food and run away."

"He won't get far M'am, not with his back and legs in that state – he'll be back by teatime."

"He says in his letter that he is going to sea."

"Well, there are a lot of ships in at Poole just now – I was round the docks yesterday, I'll go again if you like and ask around."

"Take a good horse, and if he is not at Poole go to Southampton. Here's two pounds in case you need to stay overnight anywhere, but do try your best to impress upon George that it is all our fault, we are sorry and it will not happen again."

"Right M'am, I'll take 'Carrots', and I'll tell Mr Tremblett where I am off to."

"Thank you Tom, do please try to bring him back. I'll explain to Mr Temblett where you have gone and why."

Clarissa then spent the rest of the morning doing what she did best, organising her business and working at extra pace to push a full day's work into four hours.

Back at No 18 Mrs Collins undoubted ability in the art of mendacity was about to be tested, because Dr Montrose had in fact informed the Police as to what he had seen, and as a result a young officer came to make enquiries. He was received at the front door by Rose, but Mrs Collins took over and showed him into the parlour and closed the door. The young policeman was inexperienced and he was impressed by Mrs Collins' concern.

"Yes," she explained. "George had met with an accident and since I have a sister who lives right next to the sea at Penzance, we put him on a train to convalesce in the sea-air."

"So the boy isn't actually here?"

"No. That's correct officer, he isn't here, his is with my sister, and if I may say so, in very good hands."

"Dr Montrose said he was here yesterday."

"That is correct, he was here yesterday, but we decided he was well enough to travel, and so he went down to Cornwall first class, and in great comfort – we sent a maid with him to look after his luggage."

The young policeman was taken in with what he heard. He made suitable notes and left, greatly to Mrs Collins relief. When he arrived back at the Police Station the Sergeant was 'off' for the day, so the enquiry made no further progress on that day.

Clarissa came back home from work just past twelve noon and immediately called Rooney into the kitchen and sent Rose off to do some shopping.

Rooney was on the back foot, so she started off in her usual belligerent way, but Clarissa cut her off and said, "It's no use just blaming my mother for all this. According to Rose you beat George just as much, and this was not the first time."

"Lads take no harm from a beating – it couldn't have been so bad, the first time you didn't even notice the boy was hurt."

"That is a justifiable criticism of me – I failed to notice. But Rose told me that he bled so much his shirt was stuck to him, and she had to cut if off him with scissors."

Rooney became more truculent and decided to shift the blame entirely onto Mrs Collins.

"She's in charge 'ere, everythin' she says is law, so I did as I was told, so ask Mrs Collins why she started it."

"I shall ask Mama, but I have a lot to think about and a lot to do. He is missing and I don't know where to start looking."

"Try them two maids who was 'ere before me, he wrote letters to them – they might know."

"One thing I have decided," Clarissa said, "And that is that there is no place for you here after this. So I am going to give you six weeks wages and a letter of commendation for your next employer, whoever that might be. It is not a glowing report, but it does say you are a good cook and you do your work thoroughly – it is as far as I am prepared to go."

"And what if they writes to you?"

"I shall say your behaviour towards children could be improved. So if I were you I would look for a household that does not include children. I would prefer it if you could leave today."

"I'll leave tomorrow – that's as quick as I can arrange things."

"Very well," Clarissa said. "Tomorrow will do – there is no need for you to do anything between now and your leaving – Rose will manage alone."

Clarissa then took a deep breath and walked to the parlour. She realised that as she reached for the porcelain door knob that her hand was trembling. She stiffened herself up, took another deep breath and went in. Mrs Collins received her graciously as though the topic of conversation was going to be some happy event. She sought to disarm Clarissa and simply ignore yesterday's events and also brush aside the fact that George and most of his clothes were gone.

"Boys do make rash erratic decisions but he will be back as soon as he is hungry," Mrs Collins stated.

"I don't agree Mama – I don't agree at all, he was severely beaten some months ago, I have had a detailed description of his injuries from Rose."

"No doubt greatly exaggerated," Mrs Collins interjected.

"What I saw could not be exaggerated, indeed it defied description of any sort, and if I had been George I too would have left."

"Where does this discussion get us?" Mrs Collins asked. "He is gone now, you think he will not be back so now we settle down and carry on with our lives as people usually do."

"As if nothing had happened?" said Clarissa, amazed at her mother's calmness.

"Well what has happened? – a boy was disobedient – not for the first time and he got what he deserved – there's an end of it."

"Then I must refresh your memory, Mama! Mr Tonbridge will be here in a day or two to see if George is ill. Dr Montrose says he will be going to report the matter to the Police. Dr Montrose stables his horse with us and will have plenty of opportunities to discuss George's injuries with Tom. Mr Haggle will be here to enquire about George's absence from Bible Class. Oh! Yes I nearly forgot: Dr Montrose and his wife are friendly with Mr and Mrs Hemsley. I imagine last night's events being discussed when next they meet. Dr Montrose said that in all his years as a doctor he had never seen the like of it."

Mrs Collins sought comfort by cuddling her arms around herself and gathering her cashmere shawl about her shoulders, and pretending that none of this was her concern.

She was not prepared for Clarissa's next suggestions, "I think you should leave Poole Mama."

"LEAVE – leave – I'll do no such thing – I live here and this is where I'll stay. The deeds to No 18 are in my Deed Box at the Bank – I arranged that with Mr Copeman."

"And now, all but £100 of your £1500 is repaid, I can arrange that tomorrow and then the Deeds which are now in my name and have never been in yours', can be transferred back to my Deed Box." Clarissa waited for this to sink in.

"Even so – why should I leave – you are my daughter, where else should a widowed lady live but with her daughter?"

"The daughter has a voice in this matter as well, and this is my house, and I would prefer not to share it with someone capable of inflicting punishment to the degree I saw yesterday."

"Punishment, pain, you don't know the meaning of the word, the pain I suffered losing my dear husband, the worry I had rescuing your faltering company when it was on the brink of bankruptcy, and now the pain of hearing my own dear daughter turning me out of house and home – oh! It is too much."

Try as she would Mrs Collins could not weep. She had never wept, her tear ducts had forgotten how to. She rocked to and fro desperately trying to go through a physical response natural enough to warm hearted people, but quite impossible for her. Clarissa was not convinced, and saw her mother as she was – the complete solipsist.

"We'll talk about it again tomorrow, I have letters to write now which must be posted today, but I am serious, I do not see this now as a permanent home for you. Your main interest will not be open to you."

"And what is that pray?" Mrs Collins interrupted.

"The Church of course, as soon as Mr Hemsley hears."

"Damn Mr Hemsley and the Church – I can manage without them." Mrs Collins gritted her teeth.

"So the Church is not your main interest then?"

"I just enjoyed having them all dancing on strings – spineless creatures."

"Then what is your main interest then Mama?"

"Me, of course, just like your main interest is you, isn't it the same with everybody?"

This was Mrs Collins as she really was. Clarissa didn't like what she saw and drew back as Mrs Collins tried to embrace her, as one would recoil from a boa constrictor. This was Mrs Collins first and last attempt to embrace her daughter. She moved to the door, then stopped, and said, "Within a week I'll be gone and as for what happens to you or George I don't care that," and she snapped her fingers. "I never wanted a child – I had one, and what made it even worse – I had to have you." She went into the kitchen and said to Rooney, "Go to my room and we'll discuss what to do next – we are not staying here."

Clarissa sat down at the little desk. She had two letters to write, but she was trembling all over, and she knew it would be some time before she could put pen to paper. She pulled the little tassel which summoned Rose from the kitchen. Rose came into the parlour and was most solicitous as to Mrs Eefamy's welfare, she could see that Clarissa was trembling.

"Oh! Ma'am you have had a terrible time of it, can I make you a drink?"

"Yes Rose – something to steady me up a little bit."

"I knows just the thing Ma'am, just give me five minutes and I'll be back."

Rose went off into the kitchen. Rooney had vacated it and gone upstairs with Mrs Collins to discuss their future. She made a strong mug of tea, put two teaspoons of sugar in it and a good slug of whisky. She put this on a tray with a good sized piece of chocolate cake and took it in to Mrs Eefamy.

"Oh! This is nice Rose, what is it?"

"Tea with a drop of whisky in Ma'am."

"Whisky? Is it really? I had no idea it tasted so good. And the cake, will that do me good as well?"

"I'm sure you will feel better very soon Ma'am."

"Rose, I want you to stay on here, but I am going to write to my two step-daughters who are in Switzerland, and I am going to ask them to return home. Then I am going to write to Polly and Marie – who used to be here – and I am going to ask them to come back here as well. Now that is why I started off this little speech by saying I do want you to stay. They will not be pushing you out – far from it, you will all work together."

"I did hear from Master George that Polly and Marie were very nice, so I am sure I can work with anybody who is nice to me." In fact Rose was a bit unsure, but after working with Rooney anything would be an improvement.

Rose then plucked up courage to ask "And Rooney – what's to 'appen with her?"

"She will be gone this week and probably Mrs Collins as well."

Rose didn't know what to say – her two main adversaries in life were leaving. Her face said it all. She mumbled something incoherently. Clarissa looked on in amusement – the poor girl was so relieved, happy, rescued, she was speechless. Rose curtseyed, and left the room. She was going to have some tea with whisky in as well and big piece of chocolate cake. This was a great day at No 18.

Clarissa was feeling much steadier now, after the fortified tea, and the chocolate cake and she began her two letters. One to Anne and Caroline in Switzerland, in which she was going to be quite straight about the whole affair: she knew that she had paid too much attention to her business, but had she not done so the firm could have gone under. She knew that in future she had to try to strike a more even balance in her life. She was not going to offer excuses, she was going to promise to do better and to make No 18 a happy home, and to suggest that it would be an altogether happier home if the two girls came back to it. She would also tell the girls that she had written to Polly and Marie care of the Embassy Hotel (of happy memories) to ask them to come back and work for her. Having thought all this through, Clarissa decided that the easier of the two letters would be the one to Polly and Marie. She told them quite frankly all about George and Mrs Collins and Rooney and how things would be very different from now on. She also mentioned that Tom was trying to locate George and persuade him to come back home. After an hour or so both letters were done and ready for posting. Clarissa felt as if a new and better period of her life was just ahead and if only George would come back.

Caroline and Anne received the letter with the news about George six days after it had left England. They were very concerned about George and at the same time excited by the possibility of leaving Switzerland and returning home.

Over the previous twelve months they had become very friendly with a girl from Cornwall named Thurza Paxton, she had suddenly arrived at the St Marie Finishing Academy, and had had a great influence on all the girls, and at the same time she had given the teaching staff considerable cause for concern: Thurza was way ahead of all the other girls as regards 'growing up'. She was no older; she was eighteen, but she was decidedly mature. Her figure was worrying to the teachers and in particular to the Head Teacher because her contours were so pronounced, indeed untrammelled. This combined with her ungovernable cluster of ginger/golden hair made her the cynosure for all eyes wherever she went, and Thurza knew it. She did her work at school and gained good marks, but she steadfastly refused to take part in any games apart from croquet, and often said to the young tennis coach who came to the Academy, that nature never intended her to run about after a ball. She would accompany this statement with a meaningful look and more than a hint of a naughty smile which the young man found irresistible, but at the same time, daunting, because he was employed by the Academy and had to show results.

Anne and Caroline showed Thurza the letter and they read it together. To the two Eefamy girls it meant returning home, to Thurza it meant she had to think quickly what to do next. Her father was a doctor in Penzance, Cornwall, and should have been in a comfortable position financially because he was a good doctor with a thriving practice, but he lived beyond his income, and always had. Five years previously he had absconded from Oban on the west coast of Scotland in a great hurry, leaving mountainous debts but no forwarding address. He had taken what he, his wife and his, then, thirteen year old daughter could carry, and gone by train as far as he could go. Oban to Cornwall is a long way and he was hoping that the six hundred miles would be sufficient to protect him from his creditors, who were considerable in number, and incandescent with rage once they learned that the good doctor had run out on them. Dr Paxton set up his practice in Penzance and quietly went about his work. He did not join any medical organisations and was not affiliated to any professional bodies – people can be traced via such connections: but he and his wife did join the social set and he kept two good hunters for regular meetings of the hunt, and he attended the resultant Balls, and social functions, suitably, indeed stylishly attired. Mrs Paxton too liked nice clothes, and hunting outfits, boots are all very expensive. Admittedly less expensive, if one does not pay for them.

Dr Paxton's reputation as a doctor grew rapidly. His reputation as a bad payer took a little longer to take hold. He had learnt from his experience in Oban who to pay and who to keep waiting, and he carefully rationed out his money so that tongues would not wag too freely, but after his first three years, things were beginning to catch up with him. So he asked his Bank for a £300 loan, as security he showed the Bank Manager his books, which were immaculately kept, and skilfully combined two unlikely qualities, mendacity and apparent authenticity. The Bank Manger was convinced and granted the loan.

Most of Dr Paxton's creditors received payment in full during the next week. The envelope also contained a beautifully worded letter hinting that a bequest, long awaited, had now been released by Chancery and that the doctor's financial troubles were over. More purchases were made and promptly paid for, trust was built up again. The trouble was that the trust and the debit grew at an equal pace. As the debt grew further, the trust diminished and within six months, Dr Paxton and his wife were in deep trouble. The Academy in Switzerland had written three times for unpaid fees. Suppliers of medicaments were beginning to hold back their wares. The local farrier was owed over £20. The owner of the livery stables, where Dr Paxton's two handsome hunters were kept, was owed over £50. The local shops were asking for ready money, and were beginning to exchange confidences about the precise state of Dr Paxton's account.

He did his rounds very assiduously, and no one could fault him so far as his work was concerned. One fine summer's day he was due to make several calls in a particularly attractive part of Cornwall and Mrs Paxton decided to travel with him, in his barouche, so that she could enjoy the fresh air and the views. They were on a very minor road near to St Hilary when a very heavy brewer's dray drew out in front of them. One of the full barrels of beer weighing two or three hundred weight crashed into the barouche, killing Dr and Mrs Paxton. The bemused and no doubt partially intoxicated drayman (a surfeit of liquor was always an industrial hazard for draymen) went back into the Public House to get help, but the two occupants of the wrecked barouche was beyond any help save that of an undertaker. Dr Paxton's affairs were looked into by a local Solicitor who took no more than four of five days to ascertain that the deceased doctor left little apart from a pile of correspondence, nearly all of which began with the word "unless". Mr Wellard – the Solicitor separated out one unpaid bill from the Academy in Switzerland and realised that Dr and Mrs Paxton's daughter was in for a severe shock. He continued with the work whenever he could, sometimes to the detriment of cases from which he could earn a proper fee. He sold the horses and the barouche. He arranged an auction of the doctor's medical equipment and the furniture and clothes. All this work and the desire to help had been engendered by his discovery of the correspondence from the Swiss Academy and the resultant assumption that the orphaned girl was in a terrible plight. He therefore saw it as his clear duty to raise enough money to pay for the girl's return to her native land, and he made this his first priority so far as allocating Dr Paxton's money was concerned. Despite excellent training in how to run a legal office, he flew in the face of years of tradition among Solicitors: he decided top put his fees second in priority, behind his scheme to finance Thurza's return.

Mr Wellard thought hard about the letter to the St Marie Finishing Academy, finally deciding to write to the Principal, to ask if the news could be broken to Thurza and at the same time hoping that the Academy would relinquish any hopes they had of collecting the arrears. He received a letter by return of post to say that the dreadful news had indeed been vouchsafed to Madamoiselle Paxton and that the Academy still cherished hopes that the fees would be paid as soon as the late Dr Paxton's no doubt considerable fortune was satisfactorily assessed.

The letter from Clarissa asking the two girls to return and the news about Dr Paxton arrived on the same day. Thurza reckoned up quickly what her best moves would be and she decided to hint about the desperate financial situation, now made much worse by the deaths of her parents and with the full, warm and tender cooperation of Caroline and Anne her future was assured: the two girls wrote to their Mama, Mrs Eefamy, and asked for enough money to be sent to buy three railway tickets. This was done and within two weeks the three girls were on their way to Number 18 Wellington Terrace.

Thurza wrote to Mr Wellard to thank him for all his help and to ask for any pieces of personal jewellery, trinkets and money to be sent to her at her new address.

Grief? Well yes there were token signs of a sadness, but Thurza was aware of her parents' failures, and she knew that she had been bundled off to Switzerland so that they could pursue the life of socialites. She had witnessed the shameful but shameless flight from Oban, and she knew that their selfishness would in the end consume them. In this case bad luck merely brought their financial predicament into focus three months earlier, but they were in dreadful trouble, with no way out. They were not likely to change and to suddenly become prudent in their handling of money. Thurza shivered when she thought about another headlong escape to Yorkshire or North Wales to begin another slippery slope. For Thurza it was an escape – had she returned to Penzance, with her parents still carrying on in their old ways, she too would have been dragged into their perpetual struggle to live beyond their income.

CHAPTER 2

The Great Escape

The person who was causing all this trouble, worry and change to so many peoples' lives knew nothing of what was transpiring at No 18. He had found it quite impossible to sleep on the night of the beating so he stayed in his room and sorted out his clothes. He didn't really know what would be needed but wisely decided that clothes which were warm or waterproof would be best. He had a good selection of cosy socks and two pairs of good boots. All this work took a long time and was done with great difficulty. George was in a lot of pain, and some of the cuts had opened up again and were bleeding, but he struggled on and got his bag packed. It was now about two o'clock in the morning, he went downstairs, on his bottom, walking down was just too painful. He left his bag in the hall, and went to see what was in the kitchen. He helped himself to a large pork pie, a big piece of cheese and four apples, he put them into a shopping bag and then stopped and thought. Had he any money? Yes, that was alright he had three pounds and fourteen shillings. He knew where the housekeeping box was and briefly picked it up and thought "No, I don't want THEIR money." "Keys? How do I get out?" He hunted around and found the back door key. He brought his bag from the hall into the kitchen, tapped his pocket to make sure he knew where his money was, then he went into the pot cupboard and took out a half pint mug with roses on it – his father often had his early morning drink using that mug. He popped it into his bag among his clothes, opened the back door and he was out – the fresh air hit him and he realised as he clicked the door shut that this was the start of his new life.

He thought at first that he would go to Poole Station and catch what was known as the Milk Train. It carried milk, fresh vegetables and meat to Bournemouth, Southampton and other big towns in the area. Then he thought he would be easily traced by using that method, the man in the ticket office would remember a boy of thirteen buying a one way ticket at half past three in the morning. So he set off to walk it to Southampton. He walked due north to Wimborne Minster, which is about two miles. By the time he reached the little village, the sun was up and to his great relief it was fine. But already he was very tired, the combination of the heavy parcels, lack of sleep, the beating he had taken and the far from receding pain were making progress very difficult. Suddenly George heard the friendly clip clop of approaching hooves, and soon a small cart drew alongside him

"Where are you off to this fine morning?" the driver of the cart called.

"Southampton, Sir" George replied.

"That's a fair stretch from here, but I can take you to Ringwood, that's about ten miles along the road and in the right direction." ⌐

"It would be great help Sir, I am finding it very hard work."

"You runnin' away from something or somebody?" enquired the driver.

"Yes I must be honest Sir, I am running away – they beat me so I can hardly stand."

"Just a minute let me help you." The driver said. He stepped down from his cart and took George's bag and parcels and laid them carefully on top of his load of cabbages, rhubarb, eggs and crates of chickens and geese. They all raised their own objections to this further humiliation, then the driver tried to help George to climb on to the cart.

"No please don't touch me, my back is so painful," and as George tried one or two different methods of gaining access to the seat on the cart, the driver noticed blood dripping on to the road.

"You're not well enough to travel nowhere, let alone Southampton, you need a doctor and I'll find you one in Ringwood." George didn't object, he made himself as comfortable as he could on the sacks which the driver had spread over the seat and they moved off. Fortunately it was a smooth, well made road so there wasn't too much jolting and George fell asleep. The next thing he heard was his friend the driver saying, "Here we are, this is Ringwood – I'll ask the doctor if he'll come and have a look at you." The man went off down a narrow street,

George thought quickly and his ideas went as follows: if the doctor thinks my injuries are serious he will insist upon my having attention, possibly resting up in an Infirmary, someone will find me, and I'll be taken back – perhaps to another beating. This was the spur George needed, he slid himself off the cart, gathered his parcels together, gave the horse one of his four apples and walked off towards Lyndhurst. The driver had difficulty in rousing the doctor, it was still only about half past six in the morning. By the time he returned to his cart George was gone, and he had to go back to the doctor to apologise. The doctor was not pleased and muttered something about drunken carters. The carter was not drunk, nor was he mistaken, the blood stained sacks bore witness to that.

Ringwood to Lyndhurst is about nine miles, two to two and a half hours walk if you are well, and George did feel better, he had had an hour's sleep on the cart, and he munched an apple and a bit of cheese as he walked along, but after two miles he knew he had had enough. He found a disused farm at Picket Post and went to investigate. The main buildings were in appalling condition but there was a lean-to shed full of dry straw and there was an old tarpaulin sheet. He laid this on top of the straw, gathered all his worldly goods about him and fell asleep. He slept until mid-day, he reckoned it must have been about four hours. He very creakily raised himself up and was confronted with the most hairy face he had ever seen in his life.

Hidden behind all that hirsute vegetation was a face, and it was laughing at him.

"That's my straw and my bed you're sleepin' in."

"I am sorry Sir, I didn't realise."

"That's alright – I've been out and about all night, so now I've come back I can cook some breakfast." He began to unload his capacious pockets – out came a rabbit, a pheasant and about eight eggs.

"Farmer won't miss 'em – he's got two hundred chickens, so eight eggs is nothin'."

The man went inside the shed and came out with a big pile of kindling and some paper, he had an old fashioned tinder box and soon the fire was going nicely. He rigged up a trestle and impaled the rabbit on it by passing a metal rod through its mouth and out the other end.

"Roast rabbit" he announced. "It will be served in thirty minutes," he continued. "Have you anything nice to drink in your various parcels?"

"No I'm afraid I haven't. I have three nice apples, they are very juicy, you are welcome to one of those."

"Yes that would be nice, I like a juicy apple, and while we are waiting for the rabbit to cook you can tell me your plans – I take it that you have run away from home."

George warmed to the tramp, he seemed to George to be a fellow misfit, so he decided to confide in him, and he told him that he was an orphan, unwanted and twice he had been cruelly beaten.

"Recently is that? when you were beaten?"

"Yes it was yesterday – and I am sorry to say I have made blood stains on your bed."

"Don't worry about that – I'm not fussy. So where are you hoping to go to now?"

"Southampton – where I hope to get a job on a ship, and be as far away from Poole as I can be."

"So now," the tramp said – "the problem is how do we get you to Southampton?"

"Correct" said George. "That is my problem."

"Problems are there to be solved and I think we can solve it because there is a little local train that carries goods, via Sway to Brockinhurst and then up to Southampton. It has to stop near Kingston Great Common to let another train pass, because this is a single track railway, they put it into a siding for ten minutes, that's where we make a move. Once we are on, it's free riding all the way to Southampton."

"I don't wish to be rude, Sir, but how do you know all this, in such detail."

He touched the side of his nose with his very dirty forefinger and said, " I am a travellin' man who does not like to pay when he travels. Now let's look how this rabbit is doin', he certainly smells beautiful."

George thought it was great fun having a delicious picnic, on such a warm sunny day, the rabbit really was very good. He sucked his fingers clean, his friend the tramp did the same though George trembled for him because he had never seen such dirty hands. Sucking made little impression on the colour of the tramp's fingers, possibly it removed some of the grease. The possessor of these disgraceful digits surveyed them once he had finished sucking them and he seemed to be quite happy with their condition.

The tramp suddenly said, "What do they call you?"

"George," came the reply.

"Just George? nothin' else?"

"George Eefamy."

"Never heard o' that name before."

"It goes right back, it is an old English name from hundred of years ago/"

"Well my name is George as well, so to avoid any confusion you can call me Driffield."

"Mr Driffield surely," George asserted

"No, just Driffield I don't think anybody 'as ever called me Mister – they just say, Hey – You! So Driffield will do nicely."

"I might find that difficult," George said.

"Suit yourself – now should we tidy up here? Make sure the fire is really out – I usually pee on it, smells terrible but it just makes it safe."

They gathered their meagre possessions together, Driffield picked up George's bag as well as his own and wouldn't have it any other way. They walked to Kingston Great Common, "no need to hurry" George was informed – "train ain't due for another hour."

When they arrived at the spot carefully chosen by Driffield, they were concealed behind a hawthorn hedge within yards of the first track.

"You see that part there, where there is two lines of rails, that's called a siding. The train we want will be along soon and he will go in there to allow the other train to pass".

George looked at Driffield and wondered how such a courteous, intelligent man could be reduced to being a pennyless tramp. Driffield continued, "I'll go to the guard and start talkin' to him, you find a wagon that's got a step to it, look along and you'll find one, and you just step up on to it and find something to hang on to. In a few minutes we'll be off and in an hour or so we will be in Southampton.

"Do you need to go to Southampton or are you doing this to help me?" George asked.

"Bit of both really, I have a bit of business in that direction, so the journey is of use to me – here he comes, did you hear the points? They've changed the rails so he'll go into the siding. Watch the wagons as they go by and pick one with a step and I'll join you as it sets off."

George stayed hidden while his companion went in search of the guard, who was talking to the engine driver and fireman. As soon as George heard that the conversation was underway he started to walk round the last wagon to look for a suitable perch. He found one and climbed up with great difficulty and found he was between two wagons, so if they went through a narrow tunnel he would not be knocked off. Luckily there was a suitable iron fixture to hang on to so all was well, but gaining the position had cost him dear in terms of pain and blood was dripping on to his foothold.

The train they were standing aside for was a little passenger train and he puffed by importantly, the driver gave a little whistle as if to thank the waiting driver for his courtesy. Then George heard the points clang back into position to give his train access to the mainline and they were off. Driffield timed his ascent on to George's step perfectly just using one hand and firmly gripping George's precious possessions with the other.

"Driver says we will be there in forty minutes and he is going right into the docks."

"Does that suit you as well?" asked George, ever courteous.

"My affairs takes me everywhere, and I allus travels cheaply, so it's all the same to me."

Driffield noticed that George was gradually losing his colour – "Are you all right mate?" he said.

"Not really, but I'll hang on."

"Here, just a minute I'll move next to you," Driffield said, and he put one foot each side of the step and firmly hanging on to George's iron fixture he pressed George against the wagon. George felt nothing – he had fainted. Driffield held him like that for five minutes or so until George came round – he was deathly pale.

"Did I fall asleep?"

"Just for a minute – it'll do you good, and with all this fresh air, you'll feel better, hang on to my jacket, and I'll make sure you don't fall."

George was aware, in such close proximity, that Driffield rarely if ever took a bath, but the warmth of the smell and the humanity of the man revived George and gradually his colour returned.

"Phew, you had me worried – I thought you was a gonner for a minute."

"I'll be alright – thanks to you" George said and he moved a little closer to the life saving miasma.

"Now when we gets into the Docks area, we'll be noticed – bound to be – so I'll head right for the Docks Police and you go in the opposite direction, I'll keep them talkin' while you get away."

"That hardly seems fair, we both travelled free and illegally."

"True enough, but I ain't drippin' blood all over my boots. If the Police see that they'll blame me, and you'll end up in hospital and being carted off home again."

"You do think of everything Mr Driffield," George admitted.

"Course I does, I've got a degree in thinkin'" and he winked a knowing wink at his admirer.

"That's your best way – see all the four masters over there? You go that way, and I'll go and talk to the Law.

"You will be alright won't you – they won't arrest you?"

"No, course not – they didn't see us get off the train and trespassing is not actually an offence unless they can prove damage – which they can't. So off you go young George, and good luck to you."

The ever polite George then amazed his helper by kissing him and saying "Thank you Mr Driffield, you are a gentleman." Driffield make a self deprecating gurgle and they parted.

George could see the towering masts of the tall ships, so he gathered up his possessions, he still had some cheese and most of his pork pie and he began his walk to the dockside. It was a lot farther than he had guessed and he was very tired when he finally arrived next to the ships. Choosing was difficult because he realised that his best chance of getting a real sea journey was to start as a stowaway, after all no one wants a thirteen year old boy who can't work or do anything useful for at least the next two weeks. And George was painfully aware that this was the case so far as he was concerned.

CHAPTER 3

George meets Mr Penaluna

Many of the ships were surrounded by workmen, loading, repairing or hanging over the sides painting, but then he noticed one small ship, The "Bulldog", with no one on it or near it. He walked up the gang plank, and he was on – quite unnoticed. He couldn't believe his luck. He saw a door which was open and it led downstairs. George went down on his bottom and saw another door – it opened outwards and inside were rolls of spare sails and piles of off cuts of damaged sails put at one side for patching. George closed the door of his dark den and sat on the pile of off cuts. He opened his parcel, broke off a piece of his pork pie, ate it and was fast asleep in seconds.

The ship was in fact ready for sailing, she was a privately owned barque of three hundred tons. She was about fifty years old but carefully maintained by her skipper/owner. Captain Penaluna, a Cornish man of great experience, who made his living by tramping around the European ports, especially in the Baltic. He knew the waters well and he had many contacts. Because of the Morse code and his mastery of it, he could send and receive signals and so he made his way to Copenhagen, Oslo, Stockholm, Tallin, and Riga. If he were paid enough he would go into Hamburg, but it was a fifty mile tow in and another fifty out, and Hamburg tugs were expensive, so if he could avoid Hamburg, he did so, unless someone made it worth his while. He was a self everything! Self made man and self taught sailor and navigator. He was small, neat, fifty years old, a bachelor and very dress conscious. He missed nothing, as he walked back to his beloved ship and up the gang plank he noticed spots of blood, although he wrongly deduced that it was paint. Fortunately for George there was not a trail of spots leading to the door he had used, but Captain Penaluna intended to ask about the spots, as soon as his crew was assembled.

They were saying goodbye to their wives, children, sweethearts and would be along shortly. They knew the tides and they knew that a tug was booked for four thirty. The skipper would need everyone on board by three o'clock, and no one kept this Skipper waiting. The mate, Mr Baguly, came on next and the Skipper pointed out the spots, no, Mr Baguly had no explanation. The crew filed on board, leaving distraught females ashore, some with children clinging to their skirts. The Skipper and the Mate checked the hatches, though they knew the ship's carpenter, Harris, was as reliable a man as one could find. Yes the hatches were fine. A lookout man shouted that the tug was alongside – the mate shouted, "Throw him a rope and cast off." The rope was made fast on the tug. The wailing from the dockside grew louder, and there was some sniffling on board the ship – they could be away six months.

The tug moved away from the "Bulldog" very slowly, taking up the slack, the timing had to be precise and it was supervised by the Skipper with the minimum of shouting. His crew had done it many times before and they knew better than to risk a 'snatch' i.e. when the tow rope tightens they must be cast off, fore and aft, and the tug must begin to tow its three hundred ton burden gently. The helmsman shouted immediately to the Skipper that he 'had her', by which he meant she had enough way to steer properly, and so the stately vessel followed the tiny smoky tug out of Southampton harbour. The "Bulldog" was bound for Oslo, a distance of approximately eleven hundred miles. If they had favourable winds they would dock in seven or eight days.

Once they had the Isle of Wight to starboard and Portsmouth on the portside, they signalled to the tug to cast off their rope. Then the little tug did a full circle and came alongside the "Bulldog". Mr Penaluna threw a purse with twenty sovereigns in it to the skipper of the tug who deftly caught it. Next he threw a pound of good tobacco. The job was well done, so he paid up, but he never paid anyone in advance. The Mate, Mr Baguly, looked across to the Skipper who nodded. "Set to'gallants and foresail." came the cry. The able seamen knew this routine and were already standing by, the sails cracked open, the masts took the strain, the ropes tightened and hummed and three hundred tons of ship with two hundred tons of cargo was being swept forward by the mighty but invisible wind. She heeled over and picked up speed as if she welcomed the open sea. Her crew certainly did, they loved the freedom, and the work and the fresh air, and the challenge. They had done this trip many times but every sea journey was different and they moved about their various duties with a will. It was four hours on, and four hours off for the next six months, apart from when they were tied up in port.

Mr Penaluna and his Mate Mr Baguly surveyed the scene for the next half hour, they liked to be sure that the right amount of canvas was out, not too much not too little. They called to the helmsman to make sure it was right so far as he was concerned, he knew the course he had to steer, and the angle of the sails was vital to him, so that he could steer exactly as directed and not have to fight pressure from the sails trying to bring him off a point or two.

"The stay sail would help, Sir, if you agree"

Again the hands were ready, and at the nod from Mr Baguly the stay sail was set and filled out beautifully.

"How's that for 'ee?" the Skipper shouted. The helmsman, Humpage, waved and shouted "That's got 'er – now she's really goin."

Once clear of the Isle of Wight Mr Penaluna went to his cabin to check his charts. Baguly stayed on deck – he loved the open air and had a wonderful pair of sea legs, it was as if he had giant suckers underneath his boots, he was so firm and steady. Suddenly a crack went off like a rifle "Wassat" someone shouted, "to'allant's gone – down the middle." "Get up there and fetch it down afore the Skipper sees it." Mr Penaluna was stood behind him.

"I heard it too – that's an old sail, don't ask 'Sails' to repair it – tell him to use it for patching."

Four men went down to the sail locker to bring up the replacement. They opened the door and saw George.

"I think he's dead" one man said.

"Bring the Skipper quick" another said.

Mr Penaluna came down quickly with Mr Baguly. "A stowaway eh?" the Skipper said, but he was moved by what he saw. George was a beautiful child with olive skin, dark brown hair, eyelashes any actress would have paid a fortune for. They all just stared at the peace and serenity of George slumbering quietly. Then Mr Penaluna saw the blood on the spare sails and he put two and two together.

"So this is where those spots came from, it wasn't paint, it was this boy's blood – he must be injured – look at the blood there on the sails – it's still wet."

"We'll have to wake him," Mr Baguly said. "We can't treat him down here."

He shook George gently, and as he awakened he saw all the faces looking down at him – kindly faces, peering at him, but no malice, no stern looks.

"I hope you don't mind Sir, I have run away from home and I don't want to go back – they beat me, so I thought perhaps I could be useful to you in some way – are we at sea – have we left Southampton?"

"Yes we are well out to sea, and now we must have you out of there, and we'll see if we can tidy you up" the Skipper said.

"Do you mind if I try to get out my own way Sir, I am in a lot of pain, and I might be better doing it myself."

Mr Penaluna, a fastidious and mannerly individual, took to George instantly – he loved old fashioned courtesy and this boy had plenty of it, even in adversity. George came out backwards, one or two members of the crew noticed the handsome remains of the pork pie. Slowly George came to the perpendicular and he ascended the steps very slowly, most of the crew were at the top watching the stowaway come out into the daylight.

The Skipper said, "Is the T'Gallant replaced?" The men sidled off to put the new sail up.

"We'll go into my cabin, tell the Steward to bring some warm water and some clean clothes."

Once into the cabin they tried to undress George but his clothes were glued on to him with dried blood.

"Bring Sails here and tell him to bring a sharp knife."

The Steward arrived with warm water, the knife arrived and Mr Penaluna inch by inch cut George out of his caked clothes, until he stood there naked. Everyone present was aghast.

"Who did this?" Mr Penaluna asked.

"An aunt and the housekeeper."

"Why?"

"Because I kept a kitten."

The men all looked at each other – it was beyond belief.

"We are going to sponge you down, can you stand it – do you think?"

"I'll try Sir."

Mr Baguly gently squeezed his cloth, so as to allow warm water to trickle down George's back. Removal of some of the blood revealed just how many cuts, lesions and bruises there were. He was discoloured from his shoulder down to his knees, he was yellow, purple, black and blue, and these colours were interspersed with pink and red.

"I've never seen anything like it" Mr Penaluna said.

"They should be strung up," added Mr Baguly.

"Is it really bad Sir? I can't see it."

"Pretty bad son – pretty bad, but it'll heal, if we look after you properly you'll be alright."

"I am sorry to be such a trouble to you Sir, but once I'm really well, I will work and do anything I can to help."

"I'm sure you will, but for now, just let me try to put a clean shirt on you and you can have a nap."

Mr Baguly offered to put George in a spare bunk in his cabin. George was slowly led there and he lay face down on the soft feather mattress and slept for over twenty four hours. He woke on the evening of his second day at sea, the 'Bulldog' was clear of the English Channel and was heading north-east with Holland twenty miles to starboard, it was a beautiful June day and some of the crew were on deck making music and singing. George's first thought was how lucky he was, until he tried to move, and he was forcibly reminded of exactly why he was there, and why he was lying on his bunk face down. Just as he was trying to straighten himself out and make an effort to get up, Mr Baguly, the ship's Mate came into his cabin.

"Hello there George, you've had a good sleep, feelin' better?"

"Yes Sir, I think I am, I'll get up and have a walk on deck – I liked the singing."

"Evenings is nice when you're out at sea in June and the weather's good, it makes the crew want to sing."

"I'll get up now and go on deck – if I may Sir, and do you think I could have something to eat – anything would do – I did bring a big pork pie on board, perhaps some of that."

Mr Baguly looked a little sheepish and admitted, "The pork pie is no more, we thought it might go off, pork does you know, and on a hot day like today, well we didn't want it to go to waste."

George smiled an understanding smile and said "Anything would be welcome Sir, and I hope you enjoyed the pie."

Mr Baguly swiftly changed the subject and suggested some duff.

"I have never heard of duff Sir, what is it?"

"It's a cross between bread and pudding, every ship's cook has his own ideas about how to make it. Our cook usually puts in some sliced apple or currants and raisins. Today's was like that, I'll see if there's some left."

"I'll go up on deck Sir, and have some fresh air."

"Right, I'll see you up there and you can try your first duff."

As Baguly went on deck to find Cook, the Skipper stopped him to ask him to get their speed checked. Mr

Penaluna prided himself on his dead reckoning, so regular, accurate information about the ship's speed was essential.

The Mate called to one of the able-seamen to check the speed, and then turned to the Skipper to tell him about George, just at that moment a ghostly George appeared on deck. No one said anything, they let him walk to the ship's side and lean there. George felt the evening sun on his back, and the lovely fresh air in his lungs. He was on the portside, it was warm, and he could feel the ship racing through the North sea.

"Eleven knots," Grisholme, the able-seaman called. "Eleven knots it is."

The Skipper acknowledged receipt of this information. The Mate said to the Skipper, "I'll ask Cook to bring the kid some duff Sir, and some small beer," and off he went to find Cook. Mr Penaluna went to stand near George, and asked him how he felt.

"Hungry but happy Sir – thank you."

"Cook'll be up in a minute with something for you, take your time over it, then we'll have a look at your back."

Cook arrived with the duff and a pot of milk, he decided that George was a bit young for beer, and since they were only just out of port, fresh milk was still available. The piece of duff was about six inches cubed and very solid looking. George broke off a chunk and tried it. The Cook looked on awaiting George's response, his mouth was dry so the duff was slow to go down, but a good swig of milk lubricated the mouthful and down it went. Heavy, glutinous, and cold, but very welcome for all that. As the lump hit George's stomach, he nodded and smiled at Cook.

"First food in a long time Sir – very welcome – thank you."

Cook was happy – he loved to please and never doubted the sincerity of the accolades that came his way, even though many of the crew's comments were loaded with sarcasm.

George finished his duff and his milk, and began to enjoy his first experience of being out at sea, completely surrounded by sea, no land in sight. Above him towered the three masts, all over one hundred feet high, the ropes were taut and humming with the tension exerted by the wind, and the 'Bulldog' leaned over slightly, away from the wind. Round and plump she certainly was but she went through the water like a knife. Two of the crew were perched right at the top, one on each mast, casually leaning back, and taking the air. Sometimes they shouted if they saw smoke or another sail in the distance. All sailors like to know who is around so they can take avoiding action if necessary. George heard the shouts, and tried to see where the smoke or the sail was, but he couldn't. Without him knowing it, this was his first lesson in nautical mathematics: the horizon one hundred feet up, and the horizon from the decks are very very different. George gulped in the fresh air and enjoyed the warmth of the summer sun. But most of all he enjoyed feeling safe. He knew he was amongst men he could trust. It was awkward for him when he moved, he had been standing still for half an hour or so, and moving set all his aches and pains off again. He grinned at two or three sailors who watched his slow but gallant progress back to his bunk. He instinctively felt that they were sympathetic and one certain way to a cure is to feel that someone cares. He made his way slowly to Mr Baguly's cabin, where his bunk was, and he carefully climbed into it. He lay on his face and listened to the noises which were going to be part of his life from now on: sailors singing and dancing, distant voices from aloft crying "sail, away on the port bow." The crash of water as it seemingly climbed over the gunnel and gurgled its way off via the scuppers, the music in differing keys of the ropes and riggings, and the groaning of the masts and the yardarms as they took the strain which would carry five hundred tons forward at a speed of eleven knots. Mr Penaluna or Mr Baguly occasionally added their voices to the mighty fugue by ordering slight adjustment to the sails, but on an evening as warm and balmy as this, the two experts just stood on the poop, their hands clasped behind them, feet firmly on the deck, looking aloft at the sails, checking neatness of the rigging, but finding no fault, they enjoyed the fact that, at the moment, they were masters of the sea, and the reverse was not the case. Humpage was at the wheel and he loved being in charge of this mighty but delicately responsive ship. He prided himself on keeping her just at the right angle to the wind to gain maximum speed, and at the same time keeping to the correct compass reading. He resented having to sleep or to go off duty, he just loved the feel of the rudder registering its objections to the wheel, and he loved knowing that the wheel he held was the master of the rudder.

The bells added to the various sounds. Soon they would mean a lot to George, but only two days out to sea, they seemed to add only to the beauty of the ship's procedures. George didn't realise that they actually controlled them. He slept well again that night and woke next morning with the sunrise. Mr Baguly's bunk was empty, so George rose as best he could and made his way slowly on to the deck. The day was exactly as it had been yesterday, warm and with a slight breeze. He was beginning to know his way around the 'Bulldog', and the smell of coffee drew him to the galley, where 'Cook' was in charge of various pans and baking trays and this morning, a large coffee pot.

"You after summat?" Cook enquired cheerily, obviously expecting an answer in the affirmative.

"Your coffee does smell nice Sir, and perhaps a piece of your duff – is that possible?"

"Duff's all gone but I baked these oven bottoms an hour ago and there's two left – one each."

George eyed the oven bottoms suspiciously – they were like tea cakes or barm cakes, but well scorched and huge. Cook sensed the uncertainty, so he cut one open, filled it with stewed apple and bit into it with abandon.

"Try it – can't beat my oven bottoms, they are famous."

George accepted one, his hunger overcoming his inhibitions, and two minutes later he nodded his approval to 'Cook' – his overfull mouth precluded the possibility of a more formal response.

"Told you" Cook said "Try my coffee – Skipper reckons my coffee is the best."

He poured George a cup of his black brew. George stared in disbelief, the smell was attractive but this coffee lacked mobility. Its viscosity was such as to remove its correct description from liquid to solid.

"Could I have a little milk in it please Sir" George wheedled.

"Milk, why d'you want milk – it hides the flavour, I suppose you want sugar as well."

George nodded his culpability but gained both additives and thus made the coffee (almost) acceptable.

"Very nice Sir" George said. "I see now why your oven bottoms are famous – it makes a lovely breakfast."

George left most of the coffee and made his way to the deck. There was little activity there, apart from scrubbing the deck, four of the younger sailors were hard at it, supervised by Mr Baguly – he called out to George, "You alright this fine mornin'?"

"Yes thank you Sir – I slept very well and Cook gave me a nice breakfast."

"That's alright then – take your shirt off and let's have a look at that back o'your's."

George tried to reach round but couldn't make it. He was attempting to gather the shirt together with lift it over his head but he was too stiff to be able to reach. Mr Baguly, who had witnessed the first shirt being cut from George said "Belay a minute I'll get a knife."

One of the young sailors stopped his deck scrubbing as soon as the Mate disappeared.

"Won't the shirt come off?" he said.

"I think it's stuck to me – with blood" George said.

Mr Baguly came back with a knife and cut the shirt from the back of the neck to the flap, and slowly, gently eased it off. The four lads gathered round to see the sight. Some of the cuts had stopped bleeding, but some had opened up when the shirt was removed. The colours were just as vivid and angry looking. Mr Penaluna arrived upon the scene and deck scrubbing was resumed immediately.

"It's a warm enough day, can you manage without a shirt on?" he asked.

"Yes I think so Sir – it is nice and warm."

"Stay on the poop deck, and keep away from any splashes of water, and if the sun is fully out only have five minutes at a time. The sun will help to dry it out, but not too much mind."

The poop was the holy of holies on any ship, normally only the Skipper and the Mate used it. George was really being wonderfully looked after and he knew he had struck gold when he had found the 'Bulldog'.

Since leaving Southampton, the 'Bulldog' had put behind her two hundred miles per day, now, on the third day out they were leaving Dutch water and heading up north towards Denmark. Mr Penaluna and Mr Baguly spent some time studying their charts. They had made good time and could afford to spend a day at Esbjerg in Denmark. The Skipper was worried about George's back and he thought he might be able to do some business there. He knew there would be a good doctor in such a large town, so he decided to break the journey with a short stop at Esbjerg. News got around the ship and the men were very excited by the prospect of an unexpected stop. It meant fresh provisions, an hour or two ashore, a chance to meet a girl, an opportunity to get drunk.

The weather continued fine and they docked about ten am. on their fourth day out of Southampton. Mr Penaluna was very precise in his instructions to the crew.

"We are sailing at seven o'clock tonight – so we are here for nine hours only, half can go ashore now until two o'clock, you must be back by two, to let your mates go – they must be back by six – without fail by six. Anyone late will be docked pay, and we will sail on time."

He then turned his attention to George. "You will come with me, we will find a good doctor and get you patched up properly."

Mr Baguly then stepped forward and said, "Me and Cook's stayin' on board Sir, and I'll see the men do exactly as you said."

Mr Penaluna nodded and shepherded George off the 'Bulldog' and off they went to find a doctor. Mr Penaluna was very smartly dressed and looked very prosperous, which indeed he was. George was wearing one of the two shirts which had been cut from his back – just loosely tacked together. Mr Penaluna found a doctor's house and they were shown into the doctor's surgery. Dr Schymberg came into the room, spoke Danish, and to George's amazement Mr Penaluna replied in the same language and then quickly cut the tacking stitches and revealed the reason for the visit. His glance at Mr Penaluna spoke volumes. Mr Penaluna explained the situation, how George had run away from home, become a stowaway, and here was the predicament.

Dr Schymberg examined George's shoulders, back, buttocks and thighs in great detail, and made some suggestions to Mr Penaluna, which he in turn translated to George.

"The good doctor is suggesting that your best course of action would be to stay here – ashore, so he could treat you regularly."

"How long would that take Sir?"

"About two weeks to be on the safe side."

George was thinking as quickly as he could "What about your journey Sir – when will you be back to Esbjerg?"

Mr Penaluna realised George was one step ahead of him.

"Could be six or seven weeks before I am this way again, but I will be in Copenhagen in three weeks time. You could stay here for two weeks, then hire a pony and ride across to Copenhagen and meet us there."

Mr Penaluna translated this to the doctor and it was agreed. Quite unknown to George quite a few gold sovereigns changed hands before Mr Penaluna and the good doctor parted company.

Mr Penaluna then took George to one side and explained all that he had arranged. He had no need to tell George to behave himself because he already knew that

George's manners were impeccable. But he took some time to reassure George that this was the best way to achieve a real cure for his injuries, that he was not being dumped. Far from it, Mr Penaluna was looking forward to meeting up with him in three weeks time. "Even if my business dictates that I should be elsewhere first – I will be there, I will come to Copenhagen whatever happens. See my agents, Fothergill and Jones, they will know when I am expected and if you cannot find their office, ask the Harbour Master – he will put you in the right way."

"Fothergill and Jones" George said "Will they know where you are?"

"Yes they will know, because I will come across a ship in the next two weeks which will be bound for Copenhagen and I will give a letter to the Captain – that is one of the ways we keep in touch with the World."

"Thank you Sir, I am very grateful for the way you have looked after me, and once I am well I shall look forward to repaying you by being, if you will allow, a very hard working member of your crew."

"I always need lively young men aboard my ship, so you will be welcome."

George liked the idea of being referred to as a 'young man', his first inclination was to kiss Mr Penaluna but he thought better of it and shook hands – heartily.

Dr Schymberg was a married man with a grown up family, they lived in the country on a farm about six miles outside Esbjerg. He ran his practice from home two days each week, and came into town for the other days to ply his skills. He kept a little dog cart for his commuting, so he and George were soon back at the farm where George was due to stay for two weeks. The Doctor's wife was never completely sure what would happen next, her husband was a mercurial character, so life was full of surprises. George was the latest of them. When she saw the extent of the injuries she fully understood why Dr Schymberg had offered his services. She went upstairs and rearranged the beds (they had four sons) so George could sleep alone. The Doctor took George into his surgery and the treatment began.

Within a week George was more or less cured, and was his usual active self. He had picked up enough Danish (a notoriously difficult language) to converse with the family and he was soon making himself useful, by feeding the pigs and chickens, collecting the eggs, and doing other little jobs around the farm. The start of the second week was an especial delight; the youngest son Lauritz began to give George riding lessons.

"Why do I have to take it so seriously?" George asked.

"Because we have to ride over one hundred and twenty miles to have you in Copenhagen, in time for your ship." Lauritz told him.

"Is it really as far as that?"

"Yes it is and you need to ride properly otherwise it is hard on the horse and you will ache all over."

So they did about two hours practice every day for a week, by that time the pony was used to George and he was riding quite well. Dr Schymberg examined George's back carefully each day for the first week, but after that, he was sure the worst was over and just looked briefly to

48

confirm that he was well on the way to a full recovery. What contributed greatly to George's well being was the warm friendly attitude of Dr Schymberg's whole family and the excellent locally produced food: ham and eggs for breakfast with home made bread. Thick cheese open sandwiches for lunch and in the evening a huge pork hot-pot with potatoes, onions and apples slowly cooked in the oven. During the first week, before the riding lessons started George spent nearly all the time with Mrs Schymberg in the kitchen. The Doctor was out and about attending to his patients, the four boys were hay-making, so George offered his services and Mrs Schymberg quickly realised that he really did know his way around the kitchen. He peeled the potatoes and apples, made sandwiches, ready for the voracious appetites of the haymakers, and did most of the tidying and washing up. Mrs Schymberg was a cheerful hearty lady who appreciated the help she was receiving and kept up constant, and at times, intelligible, conversation with George. So he added to the knowledge he had accumulated with the dreaded Rooney at No 18, and thoroughly enjoyed his week's work with his Danish teacher.

In between the riding practice he continued to help in the kitchen, and Mrs Schymberg had taken to him so much that she did ask her husband if there was any chance that he could stay. "He has no family at all in England – his parents are both dead and his step-mother allowed him to be ill-treated."

"Yes I know all that but I did promise the Captain that I would make sure he was cured and safely delivered to Copenhagen, so I must keep my promise."

"But will you tell him please, that if a life at sea does not suit him, we would like him back here as part of our family." The Doctor looked at his wife and put his arms round her, "Four boys and me are not enough for you – your heart is so big, you need more?"

"He is a lovely boy, and I would like to keep him" she sobbed.

"Well I will write a letter to the Captain, and Lauritz can take it with him when they go to Copenhagen."

"Will they be alright journeying all that way – they are both young?"

Lauritz is eighteen, he is a man, and very sensible, he is looking forward to it, and he will be back in about two weeks."

"TWO WEEKS – that long?"

"It is a round trip of about two hundred and fifty miles, so, yes it will take two weeks."

Mrs Schymberg had rarely been as far as Esbjerg, six miles away, so two hundred and fifty miles meant nothing to her. So she shrugged and accepted but added "You will write the letter to the Captain?"

"Yes I'll do it now, you can read it, so you will know I've done exactly as you ask."

After conversations with all his sons it was decided that seven days would suffice, Lauritz would accompany George and once he was safely delivered into

Copenhagen, Lauritz would return, riding one pony and leading the other.

Mrs Schymberg made sure the saddle bags were well stocked with good Danish food: pork pies, cheese, cooked bacon, bread and fruit, also bottles of fresh spring water. It was June and the plan was that the boys would sleep outdoors if the weather was fine, but look for accommodation if there was rain. They were planning to take a direct country route, so the horses would have good grazing at the various stops, and they would drink from streams or pools as and when they came across them. Dr Schymberg gave Lauritz a purse of money to pay for accommodation should the weather be against them, and they had maps to guide them on what was, for two boys, an epic journey. The whole family rose extra early on the vital day and by seven o'clock they were ready. Mrs Schymberg cast more than a few pleading glances her husband's way but obtained no encouragement – the boy must return to the Captain, on that the Doctor was quite decided.

"Are you sure your back is quite better George?" Mrs Schymberg asked, possibly hoping he would say "not quite". But no such answer came her way, George was sure he was better.

"Thanks to you all – I am sure that I really am cured," George said, and at the last minute jumped off his horse to kiss his generous hostess. Then onto his horse again and they were off at a steady trot.

"Not too fast," the Doctor called after them, "Consider the horses!"

The boys waved and they were gone. As soon as they were out of sight they did allow their mounts a good canter for a mile or two, but never broke into a gallop. For most of the day they either walked or trotted and by five o'clock Lauritz reckoned they had travelled thirty miles, that was enough for one day. They settled down under some trees, it had been a lovely warm day and they decided it would be an ideal night to sleep outside.

Lauritz said, "Let's attend to the ponies first, take off the saddles, make sure their hooves are alright, give them some water, tether them so they don't go missing, then we can have our meal."

George agreed, of course, and within half an hour they were settling down to do justice to one of Mrs Schymberg's pork pies. It was a lovely balmy June evening, it wasn't likely at that latitude, to go dark before eleven o'clock, but that didn't affect Lauritz and George, by eight o'clock they were both fast asleep.

The next morning George woke first, looked immediately to see that the two ponies were still safety tethered, and grazing contentedly. Lauritz roused when he heard George opening the saddle-bags to see what there was for breakfast.

"You sort out breakfast George, and I'll take the ponies to the stream for a drink." So all their early morning requirements were looked after, the two boys had a cursory wash in the stream, and by seven o'clock they were heading for Kolding, a large town on the opposite side of Jylland from Esbjerg. Lauritz was hoping to be able to camp between Kolding and Middelfart for their second overnight stop. But by three o'clock George was literally falling off his pony, so Lauritz stopped in Kolding and George was allowed to sleep for about three hours.

"I am sorry about that Lauritz, but I just could not keep my eyes open – I thought I would fall off my pony."

"I know you were tired, but you are doing very well. We'll ride now until about eight o'clock and we will have done another thirty miles. Actually they did better than that. The rest in the afternoon had done the ponies a lot of good as well and they reached Nørreaby by eight o'clock. They were now seventy miles from their original starting point. Lauritz decided to have a break in the afternoon of their third day, and then to push on in the cool of the evening, and by the evening of the third day they were on a ferry from Nyborg to Korsor. So with the help of the ferry they covered about fifty miles that day.

The weather was being very kind to them, it was bright, warm and breezy during the day, and since the earth had warmed up it did not go below 48° or 50° during the nights. They were making good time, so Lauritz decided to make for Copenhagen by a southerly route, so that the last twenty miles would be via Solrød Strand, then they would go north via the continuous beach or strand, and thus complete the journey right next to the sea.

George's injuries were now completely healed and his two and a half weeks in Denmark had transformed him. He arrived pale, haggard and thin. Now he was robust, vigorous and tanned. He loved the journey he was making now: the Danish countryside was beautiful.

The trees were in blossom, that known as May blossom in England is June blossom at that latitude and it gave off its fragrance generously. Many of the fruit trees were still covered with flowers and the meadows and hedgerows were filled with bluebells, wild garlic, cowslips and buttercups. Unlike England, continental farmers never suffered 'enclosure', so it is possible still to wander from land in one ownership to another piece owned by someone different, quite unhindered by continuous dry-stone walls, or hedges or fences. So Lauritz was able to plot a route and keep to it. Sometimes they did stop at farms for half an hour, Lauritz would explain the purpose of his journey, the farmer would realise that he was of farming stock, and so the two boys would leave the farm with fresh bread, milk and with luck a tasty pie, and a friendly wave.

They reached Køge, just south of the many beaches they intended to ride over and camped by the sea. The next morning they started for Copenhagen and just as they reached Sølrad Strand they saw a fishing boat in trouble – it was about fifty yards from the shore and it was drifting side on towards the beach. Between it and the beach were large jutting rocks. The two fisherman on board shouted that they had lost their rudder and were drifting dangerously. Lauritz found a length of rope on a beached fishing boat, and told George what he intended to do, then with the rope tied around his middle he began to swim out to the beleaguered boat, drawing the rope after him. The further out he was, the heavier the rope became, so the intended rescue apparatus was in danger of drowning its user. A man on the boat threw a rope to Lauritz, which at the fourth attempt he managed to hold on to and slowly they dragged Lauritz to the comparative safety of their vessel. Now it was George's turn: the rope reached from the shore to the boat. George tied the two horses together and by standing between them with a foot in a stirrup of each horse, he urged them forward, and slowly the boat was drawn away from the rocks, the incoming tide deposited the boat on the gently shelving beach.

The two men were speechless, but their gratitude was obvious. Five minutes later the offending rudder drifted in and was thrown upon the beach by the defeated tides. Almost as if the sea were saying, "If I can't wreck you completely you may as well have this back." The fishermen lived nearby and insisted on taking the boys back to their homes for a meal – fish of course followed by the local Havarti cheese – a cheese with a flavour so powerful the boys could taste it for days.

By mid afternoon they were at Karlslunde Strand, and there they camped for the night. They walked inland half a mile or so and found a small farm, Lauritz explained that they were on a long journey and needed somewhere to graze the horses. The farmer agreed and added that they could sleep the night in his house. Both Lauritz and George were ready for a proper bed and a bath, so they made themselves comfortable and enjoyed a cooked meal and some more Havarti cheese. They left early next morning after Lauritz had made a small payment out of the purse of money his father had given him. They carried on up the continuous beach and arrived in Copenhagen.

They found an Inn about two miles from the centre where the horses could be well looked after as well as themselves and they set off in search of Fothersgill and Jones, the Skipper's agents.

Copenhagen was by far the busiest place Lauritz had ever seen and the architecture was quite different from anything either of them had experienced. The main buildings concerned with Royalty or the Government had huge copper covered towers or spires, (this is still a feature of important buildings in Denmark today.) The city had big open squares and very broad streets, which were difficult to cross because of the traffic: horses and carriages were everywhere and the number of horse drawn carts was enough to actually achieve traffic jams at various road junctions. The two boys walked towards the worst of the traffic, having decided that it was coming away from the docks, and that is where they would find the office they were looking for.

George had been to Southampton with Mr Tonbridge, his head teacher, so he had some experience of large docks but it was all new to Lauritz. George took pride in pointing out the Schooners from the Brigs and the Snows from the Clippers. Also George knew many of the flags and he pointed out the Danish Standard, the Kingdom of Poland, the Merchants of Austria, The Blue Ensign, Greek Merchants, Malta, Naples even Peru, they were all represented. It was a very busy port, goods from all over the world were being unloaded and vast warehouses were waiting to disgorge Danish products and take in fresh ones from abroad. The smells which surrounded the boys as they walked among the ships were evidence of the variety of goods, timber from Sweden and Finland with its rich pine scent, tobacco from America, coffee beans from Central and South America. The smell of cheese was a frequent visitor to their noses.

George and Lauritz looked at each other frequently – this was a very easy place to become separated and a difficult place to find a lost partner. Almost every step they took they were in someone's way; porters carrying sacks, men wheeling trolleys and trucks or barrows, men with ponies and carts. All very cheerful, used to the jostling and making way for each other. One ship had a broad gang plank between it and the dock, and barrels were being rolled down the plank very skilfully, each one looked heavy enough to crush a man, it landed thump against a pile of sacks stuffed with straw, two men moved the barrel, just before another arrived, all perfectly timed.

Lauritz and George would never have starved as they moved about the docks: street vendors were everywhere, selling bread, cakes, shellfish, pies, dairy products of all sorts, usually carried in large wickerwork baskets suspended from a yoke. The vendor shouted out the benefits of buying from him, adding to the hubbub of the sailors and stevedores, and carters who all found it quite impossible to work in silence. Two boys about nine years old each sat astride a donkey, they were equipped with a long handled ladle and they sold fresh milk out of kits, large metal containers each holding about fifteen gallons of milk. They made for the ships which were about to set sail because they knew that the Cook or Steward who wished to indulge his skipper would buy fresh milk to put in his tea or coffee. Some of the really up to date ships carried a dry-air siphon refrigerator which worked by having ice blocks in a compartment of the galley. Just like Southampton, the confusion was added to by wives and children bidding fond farewells and further added to by Clerks from the Shipping Companies running on and off ships with Bills of Lading and other documents. Some sailors were conducted (some dragged) back to their ships by the Constabulary. It was not unknown for sailors to get drunk just before setting sail, some were well known to the Police, and since they had enough to contend with – petty thieves and pickpockets were everywhere – the Police would deliver the singing, shouting, rowdy sailor back to his ship and thus be sure that he was off their hands. Once on deck, the Mate or the Bo'sun poured cold water over the unfortunate celebrant, and locked him up below. If he was not sufficiently recovered to help when the ship was ready to sail he would have a day's pay stopped and be relegated to menial duties for a day or two.

In the middle of all this confusion George and Lauritz began to lose sight of what they were really trying to do, ie, find either the Harbour Master's office or Fothergill & Jones' premises. But at last they stumbled across the Captain's agents and went in to enquire. It was good news, the 'Bulldog' was on its way and would arrive this week. It was now Tuesday. No – they didn't know which day, but to come every day and ask. The man pointed to a spot where he thought the 'Bulldog' would tie up and concluded the interview abruptly – he was a busy man, but once 'Bulldog' was in, he would be happy to help in anyway he could. George really did want to ask more questions but Lauritz pulled him away.

"He is too busy just now – and that is all we need to know – your ship is not in yet, but she will be in in a day or two." George agreed and they made their way out of the docks and back to the Inn where they had left their ponies and resolved to come back the day after.

They called at the office on Wednesday and Thursday but without luck. On the Friday morning they decided to give their ponies a run on the beach, most horses love splashing through shallow water, the two boys were racing their ponies up an down the length of the beach. George over estimated what he was capable of so far as horsemanship was concerned and he ended up sat in two feet of water, then as he stood, he looked out to sea and pointed, "That's her" he shouted, "That's the 'Bulldog."

"How do you know?" Lauritz said. "They all look the same to me."

"How many cows have you on your farm – do you know them all by name?" George asked.

"Of course, I know everyone and we have forty."

"Well – it's just the same – you know cows and I know ships and that one is mine. Come on I want to see her dock."

"You can't go like that – we'll have to go back to the Inn to get you tidied up."

"No," George said, "I'll dry out on the way into Copenhagen – let's go now, and see her arrive – she's beautiful."

They rode into the docks area and tied their ponies up to a rail. Then they walked towards the open sea. 'Bulldog' was about six miles out and under tow.

"Why are they being towed in?" Lauritz asked.

"It is too dangerous to enter harbour under sail, a sudden squall of wind and she could crash into another ship, sailing ships cannot be handled precisely. In the old days before tugs, they used to be brought in with teams of men in rowing boats, sometimes most of the crew would be rowing their own boats as well, it is a very risky affair bringing a ship into dock."

Lauritz was suitably impressed by George's explanation and they both resumed looking out to sea, and admiring the beautiful 'Bulldog'. The sun was shining on her and even at a distance it was obvious that she was immaculate. Her black paint was spotless and the white Plimsoll line could now be clearly seen. Her sails were all furled with precision and the spars were lined up with geometric accuracy. The rigging was all just as it should be, no loose ends floating in the breeze – this was indeed a 'tight' ship, run by a keen and enthusiastic crew. George had enjoyed his three weeks in Denmark and he was tremendously grateful to Lauritz and his family for all they had done for him, but he could not wait to get back on board his ship – he knew that the call of the sea was irresistible to him.

An hour later and 'Bulldog' was entering the dock area. She created quite a stir: people were stopping to look and admire – George felt very proud – this was his ship. He ran alongside as soon as she was tied up, he was waving and shouting, but no one recognised him, how could they, he was changed completely.

"Mr Baguly" he shouted. "It's me George."

"Bless me soul - I wouldn't have knowed you. Skipper – Sir, come here look at George."

The crew ran a gang-plank down and George dashed up it into Mr Baguly's arms.

"You've growed a foot" he said.

All the crew gathered round and then broke away to let a smiling Mr Penaluna through. He stood away a little to admire the transformed little stowaway.

"You look fine George – just fine."

"Am I now a member of your crew Sir – that's what I want to be."

Mr Penaluna turned to his men and said "What do you think lads – do we take him?"

The chorus of acceptance was deafening – George was in tears. Lauritz was vastly impressed. The Skipper recognised him as one of Dr Schymberg's sons and told the crew who he was. Some said "Let's take him for a drink."

The Skipper agreed but added "Only one or two mind, we need to get this ship unloaded, as soon as the papers are cleared, so be back by four and sober."

He put him arm around George's shoulder and gently pushed him towards Mr Baguly and said "He is yours now Mr Baguly, make a sailor of him."

"I will indeed Sir – I will indeed." He took George with him. George looked around for Lauritz, he was just entering a hostelry with some members of the crew. How they would converse, goodness only knows, but one or two drinks would loosen all their tongues.

Lauritz and his fellow drinkers came back more or less punctually and if not quite sober they were at least capable. Lauritz said 'Farewell' to George who replied in tolerable Danish and asked Lauritz to convey his thanks to all at home. Mr Penaluna thanked Lauritz also and asked if he had sufficient money to see him home safely, and with a wave he was gone.

They now returned to the business of running a ship: the Agents Fothergill and Jones brought sheaves of paperwork on board. Mr Baguly sent four men to search for provisions, water and fresh vegetables, and then called to Humpage, who was third Mate,

"Mr Humpage – all our brass work could do with a good going over, set George and Oliver on it – show 'em 'ow it's done." The third Mate showed how to mix powder into colyaoil to make a paste.

"Now you need some old rags and a bit of energy, and the brass will come up lovely." The binnacle was all brass and the wheel had many brass fittings so this kept the two boys busy for a couple of hours after which time George began to wonder about food, he had been well and truly spoiled in the last two weeks, now he would have to get used to sailor's food at irregular intervals. When they were in harbour they ate local food and it was good. But once they were at sea the fresh vegetables and fruit would last only a few days and Cook could prepare only basic meals because he rarely had a steady surface to work with.

The two boys went to Cook's storeroom and found some apples and a large hunk of yesterday's duff, not ideal but it filled a gap and that was all that was needed.

The ship was now ready to leave Copenhagen. The Skipper and the Mate had spent some time with the charts, they were sailing next to Leith. Mr Penaluna had bought four sacks full of amber and he had heard that the ladies of Edinburgh had taken a fancy to amber jewellery so he intended to make a brief call there, before going north, round the Orkneys, down south via the Irish Sea to La Rochelle on the west coast of France. He had on board high quality timber of the kind used for making furniture, some would be unloaded there but the majority of it was bound for Taranto in Southern Italy where it would be used to make church furniture. The journeys would be complex during the next few weeks and Mr Penaluna was not unduly upset when the Manager of Fothergill and Jones, his Agents, came on board to say that would not be able to sail that day because all the tugs were fully engaged and none would be free until the next day. Mr Penaluna shrugged his shoulders but said to Mr Baguly,

"Don't tell the crew, we've got 'em all aboard and all sober, so have them check the rigging and the sails, we need heavy weight sails for the North Sea and the Irish

Sea, then we can change when we reach the Mediterranean."

The crew had not overheard the news of the delay but George had, because at the moment the news was imparted, he was bringing a tray of coffee to Mr Penaluna's cabin. The days delay gave George chance to think and survey his life and he decided he must write to Rose and tell her of his adventures. He confessed to Mr Penaluna that he had overheard the news of the delay.

"That's alright George – I can trust you to say nothing."

"I would like to use some of the time, if I may Sir, to write home."

"I thought they treated you badly there, I'm surprised you even think about them."

"This letter is to Rose, a young servant in the house who helped me a lot, and she can contact my two sisters and let them know that I'm safe."

"Then of course you must write. Take the letter round to the Agent's office when you've finished it, and they will post it for you."

Next morning the tug arrived early, the man on watch on the 'Bulldog' roused the Mate and soon every member of the crew was on deck. The cargo was mainly high quality timber which had to be kept dry for two good reasons; firstly salt water would ruin it and secondly the wood, if wet, would swell and wreck the ship. Mr Penaluna and the ship's joiner Harris went about covering the hatches; Harris doing it, with help, and Mr Penaluna seeing it was done properly – this was his ship and the last thing he wanted to do was spend his last days living on the insurance brought in by a lost 'Bulldog'. Three strong tarpaulins were stretched over the main hatch, the overlaps were tightly drawn down the sides of the coamings, and the corners were folded across as though they were making a parcel. The folding of the tarpaulins was arranged so that when the seas broke over the ship, the water would rush past the lugs instead of into them. This was to avoid the risk of them being washing open. Flat steel battens were then placed one on each side of the hatch and hardwood wedges were hammered into place to tighten everything down. Mr Penaluna nodded his approval. The after hatch was secured except for a corner which was left open for last minute items which would need to be stowed.

"Check the crew, Mr Baguly – if you please." Mr Penaluna called out. Everybody was on deck, so this was soon done. The Harbour Master and the Pilot were on board. The Mate shouted, "Hawser," to the tug – this was done. "Stations" ordered the Mate. Humpage was at the wheel, he swung it hard both ways, just to check the chains were in good order. The Pilot indicated that the tug could move off, and she pulled the 'Bulldog's' head away from the dock.

"Let go for'ward" came the cry.

"Slack away."

"Let go"

The orders came one after another. Mr Penaluna there on the poop in his magnificent three quarter length coat of a rich plum colour, he wore a hat not dissimilar to that used by Nelson. He had not said a word, nor did he need to, but he was in control, his training and his insistence upon discipline made this the ship it was, the trimmest, best kept, best painted, barque one could wish to see. Pride of ownership exuded from Mr Penaluna. No one observing the events of the last half hour could have doubted who was in charge, yet he never said a word.

Many on the docks stopped what they were doing to admire the 'Bulldog' as she was towed out, she was so graceful. The figurehead was a black and white bulldog with fierce eyes and a friendly grin, so you were never quite sure if he would lick you or bite you – a bit like his owner – strict and yet capable of real human warmth.

As the 'Bulldog' came out into the Oresund the tug swung her northwards, the prevailing winds in that area were of little use and tacking would be difficult especially as they reached the gap between Helsinfors and Helsingborg (in Sweden) the currents could be difficult and with barely four miles to play with Mr Penaluna opted for a tow right past that point and into the open sea. The island of Ven could also present problems, so this was an expensive day for Mr Penaluna. Eight hours out of Copenhagen the crew gathered to the portside as they were towed past what we know in England as Elsinore Castle – home to Hamlet. No one on board had read the play, nor seen it, but they felt an affinity with the place just the same.

They cleared the gap between Denmark and Sweden, a really brisk wind met them, the tug dropped the hawser into the cold sea and circled around to take off the Pilot. Farewells were shouted.

"Topsails" roared the Mate.

Within seconds the crew, who were 'on their marks' had done this. George went up the rigging too, and watched as Oliver wrestled with ropes and lee sheets Oliver miraculously did his part, showed George what to do, and still had a spare hand to grab George if he felt he was unsteady – they were eighty feet above the deck. The wind filled the sails and the men on the halyards tightened down.

"Lee fore brace" called Mr Baguly

"Look out aloft"

"Let go the bunt and hang on"

"Sheet home main topsail"

"Hoist away main topsail"

"Belay lee sheet"

All these – to George – foreign expressions were being shouted and when adhered to, they had the effect of changing the 'Bulldog' from a vessel which needed to be towed into one capable of harnessing nature and plunging forward, very much in charge of its own progress.

Mr Penaluna watched from the Poop deck as his hands went about their duties. Humpage was at the wheel and he knew the 'feel' of the 'Bulldog' better than anyone, he hated parting with the wheel and really thought the 'Bulldog' slowed up or wandered off course when he was not steering 'his' ship. The men allocated to the mainsail were in position ready for the order. Mr Penaluna was waiting for the sails which were unfurled to bring her up to speed.

"Ten knots" yelled the Bos'n.

"Loose the main-sail" Mr Penaluna called, and 250 square yards of canvas were added to the driving force of the 'Bulldog'.

"She's off now my beauty" Humpage called.

"Thirteen knots" yelled the Bos'n.

"Everythings fine now Mr Baguly" Mr Penaluna said. "Ask Cook to prepare dinner for the men if you please and join me in my cabin to go over the charts," adding as an afterthought. "I have some Danish ham and some Danish beer – enough for two I think."

"Thankee Sir, I'll join you in a minute."

Mr Penaluna stepped over towards Humpage and glanced at the compass, then looked aloft to see how the wind was hitting the sails and how the sails were trimmed.

" Thirteen knots, she'll do more but more than thirteen is hard on the bracings. If the wind stiffens, send for me and we'll shorten sail."

"I will Sir," replied Humpage. Mr Penaluna put his hand on Humpage's shoulder just for a second, he knew his ship was in good hands, and he suddenly thought of the Danish ham awaiting him in his cabin.

George's letter resided in the office of Messrs Fothergill and Jones for less than twenty four hours: a ship was due to leave for Newcastle on the next tide, and this letter to Rose at No 18 Wellington Terrace, Poole, Dorset was on that ship. Nine days later it dropped through the letterbox and was retrieved by Clarissa, who was intrigued.

"Rose, Rose" she cried "A letter for you."

"Can't be Ma'am, I don't know nobody who writes to me."

"It's her young man" Polly said.

"Haven't got one – yet" Rose countered.

"Open it, open it" Marie said, trying to take it.

"Just a minute" Rose said "I'm enjoying this, I've never had a letter before."

Then she opened it.

"It's from Denmark" she exclaimed, "It's from George!"

This last sentence came out in a strangled fashion, tears flooded on to the letter. Clarissa gently took it and read:

Dear Rose

I am now on a ship as part of the crew, and we are in Denmark, then we go to Scotland. I got on this ship in Southampton and they looked after me. The Captain, Mr Penaluna, put me ashore in Denmark with a doctor and he got me right and sent his son and me across Denmark to meet up with my ship in Copenhagen. I had to learn to ride a horse because the journey was 120 miles. I saw my ship come in and Mr Baguly (the Mate on my ship) didn't know me because I looked so well after my three weeks on Danish food.

I will write again perhaps from Italy, but I don't know how long it will be – perhaps weeks. Italy is a long way.

I will know in the future because Mr Baguly is teaching Oliver (he's my friend) and me about navigation, so I will be able to look at charts and calculate where we are going and how long it will take.

If you see Polly and Marie say 'Hello' for me. It is difficult for you to write to me because I never know where I'll be. My ship is called 'Bulldog' and she is beautiful. The Captain is a Cornish man called Mr Penaluna, and if the weather is fine he wears a lovely plum coloured coat and a sea-captain's hat. He is very strict but he helped me when I was hurt and I do like him and Mr Baguly too. The Cook is funny – he drinks too much and makes mistakes, last Tuesday he sent me to the Captain with his breakfast and it was in the middle of the afternoon. Mr Penaluna just said "That Cook!!" and gave me the tray back, so I took it outside and Oliver and me ate it.

I will write again.

Love,

George Eefamy (Sailor)

Clarissa said "It is all a bit confused but he does seem to be happy and that is the main thing – his sisters will be home to stay permanently in the next few weeks, and I would like to show them this letter – if you have no objections Rose?"

"No. Course not Ma'am, but I would like to keep it in my room so as I can read it when I feel like it."

"You do that Rose, but don't cry on it anymore or we won't be able to read it when Caroline and Ann come home."

CHAPTER 4

Bonny Dunoon

Number 18 became home to seven ladies: Caroline and Anne were newly returned from Switzerland with Thurza Paxton, and Rose, Polly and Marie were the staff. The household was headed by Clarissa. As soon as they had definite news that they were needed and confirmation that both Mrs Collins and Rooney had gone for good, Polly and Marie went to see the Manager of the Embassy Hotel and explained their position. They had enjoyed their stay but the Manager's son was due to return from his tour of duty in Scotland and as Polly said to Marie "Once a bottom pincher always a bottom pincher" and they didn't want to risk that. So their return to No 18 was soon arranged. Clarissa was happy about it, her income was sufficient to sustain a home with three servants and they all lived well and, more importantly, happily together.

Mrs Collins and Rooney, two of a kind, went to Scotland together and had to set up house. They decided upon Dunoon which was at that time just becoming known as a holiday resort, with many amenities, and a mild climate. They found a small house overlooking the sea at a reasonable rent, it was partially furnished, and the local Estate Agent ran a monthly auction. As he put it; of high class furniture from nice country homes, so their requirements were catered for at little expense. Mrs Collins found it impossible to quell Rooney – she was determined NOT to be regarded as a servant any longer. She had money of her own, some of it not come by legally, but be that as it may, she was not far off being as 'comfortable' as Mrs Collins, and she was not going to be an underling any longer. They agreed to share the work in the house, they would look after their own rooms. Rooney would do the cooking, Mrs Collins would attend to the shopping – she arranged this craftily by only selecting shops who would deliver. So even if it was lowly kippers for tea, they were delivered.

The system worked well enough, they got on quite amicably together and always did the washing up as a pair. Rooney was an excellent and economical cook; chicken carcasses were boiled up to make broth, left over meat from roasts was used up in Shepherd's Pie, so they lived cheaply. Their total assets were not huge, and with interest at 3%, their income was about £120 per year. But at the time the average weekly wage for a working man was approximately £1, and on that he would have to keep a family, so Mrs Collins and Rooney had what Jane Austin referred to as a competence.

Mrs Collins could never really settle to the notion that someone who had been one's servant could, overnight, become one's equal. Mrs Collins was very class conscious and Rooney's new 'promotion' in society was not fully accepted by Mrs Collins. After some months of living together little things began to annoy Mrs Collins: Rooney would get up early and have her breakfast, and then start doing the grate or using metal polish. One morning Mrs Collins came down at about 8.30 am and found the kitchen table covered with brassware, a strong smell of metal polish pervaded the kitchen and this Mrs Collins, found, not unreasonably, to be unappetising.

"Really this is too much, one can't eat with such noxious smells, you could at least wait until breakfast is out of the way."

Rooney was quite unperturbed and she continued to polish up the brass candle sticks.

"Breakfast was ready at 8.15 am, it is now nearly 9.00 o'clock and jobs must be done or we'll never keep straight."

The look of virtue on Rooney's face Mrs Collins found annoying but Rooney was right – and that was hard to swallow. It also meant that Mrs Collins would have to get her own breakfast ready – which she did grudgingly. She just made toast and a cup of tea.

"I wouldn't have minded a cup of tea," Rooney said as she watched Mrs Collins taking her tray into the parlour away from the smell of polish. Mrs Collins gave her a look which said it all. Rooney knew there would be no tea – but she would not forget.

So, after just a few weeks of living together, tension was the dominant factor in their lives. Both were strong characters who regarded happiness as a luxury they could manage without. Indeed it was something which had passed them by for most of their lives and it was doubtful if they really knew what happiness was. Their life together meant financial security but nothing more than that.

Rooney broached the subject of wills one day with Mrs Collins.

"If I die tomorrow, what would happen to my money?" Rooney asked, out of the blue. Part of the idea obviously appealed to Mrs Collins, and a ghostly smile passed across her face as she savoured the prospect. She enjoyed Rooney's next supposition rather less, "Or you for that matter, what would happen if you went?"

"I suppose my daughter would inherit mine."

"Exactly, and mine would go to the Crown or stay in Chancery – which is much the same thing, and financially neither one of us could manage without the other."

They both sat silently for a few minutes as the weight of this information sank in. Neither was capable of any warm feelings, so gratitude was foreign to their natures. Their interdependence should have engendered a gentleness and a feeling of care one for the other, but it didn't, it merely gave rise to resentment. The topic of a will was from now on very important to them and more pressing still was the prospect of who would be the recipient and who the donor. They both knew which was the preferred option and as a result they began to examine each other and to look for signs of infirmity. In fact they received little to encourage them: Dunoon has a healthy invigorating climate, this combined with good plain food and their natural strong constitutions meant that both women, though in late middle age were surprisingly

vigorous. Perhaps the process needed a little help
…………..

Mrs Collins had never taken an interest in flowers or gardens, but she did decide that their little patch at the front would benefit from some careful attention, and whilst out shopping or to be more accurate – arranging for comestibles to be delivered, she called in the hardware shop to enquire about garden tools and plants. The owner of the shop was very helpful and he promised to send his son Andrew round that very evening to see what could be done to arrange for some colour to be added to Mrs Collins' front garden. Andrew was employed at one of the large estates in the area as a gardener and handyman, so he was ideally suited to the task of improving the appearance of the good ladies' gardens. He arrived with his tools in his wheelbarrow, and having made himself known at the front door, began the task of making the centre patch of the garden a more hospitable place for some auriculas. He explained to Mrs Collins and Rooney that they were all the rage, and auricula societies were forming all over Great Britain they were so popular, and of course he had some for sale.

This all took place in late April. Ideal time, according to Andrew for plants to be transplanted and the April showers would help them to thrive. Mrs Collins bought a small trowel and a watering can, and asked Andrew to put up a shelf in the coal shed cum out house at the back of the house, this would be the place where Mrs Collins could keep her gardening equipment. Once a week Mrs Collins donned her gardening apparel; winter boots, an old pair of gloves and a hat of the type no longer in fashion. She collected her watering can and her trowel and thus equipped she made her way to the front garden. She made sure that Rooney knew of this undertaking: little else was mentioned on the appointed day. Conversation consisted of, "I'll be attending to the garden late this morning" or, "After I have tidied up the garden I will go and do the shopping. Later in the day it was a case of. "Yes I spoke to Mrs Jamieson as I was doing the gardening."

Rooney writhed with agony, but had to admit that the results were good. A rose was planted in the middle of the six foot square bed, and about fifteen auriculas surrounded it – this was the garden. Imagine Mrs Collins indignation when she arose one fine morning in late May to find a new plant had taken up residence amongst her treasures. Her trowel was urgently needed and of course she could not undertake the summary removal of this insurgent without the suitable apparel. She noticed this unwelcome addition just after breakfast and prior to washing up. She excused herself from any post prandial duties on the grounds that she had urgent work to attend to outside. She adopted her horticultural garb and went into the outhouse for her tools, nothing less than her total array of weapons would suffice, so armed with her watering can and trowel she advanced on this contumacious invader. Chickweed is soon defeated and Mrs Collins was disappointed that it didn't put up more of a fight. She plucked it out between her thumb and forefinger and the battle was over. She deposited it ceremoniously in the dustbin (usually known in Scotland as the bucket) and that was it – finished. So she watered the rose and the auriculas, put her tools away and went back into the kitchen to apprise Rooney of her adventures. She could hardly have found less receptive ears. Rooney was not interested in the garden. Her main interest was wills – to be precise Mrs Collins' will and the chances of her – Rooney – benefiting from it.

As the season progressed weeds became more of a problem. Part of the front garden and the whole of the yard at the back of the house were paved with large granite setts about nine inches square. This left a lot of cracks and weeds do love cracks. Neither Mrs Collins nor her trowel were equal to the task, and so she called in to see the hardware man to enquire about a solution.

"The weeds are everywhere," she complained. "And they are held tightly between the cobbles, so I can't pull the roots out."

"Yes, I know exactly what you mean, they are awkward: why not try some weed killer?" Mr Denness suggested.

"Weed killer? Does it work?"

"Oh! Yes. Andrew uses a lot of it on the estates path and drives – it really is the modern way to tackle weeds. Try a small tin, it's only one and six pence, and it does save a lot of stooping. Read the instructions on the tin, mix it in your watering can and water the weeds with the solution. In two or three days they'll be dead and all the dead stalks can be swept up – perhaps you'll need a yard brush – I have one here with nice stiff bristles."

Mrs Collins returned home with her little tin of weed killer but asked if the brush could be delivered. She didn't want to be seen carrying a brush, she imagined that she had some social status and a yard brush was just not her. She mixed the weed killer as soon as she got home, and went around the back yard and the surround to her auricula bed at the front. Two days later it was all as Mr Denness had said – the weeds drooped and became discoloured, and the new yard brush did the rest. There followed a dry spell and early morning announcements to the effect that watering took precedence over washing up or other domestic chores. Unfortunately Mrs Collins had not read the small print on the tin which said "Please be sure to carefully rinse out the watering can after using it with weed killer." In two or three days the rose and the auriculas faded and died. In high dudgeon Mrs Collins berated Mr Denness at the hardware shop. He pointed to the small print and added "Perhaps it is best to have two cans, one for watering and one for weed killer, that way it can't happen again."

"It's a very expensive solution for me."

"I've just received delivery of some new ones and they are a little cheaper, could I show you one of those?"

Mrs Collins agreed, but still determined to show who was in charge, she asked for it to be delivered.

"Andrew could deliver it this evening" and then asked tentatively "Would you want him to replace all the plants Mrs Collins?"

"Yes – at a reduced price."

Mr Denness smiled acceptance of these rigorous terms of contract. The auricula season was over and would have to be replaced with nemesia which were cheaper anyway, so no one would lose.

That evening Andrew came round with his barrow, the watering can, nemesia and a rose and began his little job. Mrs Collins and Rooney came out to inspect the finished article, it all looked smart again. Mrs Collins asked about the weed killer, Andrew confirmed that even the slightest trace would kill the plants.

"We have separate watering cans on the estate and we paint one set red – red for danger you see. We made a slight mistake once and splashed a lettuce with a few drops, so we plucked up the lettuce and threw it on the compost heap but some rabbits found it and a few days later we picked up four healthy looking rabbits which had just died of unknown causes, but we think it was the lettuce – it is a very strong poison – so be very careful."

Dunoon season was about to begin and posters went up all over town to announce the arrival of the Henry Sturgess Theatre Company. They were going to stay for ten weeks and provide ten different plays during that time. Mrs Collins was surprised at Rooney's enthusiasm.

"Oh, yes" Rooney said, "I had a position once in Brighton and I loved going to the plays – I like the tragedies best, like "The Silver King"."

"Well I won't be wasting my money on them – I'll stay with gardening as my main form of entertainment."

"Yes, I agree, everybody is not alike, but I think I'll go to the first one, and see if they are any good, and if they are, I'll book for the season.

Next day, Rooney didn't feel too well, so she went for a walk on the promenade. She sat on one of the benches overlooking the sea and began to think carefully about the events of the last few days. Mrs Collins had suddenly taken more than a passing interest in the kitchen, and she had taken the trouble to brew extra cups of tea mid morning or mid afternoon.

Rooney was by nature a criminal, her present financial position was almost entirely due to her handling of the housekeeping money at No 18 and to her methods of disposing of other peoples' goods at her various places of employment. So she had a criminal's mind. In that mind there had developed over the last few weeks a certainty that she would be happier if Mrs Collins were not around, but there was not enough money to manage on her own. If by chance all their combined wealth were to be owned by one person only, then the result would be comfort and life would be altogether more pleasant. Rooney's mind continued to work, and to her the connection between the conversation on wills, the arrival of weed killer, Mrs Collins' sudden interest in the affairs of the kitchen and Rooney's upset stomach, these four facts came together, and Rooney concluded that special care would be needed from now on. A competition was just starting, she knew Mrs Collins well enough, she had witnessed the beatings George had suffered. This was a powerful opponent, and Rooney was determined to win. She rose from her bench and began to think about her upset stomach – Mrs Collins brewed very powerful tea, could the strength of the brew be a deliberate ploy to hide the taste of the weed killer?

She called at the chemist's shop on the way home and bought a bottle of something for indigestion and took it home. She plonked it in the middle of the table and announced that the chemist had advised her to leave tea alone for two or three weeks and just have hot water to drink. She examined Mrs Collins closely during the imparting of this information and detected a slight twitching of the lips. She knew enough about the reading of facial expressions to be sure that this particular movement indicated frustration. The two ladies were living quietly in sunny Dunoon, on a comfortable income in the kind of circumstances most ladies in Britain at that time would have envied, but these two ladies were at war.

Within a few days the fresh air at the front, drinks of hot water, and Rooney's iron constitution had won the day, and she felt well enough to go to the first play. It was a comedy, designed to get the season off to a good start. In the interval Rooney felt like treating herself and went into the bar. Ladies, at any rate unaccompanied ladies, did not go into the bars at theatres but Rooney had little time for convention and she fancied a small gin. Having been served she noticed there was only one seat left, and that was at a table where a rather distinguished looking man was sat. Rooney recognised him as a member of the cast. He had played a very small part in the first act as a butler. Rooney politely asked if she could join him, he gestured to her to take a seat.

"You're not drinking" Rooney said. "Is that management rules?"

"No, not management rules, management stinginess – they don't pay enough to give anyone a chance to have a drink."

"Please allow me to buy your one – I'd love to, I do enjoy plays and it would be my way of giving something back."

At that moment a waiter was passing the table and Rooney stopped him, "Now what would you like?" Rooney asked the actor.

"A double whisky please."

Rooney hadn't expected her generosity to be exploited to quite that extent, but she made no comment. They spent the rest of the interval discussing the future plays and Rooney decided to book for the season, it was cheaper too, that way – you got ten plays for the price of eight.

The next time Rooney went to the theatre she felt more at home with the situation, and was quickly down to the bar in the interval for a gin. Her actor friend was there, again looking rather disgruntled. He confided in her that he had hoped to be given the lead in the new play, but again he was relegated to a small part, and small parts meant small wages. Rooney ordered him a double whisky and tried to engage him in conversation. At the end of the interval she had ascertained that he was married but separated, had never really had any big parts with any major theatre company. He had been in the Army for a few years but that had not worked out. In fact he had been cashiered: his post in the Army had been as a Pay Officer, and he had tried unsuccessfully to work the old dodge of having a few 'invisible' men on the camp who were not actually there, not in fact anywhere, but their names did appear on the pay sheets. So Captain Scroll, as he was then, pocketed the money every week. This scheme could be made to work very well but if the Sergeant was not brought into the arrangement, he could be difficult. Captain Scroll was greedy and wanted all the cash. He failed to take his Sergeant into his confidence, and paid the price. The Sergeant was promoted and from then on was better able to work the system for his own benefit.

So Osbert Scroll, of distinguished appearance, took up acting. Because he was so handsome he could always obtain work but the companies were run by actor/managers and they always kept the best parts for themselves. Osbert was reduced to small parts and small pay, so the occasional double whisky from an admirer fed his ego and saved his pocket.

By the time the fifth play came along Rooney and Osbert were old friends. He never offered to buy a drink for Rooney and seemed to have no feelings of guilt about accepting drinks from a lady old enough to be his mother. They met as usual in the interval and Osbert confided in Rooney that he was particularly hard up this week, because some articles of clothing had been lost and the Manager insisted that since they were part of Osbert's clothes for the part he was playing, he must have lost them, and the cost of the replacements was deducted from his weekly pittance. Rooney reached into her purse and produced two half crowns and slid them across to Scroll. He accepted with a mumbled thanks and offered an assurance that she would be repaid as soon as times were better. Rooney knew there was no chance of that, and she also knew that she owned him – if he could be bought for five shillings then he would be putty in Rooney's hands for a few pounds.

Over breakfast next morning Rooney broached the subject of interest on their capital. It still stood at 3%.

"What would you say if I told you that I have made contact with a Bank which pays 4%?"

Mrs Collins was interested "How much difference would that make to our income?"

"At the moment we receive just over £120 per annum in interest. Now at 4% we would receive £160 per annum, and that would work out nearly a pound a week extra."

The working man at that time earned between fifteen shillings and a pound per week. So a pound each week extra, was indeed a big temptation.

"What do we have to do? " Mrs Collins asked.

"I have met this Bank Manager at the Theatre, they are going to open a new branch in Dunoon, and he is in town looking at premises. If you agree I'll ask him to come round next week and talk about it."

"Why next week – ask him to come today."

"He is a very busy man, he has many people to see, but I am sure he will come next week." With that Rooney concluded the conversation and started to tidy up the kitchen.

During the interval of the next play Mr Scroll mentioned to Rooney that he wasn't required at all during the next part of the play. Rooney took the hint and the opportunity and stayed with him. She ordered extra drinks and got into a huddle, she had much to impart and after half an hour she had a very willing conspirator. As they parted she unobtrusively passed Scroll a half sovereign, then she made her way home.

"Oh you're a little early this week was it a short play?" Mrs Collins asked.

"No, the play wasn't shorter, but I met the Bank Manager during the interval and he told me that his company has now settled upon premises in the main street in Dunoon and they will be open for new business next week. So I thought I would come home and tell you about it."

"What do you think we should do next?"

"I think we should draw our money out on Monday of next week, and go straight to the Bank with our money, and put it in the same day. He said afternoon would be best because he is hoping to deal with some big business accounts in the morning, but he will be free from 3 o'clock onwards."

"That all sounds very satisfactory. Do you really think they are reliable? Can we trust them?"

"I have asked Mr Scroll, the Bank Manger, to call here tomorrow morning – it is only fair that you should meet him. I think you will agree with me that he is just the right man for the job."

At ten thirty next morning Scroll turned up looking a million dollars. He had borrowed a very expensive morning suit from the theatre wardrobe and he came complete with carnation, topper and silver handled walking stick. Mrs Collins was completely taken in and was so flattered by the presence of this exceedingly handsome man, that her usual caution in all matters financial failed to operate. Scroll, it must be admitted, carried off his part in a manner which indicated that he really was a talented actor. When he first appeared Rooney was a bit apprehensive in case his performance went over the top. But though he was dressed as a dandy, his manner was subdued and thoughtful. After fifteen minutes or so he pulled out a very heavy 'gold' pocket watch which was actually a stage prop that didn't go, and announced that he had a meeting with a shipping company and he must be off.

"I look forward to seeing you two good ladies next, (at this point he extracted from his pocket a very expensive looking diary, four years out of date) – Monday – Ah yes, I have it here. Shall we say three o'clock? Good – I'll bid you good day Mrs Rooney and Mrs Collins, and we look forward to a prosperous business relationship."

Mr Scroll made a grand exit and from the front door the two 'good' ladies watched him striding out towards his new premises, every inch a successful business man.

In fact he <u>was</u> going towards his 'new premises': as instructed by Rooney he had rented an office on the main street and was going there to make it look as convincing as possible. The Auction Room had lent him some quite passable furniture on the promise that he would buy extensively from them once he was settled in the town. He told the Auction Room Manager that his Head Office had been a little slow to react when he found the new office and therefore more furniture would not arrive for two weeks. Among the large store of theatre props he had found a sign board, which read CARLTON STEAMSHIP COMPANY. He had painted out the middle word and substituted the word BANKING, it wasn't entirely successful but he thought it would pass muster. So he had done his part. It was now up to Rooney to do the rest.

On the agreed day Mrs Collins and Rooney set out for the Bank. They had their Bank Books with them and they asked for withdrawal forms. This was a perfectly normal procedure but when the clerk on the till saw the amounts involved he was very shocked.

"Are you sure ladies – this would effectively close your account with us?"

"Yes we are sure," came the answer. The clerk slipped off his stool and went to speak to the Bank Manager. Rooney took the opportunity to say to Mrs Collins "Say nothing. He'll want to know why and how etc etc. It is our money and we will bank where we like but say nothing – this is our business." Mrs Collins nodded – she was thinking of the extra £40 per annum in interest.

The Bank Manager came out of his office trying to conceal the panic which he felt. Head Office had to be notified of all major withdrawals and they required detailed explanations.

"Please come this way ladies," he said guiding them into his office.

"Have we in any way fallen short in our handling of your affairs?"

This was a perfectly fair question and he looked from one to another and back again time after time – rather like someone watching a tennis match. The two faces gave no inkling as to the motive.

"Please ladies. Please let me know, have any of my staff been less than courteous?"

At last Mrs Collins said, "We thought we would like a change."

"Yes, that's it," Rooney said. "We thought we would like a change."

The Bank Manager had heard thousands of reasons for unlikely transactions in his forty years in the bank, but this left him speechless and almost apoplectic. His job and his pension might depend on this – Head Office would never accept the explanation.

"Are you moving to another area?" he asked, now desperate to retain the business.

"There is probably a branch of ours in the town you are going to."

"We are not moving out," Rooney said "We don't have to give any more reasons. It is our money and we have decided." She looked at Mrs Collins and gained a firm nod of assent. Mrs Collins' greed had conquered her usual sense of business and totally banished any vestige of caution.

"Is there nothing I can do or say to persuade you two good ladies – ours is the oldest established bank in Scotland – it's reputation goes back over one hundred years."

Rooney was getting bored and edgy. "We'll take the money now in five pound notes and sovereigns, mainly five pound notes. Sovereigns are too heavy for us to carry if there are a lot of them."

"Am I not to receive any explanation for this unusual behaviour?"

"You did not ask for an explanation why we put the money with you, and you'll get none when we take it out."

"I could be a broken man because of this," he stated, looking at the two faces in front of him for traces of sympathy, but he found none, because there was none.

He stumbled out of his office and went to the clerk on the till and instructed him to make the withdrawal in the manner described by Rooney. It came to just over £4,100, it was mainly in five pound notes but there were over 400 sovereigns. These were divided more or less equally into the leather bags the ladies had brought for the purpose. Rooney had thought of everything: there was a cab waiting outside. "45 High Street" she called out as she and Mrs Collins lugged out their precious life savings.

They arrived at the 'Bank' only to find it shut. The man who kept the shop next door came hurrying out and announced, "The Bank Manager told me to tell you that he is very sorry but he received a telegram instructing him to go to a meeting in Glasgow but he will be here tomorrow morning at 10 o'clock prompt."

Rooney quickly turned to the cab driver and said, "Wait for us we'll only be a minute." This gave Mrs Collins time to weigh up the premises – they looked quite convincing as a small branch office of a bank. Rooney continued to talk to the shopkeeper, when she had extracted all she needed to know she said to Mrs Collins, "The shopkeeper says some furniture has arrived and some carpets, and the new manager has been in and out several times."

"Oh well," said Mrs Collins, "We have lost a day's interest, but I shall insist that the transaction be backdated."

"Yes that is a good idea – after all it is not our fault he's not here – come on we'll go home now."

So the two ladies climbed into the cab and were driven home. Once there, the driver stopped, applied the brake, and offered to help with the heavy leather bags.

"What's in here?" he asked, "the Crown Jewels – judging by the weight of it."

"Never you mind – we'll look after them," Mrs Collins said. And the two ladies struggled inside and put the bags on the kitchen table and set about making their tea.

"Where are we going to put the bags for the night?" Mrs Collins asked. "Do you think the cab driver knew what was in them – he did drive us from bank to bank and he did try to carry them in for us."

"Yes that's true. Cab drivers go in Public Houses and if he starts to talk, the wrong sort of person could overhear."

Mrs Collins said, "We will have to think where to hide the bags overnight – in our bedrooms I would think."

"No, not bedrooms – if we are broken into and God forbid – that is just where they will look. I think the food cupboard would be best – no one would look there – so the money will be safe."

The bags were stored in the food cupboard, the vegetable and fruit rack was positioned in front of them, and this Rooney piled up with pan lids.

"If anyone disturbs them, they will fall on the stone floor and wake us up."

"Wouldn't we be better sleeping in the chairs in the kitchen?" Mrs Collins asked.

"No, I don't think there is any need for that, but we will pile up the dining chairs next to the front door to make sure no one gets in."

"And the back door?"

"Before we go to bed – we'll push the kitchen table against it – that should do it."

So full siege arrangements were made – now it was time to feed the garrison, and so Rooney and Mrs Collins began to cut bread and butter and to make tea.

Their usual time for bed was about half past ten, they had completed their security system, and reluctantly they thought about going to their respective bedrooms – they neither liked to put too much distance between themselves and the leather bags. Rooney suggested a nightcap. Mrs Collins since arriving in Scotland had acquired a taste for a 'wee dram' but there had to be a reason which would salve her easily assuaged conscience. Rooney offered one.

"We have both had a worrying day, so a teaspoonful of whisky in our tea would do us both good." Mrs Collins and her conscience were happy with this and Rooney did the preparation: four spoonfuls for Mrs Collins but not for herself.

Mrs Collins applauded the idea after the first sip – "It seems quite potent," she commented.

"Aye it's malt whisky you know, it has the flavour."

Mrs Collins tried again – yes indeed it did have the flavour. They went to bed or at least Mrs Collins did – Rooney closed her door but remained fully dressed. She waited about fifteen minutes, gently she opened her door and carefully trod across the passageway, avoiding any floor board which she knew could creak. The tell tale signs were there: Mrs Collins was well away. But to be on the safe side Rooney slowly went back to her own bedroom and waited another quarter of an hour. Again she listened: Mrs Collins sounded like a bronchitic water buffalo, she was soundly asleep.

Rooney went downstairs on her bottom, and walked towards the front door. She alone had piled up the chairs and she had been careful not to lock or bolt the door – thus reducing the noise when she made her next move.

She carried the chairs to the bottom of the stairs and then went to the food cupboard. She picked up the pan lids one at a time and wrapped each one in a towel and carefully laid them on the table. She then removed the two leather bags – looked inside – just to check that they were indeed still full of money. She walked slowly and steadily to the front door, eased it open and began her four hundred yard walk to the Railway Station. She knew there was a midnight train to Glasgow and she also knew that trains left from Glasgow for Perth, Aberdeen, Dundee, Edinburgh, Carlisle, Bristol, Manchester, Leeds, Birmingham and London.

Rooney arrived at Glasgow Station at about 2am and went to the first class ladies waiting room. She placed the bags of money carefully between her feet. There was a nice fire blazing and she was very comfortable. A porter came in to see if he could be of any help, and Rooney gave him a two shilling piece and said, "I would like a large pot of tea and some buttered toast please, you may keep the change."

The porter thanked Rooney and moved a small table a little closer so it would be handy for the tray of tea. Rooney ate and drank her little nocturnal treat very slowly, she was using it as a means of keeping awake. It was more or less successful, though she did doze off two or three times. Each time as she awoke, she checked that the precious bags were still there and intact. By 6.30 am the station was busy and the office was open. There were ten apertures where tickets were sold. Rooney went to the first one and bought a ticket for Perth – a single – not a return. She then moved to the tenth one and bought a single for Birmingham. Then to the second one for an Edinburgh ticket and to the ninth for Bristol. Using a different window each time she bought in all ten tickets all to different cities all over England and Scotland. She then went to the ladies room and in the privacy afforded by such an amenity she examined the ten tickets, selected one, flushed the other nine away, boarded the train appropriate to the one remaining ticket and was never heard of again.

CHAPTER 5

Muckle Flugga

Mrs Collins awoke next morning at about 8 o'clock. She went downstairs and was confronted with the obstacle of six dining chairs, all on top of each other. The front door was wide open, she threw the chairs into the parlour, rushed into the kitchen. Her worst fears were confirmed, the food cupboard was open and the bags were gone. She got dressed and went to the local Police Station. Dunoon Police Force did not include a detective on its staff, and it took a long time before anyone could be found who could deal with Mrs Collins' case – in those days £4,000 was grand larceny. Slowly the details were taken down, the actor Mr Scroll was repeatedly interviewed but it became increasingly obvious that like Mrs Collins, he was just a pawn in the game. He had actually been promised £100 but he never received it, and he was saddled with the rent on the 'Bank' which made it all doubly hard to bear.

Enquiries were made at Dunoon Railway Station and a lady had bought a ticket for Glasgow. The enquiry then moved to Glasgow's massive railway station and after interviewing all the ticket clerks it was confirmed that a lady had bought at different windows from different clerks at least seven single tickets, which meant she could be in

Aberdeen, Manchester, Leeds, Perth, Bristol, Dundee, Carlisle, in fact anywhere in Britain.

Mrs Collins was penniless. Rooney had picked up the housekeeping money and Mrs Collins purse just before she left the house, so there was no money in the house at all. Mrs Collins wrote to her daughter Clarissa at No 18 Wellington Terrace and two days later Clarissa came up to Dunoon by train to pick up the pieces. Mrs Collins' preferred solution would have been to return to No 18 with Clarissa, but now she was not in control and Clarissa valued the peace and happiness which prevailed in her home and she was not going to jeopardise it. She took Mrs Collins back to the bank where only three or four days previously she had withdrawn her savings and opened a new account in Mrs Collins' name for £100. Clarissa then gave her mother £20 in cash and promised that the £100 would be topped up every year, provided that it was handled prudently.

"But can't we see more of each other – I would love to come and stay with you?"

Clarissa answered gently but firmly, "Yes Mama, of course you may come and stay with me – but let's get all this over with – become used to your new way of life and then we'll see."

"Please promise me that you will never utter a word of this to anyone – it is so undignified to have been duped like this – I couldn't bear it."

"No, I promise I won't say anything to anyone."

With that Clarissa left her mother and began the long journey back to No. 18.

Just as Clarissa was settling down in the corner of a first class carriage and taking out a thick leather wallet full of accounts documents, George on board the 'Bulldog' was entering Leith Docks. Mr Penaluna needed to stop there to restock with fresh water, fruit, vegetables, meat etc and he wanted to travel to Edinburgh to sell his amber to the jewellers of Princes Street.

"Shore leave is in order Mr Baguly, AFTER" and Mr Penaluna emphasised the word after, "After the heavy duty sails are in place, we will change back to the lighter ones when we reach the Mediterranean."

The men hated the heavy duty sails which were stiff and awkward to handle, but the lighter ones would not stand up to what would be required of them for the next 2000 miles. Before he left for Edinburgh Mr Penaluna, as an afterthought, came back on board and spoke to Mr Baguly, "Buy good provisions, and make sure we have enough for four weeks but if you can, be gentle with my purse." And with that he left for his trip to the jewellers of Princes Street.

Mr Baguly was left to deal with the Victuallers. Mr Penaluna said he would be away for two days, this gave the crew some free time to investigate the delights of Edinburgh and Leith, eat too much, get drunk, have a few fights and return to their beloved 'Bulldog', happy, much bruised, probably with a hangover but without any money. Mr Penaluna returned from Princes Street, unlike his crew, a richer man, things had gone well with him and he had learned a lot: amber with a tiny fly inside it was worth more than an unblemished piece. That surprised Mr

Penaluna but he learned quickly and would be on the look out for unfortunate flies who, 10,000 years ago became locked into a globule of resin and would spend the next 10,000 years staring steadily forward, trying to find a way out of their prison.

Mr Baguly kept George with him all the time they were in Leith. He didn't want the bad influence of the crew to reach George, so he kept him busily engaged in checking the food aboard and stowing it safely below. Leith was a busy fishing port, so they were well stocked up with salted cod and kippers as well as some fresh fish for immediate consumption. Mr Baguly was amazed how much George knew about food, so George explained to him how at No 18 he had been for three or four years the unpaid second cook.

At last they were ready to go. Mr Penaluna and Mr Baguly had studied the charts, especially so far as prevailing winds were concerned and they decided to go north so far as the Shetlands before heading west, then keeping well clear of Lewis and Harris, they proposed to come south through the North Channel, into the Irish Sea and then via St George's Channel and head for Côte de Leon, Brest, and call at La Rochelle for supplies before doing battle with the Bay of Biscay. This was a journey of over 2,000 miles, but Mr Penaluna reckoned they could average eight or ten knots this way, he calculated 200 miles per day and thought that even with a poor run of luck he should do it in fourteen or sixteen days. He had told Mr Baguly to provision for four weeks so he was on the safe side.

Mr Penaluna was interested in light houses and he had read that one family – the Stephensons, had built most of the lighthouses around the Scottish coast, including one at North Ronaldsay on the most northerly tip of that storm ridden island. Mr Penaluna had passed it a few times earlier in his career, usually it was engulfed in fifty foot seas, and he was so intrigued that he wanted to take a closer look.

"It's not the quickest way to Italy" Mr Baguly felt it his duty to point out.

"Quite true Mr Baguly, but I think this life is not just about making money, I feel the need to do this trip and do it properly. I know too that the Irish Sea can be treacherous, so we must watch out for Lambay, a small island just north of Dublin."

"Why Lambay Skipper? What's so special about Lambay?"

"Ever heard of the 'Tayleur'?"

"No, can't say I have."

"She was built in the upper reaches of the Mersey near Warrington. She was the largest merchant sailing ship to be built in England and her work was to be as an emigrant ship and to take people to Australia – it was big business in the 1850's. She was two hundred and twenty five feet long, and could carry four thousand tons of cargo, and over six hundred passengers. Ships were made to established designs and the owners had such confidence in the designers and builders of ships that sea trials were unknown at that time."

Mr Baguly punctuated his Captain's dissertation with various expressions of surprise. Little wonder: he was hearing about a ship that was seven or eight times as big as the 'Bulldog'. Suddenly he said "Yes, I think I did hear of her, wasn't there something odd about her rudder?"

"You've got it Mr Baguly – it was said to be of unusual design. Perhaps that was the undoing of her. Anyway she set sail for Australia with seventy- one crew and about five hundred passengers and almost as soon as the tugs had left her off Anglesey there was trouble, she wouldn't answer to the rudder and a storm blew up.

"But fancy setting out for Australia without giving her a good sea trial."

"It's money Mr Baguly, money – that was the reason. First class passengers would have to pay about £50 each for comfort. Second class about £25 and Steerage £15 and don't forget there were 500 passengers. If you run that kind of business you soon have your outlay back in your hand.

"And on the trip home it would be packed with wool I suppose?"

"Exactly, Mr Baguly, so they couldn't lose, unless they decided to be too greedy. The 'Tayleur' was not seaworthy, and she went out of control on to the rocks near Lambay. About four hundred people were drowned, and this is perhaps the worst part of this episode: very few crew members lost their lives."

"So they looked after themselves instead of their passengers?"

"I'm afraid that is so Mr Baguly and it does not reflect well upon people of our calling when that happens."

"We have no faulty rudder on the 'Bulldog' Sir, and I reckon we'll pass by Lambay quite safely."

"Please God it is so – the Irish Sea can be very fierce – we will be there in a few days time – but for now I'll go to Harbour Master and arrange for a tow out – make ready to sail Mr Baguly – we are going to Italy."

The hatches were battened down and checked by Mr Penaluna, who nodded his approval, he could see the heavy sails were in place, ready for the storms. The tug was alongside, and the procedure was followed exactly as before at Copenhagen. Mr Penaluna was a great one for precisely following set routines. Only a short tow was needed as far as Crail, then Humpage became his true self – the helmsman, and the gallant 'Bulldog' set out for 2000 miles of open sea. George stood by the rail and watched the coast of Scotland disappear. He had had a wonderfully gentle initiation in his seafaring life, he had never experienced really heavy seas, but that was about to change.

They were no more than two hours away from Crail when George heard the Skipper say to Mr Baguly, "I think it's beginning to blow Mr Baguly."

"Aye, Skipper, but nothing the 'Bulldog' can't master with a little help from us."

"Fasten up some rope, and be on the safe side."

"Aye, aye Skipper."

Mr Baguly then shouted to four of the men to lay out ropes in strategic places to ensure that as the crew moved from one deck to another they had something to grip onto. Once overboard in these seas and a man was gone for ever.

The 'Bulldog' was running under topsails and foresail only, the mainsail was reefed up but she was still making thirteen knots (Mr Penaluna's maximum). Humpage was constantly working at the wheel to keep on course, wrestling as the pressure on the rudder worked its way back to him and his precious wheel. He always looked forward, never aft, had he glanced he would have seen a wall of water, curling ready to strike, and deposit 100 tons of water onto 'Bulldog's' deck. The ship seemed to stagger from the blow, the water ran off through the scupper holes, she came up again out of a trough only to receive another wave from behind just as threatening as the previous one. Mr Penaluna and Mr Baguly stood on the Poop deck, sacred territory reserved for Skipper and Officers only, both loved this experience, confident that they would win the day. The men were moving about the ship, if not with ease, at least with safety, now that ropes were lashed along and in some cases across, the deck. 'Bulldog' passed Inchkeith lighthouse, then Isle of Moy and finally Bell Rock, all three were within seventy miles of Edinburgh. All three proved how tenacious and enterprising the Stevenson family were. Mr Penaluna looked at the rocks upon which the lighthouses were built and could hardly believe that fifty or more builders could be found who would be prepared to put up with such conditions in order to earn a living. He was overlooking the fact that he and his men were living under very similar privations and most, if not quite all, were enjoying it.

Three days out of Leith and the 'Bulldog' was fighting her way past the Shetlands, the most northerly of the Scottish Islands, and subject to the full might and wrath of the North Sea. Mr Penaluna knew the Stevenson family had built lighthouses (and the same family produced R L Stevenson the novelist, who had in fact trained as an Engineer) all around the Scottish coast. The one called Muckle Flugga was perhaps their greatest feat of engineering: it was on North Unst and it was built at the insistence of the Admiralty who had had schemes to blockade Archangel and Murmansk during the Crimea War but were acutely aware that in 1811 three battleships were lost in this area and two thousand men died. The rock upon which the lighthouse was built is 200 feet high, but the seas are so violent that it is often covered with giant waves. Mr Penaluna wished to see this and was hoping that the seas would do their worst once he was in sight of it. He was not disappointed. He brought out both watches to ensure that enough men, and more than enough, were on deck to wear the ship urgently should circumstances demand it. He put an extra man on the wheel with Humpage and kept two miles away from the rocks. Slowly they made their way around Muckle Flugga, the light shone out bravely, as the lighthouse was shrouded in mist, spray and enormous waves. A constant warning that to be cast upon these rocks was a disaster with no hope of rescue.

George stood at the rail in his waterproof clothes with a good pair of sea boots on. He and everyone else was covered with water, heavy seas were running, and the 'Bulldog' lurched and swayed. George loved every moment of it. He looked across at Humpage and his helper Cartwright, as they grappled with the wilful wheel. Humpage had no hand to spare for a wave to his little friend and a nod had to suffice. George smiled a response, or managed as much of a smile as his ice cold features could muster. Six days before this, he had sent a letter to No 18 and as he stood at the rail and looked out upon this bleak and indeed terrifying scene, his letter was delivered on a warm bright June morning nine hundred miles away, and it was pounced upon by Rose to whom it was addressed.

Rose ran into the kitchen with the letter. Polly and Marie were tidying up. Anne and Caroline came in from the dining room – Clarissa was already at work, so she would not learn of George's latest news until midday.

Leith Docks Near Edinburgh

Dear Rose

We are here because our Captain has started to deal in amber and he is trading it to the jewellers in Edinburgh. I am going to help Mr Baguly to buy the food for our next journey which is to Italy.

"To Italy?" "Imagine that" Anne cried. "George going to Italy!"

"Shush Anne" the others said and Rose carried on with the letter.

.

When we leave Leith we are going north, because Mr Penaluna (Our Captain) is interested in lighthouses and we are going a long way north to look at …….

Here Rose stopped and stared "It can't be called that, surely" she said, and pointed to the words "Muckle Flugga" in George's letter.

"Well never mind" Rose said. "Just carry on with the news."

We have had to stock up with food because we might not find another good port until we reach La Roshell (I think that is how you spell it) on the west coast of France. Mr Penaluna says we might be there in about sixteen days, but he told Mr Baguly to buy food for four weeks – you can't be sure with sailing ships – it depends upon the winds and the currents.

I will write to you as soon as I can but my next letter will be from France. I'll write to you in French, and then in Italian when we reach Taranto – I hope we don't go to China.

I will write as soon as I can. Perhaps you could send a letter to Fothergill and Jones – Our Captain's Agent – they have an office in Southampton Docks.

I do miss home but I love the sea.
George (Midshipman).

The three girls were in danger of tearing the precious letter to pieces, but Caroline came to its rescue and gave it, more or less, intact back to Rose.

"We all have a little job now, and that is to write a letter to George and to find out exactly where the Agent's office is."

Reading George's letter were Polly, Marie and Rose, as well as Caroline, Anne and Thurza. Caroline's letter to No 18 asking for train tickets for three had included a full explanation about Thurza's plight, and Clarissa, ever responsive to the girls' requests had arranged for three tickets to be sent. A week later the three girls arrived at No 18, and though Thurza's arrival initially caused a stir, things soon settled down. Women do not take kindly to having a lady of outstanding beauty wished upon them. It is natural enough: the World is a competitive place and here, suddenly, was someone equipped, even destined to win. Thurza knew she had landed on her feet, this was a nice home, full of pleasant people, there was no debt here, no likelihood of quick exits being arranged to elude creditors, and she was determined to help in any direction to fit in with what she quickly realised was a very busy regime. She saw that Clarissa, head of the house, was the hardest working of them all and Thurza respected this fact.

At twelve noon sharp the ever efficient Clarissa arrived home from work. She was delighted by George's letter, but quickly moved on to what interested her even more – Business. She asked Anne and Caroline to join her in the dining room. Rose and Marie were trying to lay the table for the mid-day meal, but Clarissa had papers spread over a large area of the table.

"Just leave the cutlery on the sideboard and the food, we'll help ourselves." Clarissa said, then she continued hardly stopping for breath, "Look at this opportunity – a milliner's shop has come up for sale in Poole and it is a haberdashery as well." Anne and Caroline looked at each other in disbelief – what were they hearing? Mama continued.

"Two sisters own it now, both ladies in their sixties and local gossip has it that they have a nice fortune each, and all made out of this little business. It is in the terms of the sale that they will stay on (free of charge – mark that – free of charge) to help training the new owners. What do you think of that?"

"Do you want us to work in a shop Mama,?" Caroline said combining indignance with incredulity.

"There is a big difference between owning a shop and merely working in a shop. You will decide what to stock and how best to sell it and within a year or two, if you are successful, you would be financially independent. It is a nice feeling to be made welcome in a bank, I know because I have made our business profitable, and its given each day a special feeling."

"But we don't know anything about shops, or hats or business, we would be lost."

"The two ladies have agreed to stay for as long as three months if necessary to ensure that you do know the business, and if you do not do this – what are you going to do with your lives? You can't just wait about hoping to get married one day. You have to take hold of life and do something with it."

These theories were quite new to Anne and Caroline, indeed they were revolutionary for the time. They had been taught in Switzerland how to be young ladies: how to dance, speak French, draw tolerably well, they were taught about art, but no mention was made as to how to make a living because it was assumed that their living was assured, and they would, in three or four years be married. The two girls knew Clarissa well enough by now to know she was a very determined person, and there was little chance that they would escape from her plan. Clarissa looked at the two girls, and realised she had won the day. She decided she would offer just half the asking price, and with that, she tidied up the papers and set about the mid-day meal, already thinking about having to buy the stock of the little shop, and wondering whether or not to include this in her offer, therefore acquiring the stock for nothing. She was miles away during the meal, Anne and Caroline exchanged meaningful glances, but by the time the meal was over Clarissa's mind was on horses – should she buy two or three more and try to bulk up the haulage side of her business? She had the grace to apologise to the two girls for being so distant, adding, "Business is just so interesting, once you really are involved it's like a drug." As if to prove the point Clarissa forgot to drink her tea or to say 'Good Afternoon', as she left No 18 to go back to her pottery.

The two girls drifted back into the kitchen, their relationship with Polly, Marie and Rose was (almost) that of sisters or at any rate friends, and they all sat round the table with an extra cup of tea, there was much to discuss. George's letter was passed around the table and then Anne and Caroline came on to the subject of the shop. Marie's attitude was guided by the fact that she had, since she was twelve, worked for her living and she thought it was a lovely idea. She was a skilled needle woman, and did all the darning and linen repairs in the house, with such skill as to make the repair invisible. She said, "I would like to work in a shop like that, perhaps I could be taught how to make hats – I'd love that."

Caroline and Anne looked at each other – perhaps this was the way forward: Clarissa had occasionally said that three housemaids were really too many. The idea formed that Marie could work in the shop, say two days each week. Another cup of tea was called for and the six young women, all good friends, and fond of each other began to thrash out exactly how it could be arranged. They did not actually say it in words, but they knew that Clarissa would not take 'no' for an answer, and they would have to make the best of it. So, facing up to the inevitable, within an hour and a few cups of tea it was settled. Caroline and Anne would run the shop, Marie would help, as required, and Polly and Rose, who admitted that they were not over-burdened could manage very well.

Thurza decided, quietly, that she would ask Clarissa if she could be found work in the offices, she had helped her father to send out bills to patients and also she had collated his papers which were concerned with suppliers' invoices, so it would not be completely new to her.

At six o'clock that evening Clarissa arrived home at No 18 and was met by the six young ladies. Caroline outlined the discussion they had had, and Clarissa said, "There. I told you it was all quite simple, we'll go tomorrow and fasten up all the arrangements, and I have decided to buy three more horses. Now what are we having for tea?"

After tea George's letter was passed round again, and Clarissa, who was in top form as an organiser on that particular day, said, "Right, let's get out paper and pens, and we will all write to George." With that she left the kitchen and went into the parlour to write her letter. Once the door was safely shut, Polly said. "I'll bet she tells George she's decided to buy three more horses for the haulage business." The girls laughed about it and with varying degrees of accuracy, tidiness and invention they started their letters to George. The six letters were gathered together, Clarissa read them all, Polly's spelling was appalling, but it didn't matter, it was from the heart, as they all were. They formed a little package and Clarissa promised to have it delivered to Folthergill and Jones via one of her team of delivery men. The letter was addressed to George Eefamy, C/0 Captain Penaluna of the 'Bulldog'. Mr Fothergill sent a note back to Clarissa to say that another agent, who was a friend of his, specialised in business with French coasters, and he thought the letter should arrive in La Rochelle in about ten days time – this would be well ahead of George's estimated time of arrival. Indeed George's progress for two or three days was nil and Mr Penaluna was beginning to wish that he had never heard of the Stephenson family and Muckle Flugga. The 'Bulldog' had battled to come around Unst, the most northerly of the Shetland Islands, but the winds were so changeable that Mr Penaluna could not find a way that was really safe. Some of the time he was actually sailing due south past Fetlar and Yell, trying to pick up a wind which he could use. At last a wind came from the east, and at (for him) high speed, with look-outs posted day and night, be came now to his precious lighthouse, he saw it flicking its light out towards him derisively. He shouted out and raised his fist "I've beaten you – we're round now and going south." Suddenly a west wind filled the sails and warmed the crew. The whole ship became a more cheerful and orderly place to be. The ropes lashed here and there for safety were taken down and stowed. The holystones came out and the slippery decks were cleaned of the dangerous slime. All the brass work was polished up and the crew, more or less on emergency stand-by for the last ten days, resumed their normal 'watch' duties of four hours on four hours off.

CHAPTER 6

George and Longitude

Like most well run sailing ships, the Mate (in this case Mr Baguly) took the port watch, and in theory the Skipper took the starboard, but in fact the Second Mate took the Skipper's turn and this was the usual case. If there was a Third Mate, he kept part of the Mate's watch. So the hierarchy of the ship ran; the Skipper, the Mate (who in naval terms was the First Lieutenant), the Second Mate and the Third Mate. These were all men capable of commanding a ship, and they were gaining experience which would be marked on their 'ticket' and in time they would be promoted.

In addition to George on the ship, there were two other boys: Oliver who was fourteen and Matthew who was sixteen, they were the three Midshipmen who were being trained up by the Skipper and Mr Baguly – they had regular sessions of trigonometry and navigation.

The rest of the crew were Able-seamen, who were on the way to being Mates, and Ordinary seamen who were really labourers with no ambition outside of doing a job, getting paid and, if possible, drunk. Then there was the ship's carpenter who was responsible to the Captain, he usually spent his time making wooden furniture for the Captain's cabin and indeed for his home, he also made wooden toys, some of which he would try to sell at the ports they called at. But his real job was to repair the masts and spars if they were broken in a storm. If the ship was holed for any reason he would make good the damage, in some cases temporarily, with baulks of timber and thick canvas – anything to keep the sea out of the hold and away from the precious cargo. Soft woods were used for repairs so they would swell and tighten.

The Sailmaker repaired sails which were torn in storms or because of fair wear and tear. He would overhaul the second set, whilst the first was being used, because he knew he was going to face the rigours of the North Sea, the Irish Sea and the Bay of Biscay. The lighter set would be carefully examined by 'Sails' as he was usually known, and they would be patched and repaired, ready to be changed over at La Rochelle, on the assumption that the lighter weight sails would be adequate for the journey across the Mediterranean.

George's pay was £6 per year, Oliver and Mathew received slightly more because of their seniority, an Ordinary seaman about £2 per month, an Able seaman £3 or £3.10 shillings. The Mates about £5 a month, and the First Mate about £10 per month. If the men were married, arrangements would be made with the Agent, in Mr Penaluna's case this was Fothergill and Jones, and every two weeks, when their husbands were away at sea, the wives would call at the office and pick up two week's pay. In the case of the unmarried members of the crew, should the sailor agree to it, a relation would call for an agreed amount of money. Otherwise single men could after an unusually long trip, come back to eighteen months pay, to the delight of the local harlots and innkeepers.

George was picking up all this information as he gradually learned his trade and became a member of the crew. He also became used to the food. The ship's cook was good, and because Mr Penaluna was not as mean as some Skippers, fresh food was bought if possible. It was coffee and some kind of porridge for breakfast, about mid-day it was meat, usually pork, potatoes and if the fresh vegetables were still available, cabbage or carrots. Some tinned vegetables were used also, mainly in soups and stews. For most of the crew it was at least as good as they would ever get at home. Mr Penaluna was used to better, and the cook saw to it that he was specially treated: bacon and eggs was a strong possibility three or four times a week. They had two dozen chickens cooped up on board, also two sheep, and a goat, the latter, because Mr Penaluna liked milk in his tea and coffee. The sheep were kept in case the meat ran out on a long trip. The cook and the Bos'un saw to the slaughtering, and the whole crew (seventeen) would benefit for a day or two after the sheep was killed. One of George's daily jobs was to feed and 'muck out' the chickens and the animal pens. He also collected up the eggs – chickens do respond to conditions, and would display their indignation by not laying if the seas were too rough, but usually they managed ten or a dozen eggs each day, and if the stock of surplus eggs built up they would be used in the duff. Duff was always a vital part of the sailor's diet, and it had been so since Nelson's time, a hundred years before. Duff was a pudding boiled in a cloth and all sea-going cooks were judged by their duff.

One morning George took the mornings collection of eggs into the galley. Cook had a fiery temper and George had chosen the wrong day to be familiar.

"Get out of here" Cook shouted. "There isn't room for one, never mind two." Cook was right about there not being much room: he was expected to cater for the ship's crew in a galley barely six foot cubed. He was especially short tempered this particular morning because he had arrived in his galley expecting to see the fire lit in his stove, but it wasn't. Nor was any kindling laid handy for him. Usually one of the Ordinary seamen would cut firewood and get the fire going nicely in the stove, so the Cook would not have to rise at 4.30 am to ensure that the galley was fully active by 5.00 am, but yesterday's main meal was a failure: greasy pork, half cooked and hard peas of a peculiar colour. The crew had objected but the cook could find no fault with it, and a brief exchange of expletives had ensued. Usually if the food was good and the duff acceptable, Cook could confidently expect his galley to be fired up by the time he arrived. Not so this morning, hence his rebuff of George's jocular greeting.

"If you are short of wood, I'll cut some for you and bring it up," George volunteered.

"Makes no difference what you do now, the Skipper's breakfast will be late and I'll get it in the neck."

"I'll take his breakfast to him if you like – he doesn't usually shout at me, and I'll explain why it's a bit late."

"Go on then you take it, and I'll make you an egg sandwich as a thank you."

George was happy with that, a fried egg sandwich was indeed a treat.

George delivered the Skipper's breakfast, Mr Penaluna looked surprised, but he was so delighted at the prospect of muscling in on three fried eggs and four rashers of bacon, that he forgot to ask why it was late. George went back to the galley to claim his reward: Cook had fried the bread (actually slices of yesterday's duff) and slapped two fried eggs between the thick slices – a feast indeed. George carried his treasure up on to deck – the smell of it wafted about and Oliver came to find out the source of this glorious scent. George offered it to him, whilst retaining a firm grasp. "Take a bite – not too big though." Oliver bit as much as was decent and at the same time filling.

"Who gave you that?" Oliver asked.

"Cook – I helped him – so I got this."

"What are you two doing?" the Bos'un shouted.

"Just finishing this off – then I'll be with you Sir." George replied. Bos'un on board ship was a kind of General Foreman.

"Do you know what all these ropes is called?" Bos'un asked – collaring George and Oliver, and indicating the scores of ropes which ascended from the deck to the sails and to the tops of the three masts.

"Some of them we know," Oliver said.

"Some of 'em – some of 'em is no good – if Mr Baguly shouts, "haul in the clew garnets – which would you go for?"

"This one," said Oliver grabbing hold of a rope.

"And the port mizzen royal clewline?" Bos'un asked. A blank expression occupied both faces

"Now you's in trouble, 'cos if you don't know you're no use to nobody." Bos'un surveyed his two pupils. "Right we'll go round the ship and look at all the ropes and you'll see just why and how they gets their names and I'll expect you to remember 'em all in a week."

There are over two hundred ropes on a sailing ship and they all have a name. The passage down from Unst was calm and the weather fair, so the two boys had spare time to go around the ship and to climb up aloft to find out exactly what each rope was called and why. Every rope had a precise purpose, and by following the rope, by eye or by actually climbing from the deck to where the rope was fastened aloft, the logic of the naming system dawned on the two apprentices.

They spent a beautiful Sunday morning gathering information and enjoying the fine weather, they were making rapid progress southwards, well to the West of the Shetland Islands. The Skipper then plotted to make for the North Channel between Rathlin Island and the Mull of Kintyre, passing Stranraer and keeping to the west of the Isle of Man. They were making good time, the favourable west wind coming at an angle to the 'Bulldog' suited her best, her lee rails were under water as she made a steady ten knots, at this rate over two hundred miles per day. The Mate decided to check the speed and roared, "Heave the log". The Third Mate, Collins, took the fourteen second glass out of the companion and went aft with it. Humpage, who for once was not at the wheel, took the log reel off its hook and another Able seaman stood by for hauling in. The log reel consisted of about four hundred feet of quarter inch rope and at the end of it was a conical canvas bag, with a peg attached to keep it open at the wide end. The bag was held with the mouth open so that when it was thrown overboard the sea rushed into it and carried it away at the same speed at which the ship was travelling. A piece of white cloth was tied to the line forty feet from the bag, when this was pulled overboard it told the crew that the bag was well clear of the eddy under the stern of the ship.

At twenty four feet from the white piece of cloth, some fishing line with one knot in it is tied to the line. At the same distance again another piece of fishing line with two knots is tied on, and so on up to fifteen knots. So all was ready for the exact calculation of 'Bulldog's' speed. At the moment the bag hit the sea, the line sped out and in two seconds the white rag flew over the rail. "Turn" snapped Mr Baguly. "Turn" replied Humpage as he inverted the fourteen second glass. Mr Baguly counted the knots as they disappeared over the rail. "Stop" yelled Humpage as the glass ran out. Mr Baguly roared "Thirteen knots." The Able seaman jerked the line, this reversed the cone and it was hauled in.

"That is fast enough for anybody," Mr Penaluna said. He had been standing nearby watching this exhibition of a seaman's craft. He spotted George and Oliver who had also been watching. "Did you follow the mathematics of that?" he asked his two apprentices. George looked at Oliver, hoping for inspiration – he found none. "No Sir" they both confessed.

Mr Penaluna began his lecture.

"The log-line works like this: twenty three and a half feet (twenty four allowing for wet shrinkage) bears the same proportion to a sea mile (6,080 feet) as the fourteen seconds in the sand glass bear to one hour. So the number of knots on the log line that run out during the fourteen second equals the number of nautical miles the ship does in one hour."

"Did you follow that?" Mr Penaluna asked. George and Oliver nodded. He continued,

"Knots are therefore just the speed, it is not a measure of distance. So to say thirteen knots an hour is wrong and to say two hundred and fifty knots in a day is even more incorrect." Miles at sea are nautical or geographical miles – six thousand and eighty feet and not statute miles which are five thousand two hundred and eighty feet. This is arrived at by taking one minute of longitude along the Equator and this is six thousand and eighty feet – in British practice – there are German, Scottish and even worse, Irish interpretations of how to measure a mile, but we will keep to the British one. "Mr Baguly" he shouted, signalling to the Mate to come closer. "We must spend more time on navigation and mathematics with these two, they know nothing."

"Aye Aye Sir" came the answer, and Mr Baguly smiled benignly at his future pupils.

George's watch was due to end and with all those figures rattling around in his head, he was ready for his bunk. He and Oliver shared a tiny cabin, because he was the younger of the two he had the lower bunk. He dropped into his bed, he thought briefly about No 18, his Mum, Rose, Polly and Marie, one or two tears escaped from his far from manly tear ducts, and he was fast asleep for three and three quarter hours – the longest stretch he was likely to have for some weeks to come. It could be fewer than three and three quarters, but it was highly unlikely that it would ever be more. The watch system did not allow it.

Sunday came and to George's surprise the Mate, Mr Baguly, shouted at him and said "Get tidied up, and your best clothes on, you and Oliver is 'avin dinner with the Skipper and me and it's mutton today."

George was intending to ask why there was only one of the two sheep in the pen. He had noticed it when he was 'mucking' them out. Now he knew. George went in search of Oliver and told him the good news. Mr Penaluna did provide his Midshipmen with smart Sunday best consisting of white trousers, a blue jacket, white shirt, a kind of floppy bow-tie, and canvas shoes. The two boys went back to their cabin, used some of their precious water allowance for a thorough wash and presented themselves on deck in their full regalia. It was Sunday and a calm breezy day so most of the crew were on deck. "Oh my!" shouted Humpage. "Look at these two little chickens." The crew gathered round and would have scragged the two boys given half a chance, but Mr Baguly came along, "Come on lads, be gentle to 'em, the Skipper wants to see 'em nice and tidy." There was no real harm in the crew but there was certainly a lot of mischief, and perhaps just a little envy: they might well have some sort of mutton stew for dinner, but they could smell the roasted legs which the two boys were going to have.

The Skipper's cabin was a grand affair, panelled in mahogany, with a white ceiling, picked out with gold, upholstered settees in green, and revolving chairs. A big sideboard and a bookcase on one side, and a desk where Mr Penaluna did his reckoning. The mizzen mast ran through the cabin, and this was surrounded by a rack filled with muskets. There was a tiny fireplace for cold evenings, and most welcome of all to the boys, a good sized table. The table was drilled at regular intervals so fiddles or galleries could be inserted to keep the plates from sliding about as the ship rolled, but the ship was fairly steady this particular day so the Steward had wet the damask cloth before he laid it on the table and the dampness of the cloth would keep the plates in place.

The Steward too had dressed for the occasion, he wore a smart blue jacket with epaulettes and fancy buttons. Mr Baguly was squeezed into a very tight fitting suit thirty years out of date and Mr Penaluna wore his favourite plum coloured full length coat. The dishes were presented at the table with a flourish and the silver domes were removed one by one by the Steward almost as if he were a magician. The aroma whetted the appetites, and Mr Penaluna began to cut at the whole leg of mutton. As the plates were loaded they were passed around, somewhat gingerly as they were very hot, but also with reluctance in case the one passed on was better filled than the one arriving. Finally all the carving was done. Mr Penaluna laid down the knife and signalled towards the roast potatoes, the carrots and onions to indicate that everyone should help themselves, he surveyed the situation with benevolence as the boys loaded up their plates.

"Salt or pepper?" Mr Penaluna asked his guests.

Mr Baguly offered the opinion that there was no room on George's plate for either. George looked up apologetically wondering if he had taken too much, but was reassured by the smiles he saw on his superiors' faces. The Steward brought in bottles of beer and ginger pop for the boys, and then stood back like a butler in a stately home awaiting instructions.

Mr Penaluna waved him out, and said, "Come back in half an hour." He knew this would give the Steward enough time to eat his own dinner.

So the battle began, would the boys be able to finish? Yes they would, and their plates were eagerly proffered when Mr Penaluna posed the question, "A little more meat?" George's and Oliver's plates shot forward, and more meat was cut, more potatoes and vegetables were made welcome, gravy too and the second helping seemed to be tackled with undiminished enthusiasm.

"Don't forget there's plum duff and custard to follow – leave room for that," Mr Penaluna said as he watched his table being emptied of all that was edible. The boys nodded and their grin told Mr Penaluna that he need have no fear that the pudding would be neglected. The conversation was led by Mr Penaluna and Mr Baguly, it was mainly light hearted, and added to the occasion. George and Oliver spoke only when directly spoken to but they both enjoyed the atmosphere as well as the food.

There were nuts and apples on the table and the tradition was that the two boys would be expected to steal as much as possible of these treats, to give to those who had not been invited to Sunday dinner. Opportunities arose as Mr Penaluna looked around the cabin for his pipe or when Mr Baguly's napkin fell on the floor. One way or another Oliver and George contrived not to disappoint those awaiting the little extras, and once the meal was over, they quickly changed into their working clothes. Sunday was like any other day: the 'Bulldog' needed her crew, and the masts were due for painting and by three o'clock they boys were hard at it sixty feet above the deck.

They proceeded south, and to the west of the Isle of Man. At the appropriate point Mr Baguly regaled the crew with the gory details of the 'Tayleur' and the disaster at Lambay, and made the point about lookouts being fully awake to their responsibilities. The 'Bulldog' was still making good time. The Irish Sea was kind to them, and though they had a lot of rain, it was warm and the wind was from the west, they were making two hundred miles a day. Mr Penaluna decided on a course to the west of the Isles of Scilly. This brought him well out into the Atlantic and into waters where whales were usually to be seen – they were not disappointed. Whales do seem to respond to fine warm weather, and the crew assembled on one side of the ship as they passed by eight whales all apparently taking the sun, and blowing spouts in the air to celebrate the glorious climate. Some displayed the huge flipper as they descended. Six members of the crew had worked on whaling sips, but none regretted leaving that industry, indeed they assured their mates that it was a ghastly business and not nearly so well paid as the adverts tried to make you believe.

The 'Bulldog' arrived at La Rochelle on a fine day, in glorious sunshine, they had made the trip from Leith in twenty-five days, so it was now July, the weather was hot and any ideas the men had about a few lazy days in port were dispelled by Mr Baguly's instructions to change all sails. This was a massive job: George hadn't seen this done before, but he played his part, showing willing and did as he was told. The first part of the procedure was to take all the lighter weight sails out of the compartment where 'Sails' had stowed them. 'Sails' himself supervised this, and checked that all the lighter sails were in good order. One or two needed slight attention and these were laid to one side. The crew was divided into three teams – one to each mast, George and Oliver were on the main mast team, and the idea was to take down the most lofty sail – the top gallant and safely deliver it to 'Sails'. He would have the lighter t'gallant ready and the exchange would be made. 'Sails' was a handy man with a needle and he had embroidered on each sail in coloured yarn the mast and the sail position, so all the main mast sails had a green sign and in the case of the t'gallant the letters 'T.G' were used. Mr Baguly was nominally in charge of the whole operation, but in fact he left it to 'Sails' who did not need overall supervision and would have resented it.

The three teams vied with each other to see who could be first to effect a change. 'Sails' would not be hurried. "Don't rush me or you'll have the main sail right up the top and the fore and aft – I don't know where." So the race faltered at the first fence – 'Sails' would have none of it. "We'll have it done all ship shape and Bristol fashion" was how 'Sails' described it and the Skipper agreed. He had been watching and approving and said to the men, "Take note of what 'Sails' says, and all will be well." He then addressed Mr Baguly, "I'm going ashore now to find an Agent who has connection with mine, and I'll enquire about victualling the ship – keep 'em at it," he added, indicating the sails, "I may sleep ashore – but I'll be back tomorrow morning at the latest." Mr Penaluna went down the planks in his smartest clothes in spite of the heat he wore his plum coloured coat and his 'Lord Nelson' hat. When he was out of earshot, one of the men said, "It's alright for him, he's gone after a bit of fluff, and we're here changing sails." Mr Baguly heard the remarks and said, "Well if you owned the ship yourself what would you do?" The man did not choose to continue the argument. Mr Baguly was not one to be argued with. He knew his place, and as First Mate he had a good job, but it was a long way from being a ship owner.

Two hours later, and Mr Penaluna was back with a packet of letters. One for Humpage, one from Mr Baguly's unmarried sister, one each for Oliver and Matthew the other two ship's boys and a small package for George. The letters had been forwarded by Mr Penaluna's Agents Fothergill and Jones and though there was no money to be made out of the system of forwarding mail, it was kept going for many years and was greatly appreciated by those lucky enough to be on the receiving end. Some members of the crew gathered round unashamedly to watch George open his packet: six letters came out. One of the Able seamen reached forward to grab one. "Let me read this one," he asked pathetically – never having received a letter in his life. Humpage stopped him and said, "Come on Bill – it's the kid's first contact with home – leave him alone."

George went to his cabin and opened the letters one by one, they were from Polly, Marie, Rose, a combined one from Ann and Caroline and finally from Clarissa. The first three, although separate, could have been carbon copies. The three girls were not used to writing letters but they managed to engender in George a real longing for No 18 by their simple and direct message of affection. Caroline and Ann's letter told him of their return from Switzerland and how they were now the owners of a little shop in Poole where they sold hats, ribbons, lace and haberdashery. Clarissa's letter contained a £5 note! Something George had never seen before, and a long letter asking him to come home and pleading to be forgiven for allowing him to be so badly treated. George had made so complete a recovery, both physically and mentally that he never gave the two beatings a thought. He was enjoying his life at sea and bore no ill will towards anyone – he never even thought about Mrs Collins or Rooney. Clarissa offered George the chance of private tuition with a view to gaining a place at a University or to buy him a commission in the Army or to make him a full partner in what was originally his father's company. None of this meant anything to George, he had made his choice and by sheer good fortune it was perfect for him – he loved the sea and he had fallen on his feet as far as the 'Bulldog' was concerned. He read the letters again very carefully, crept on to his bunk and clutching his letters cried himself to sleep. He was after all only fourteen, and many a man would have done the same.

Oliver came into the cabin a little later and saw the crumpled paper in George's hand and one piece of paper on the floor. The letters were in George's grasp but the £5 note had fallen on to the floor. Oliver picked it up and let out a low whistle. Roughly speaking it was a year's wages for him. He tucked it under George's pillow and went on deck, he told other members of the crew what he had seen, Mr Baguly wanted to know what all the talking was about – he quickly summed up the situation and said, "Carry on getting these sails swopped over – I'll deal with this." And he went off to tell Mr Penaluna of George's good fortune.

"You did right to speak of it Mr Baguly," was Mr Penaluna's response. "I think our crew are a good lot, but £5 is a very tempting sum – tell him to bring it to me and I'll look after it for him." Mr Baguly went in search of George, but he was not with his usual 'watch' where he should have been. He asked Oliver who said, "He wasn't feeling so well so I changed with him – I'm doing his watch – is that alright Sir?" Mr Baguly knew a lie when he heard it, but guessed it was for the best of reasons, and so he accepted it. "Tell him I want to see him as soon as he is feeling up to it."

"Yes Sir I will" Oliver replied.

An hour or so later George woke up and realised that he should have been working with 'Sails' on deck, he put his letter into his box, did not notice the £5 was not among them, and scrambled up into the fresh air as quickly as he could. Oliver grabbed him and said "You're alright I covered for you." George smiled his gratitude and together they began work again stowing the sails which had been brought down from aloft. Once the heavy sails were all neatly stowed away, and the light ones all in place the men came together on deck and began to entertain themselves; two could play penny whistles tolerably well and one very old member of the crew, he was over fifty, and that was very old for an active sailor, he played the fiddle, with some dexterity. They all had the natural facility to play in key as well as in tune and dancing began, some 'ladies' were enticed aboard, somehow the men had managed to obtain a good supply of wine and rough cider. No one on board apart from the Skipper spoke any French but everyone seemed to be able to communicate and the dancing, drinking and kissing went on for two or three hours.

George and Oliver were sent below by Mr Baguly as some of the behaviour became raucous and wanton. The two boys were tired and ready for sleep, and not really old enough to understand what was going on. The Skipper kept to his cabin and did his reckoning. Mr Baguly had an early night, and everyone else danced, drank and romanced the night away. At 6 o'clock next morning Mr Baguly went around all the likely spots and kicked the sleeping couples, many of the 'ladies' were naked. He threw their clothes at them and using a large yard brush, gradually rid the ship of females and got the men to their feet.

Cook had been primed by Mr Baguly and he had a good supply of hot strong coffee ready to dish out to the crew. Mr Baguly advised those who felt well enough to go overboard for a swim. The ones who didn't feel quite up to it, he had the Bo'sun turn the pump on them to liven them up. By seven o'clock the crew was assembled, George and Oliver too, and the Skipper came to address the men.

"The victuals are ready to be brought on board," he said. "So I want eight men to come with me – pick me eight sober ones please Mr Baguly and then we will begin the day's work. The tone of this little speech indicated that the previous day's events were well and truly over and progress was now uppermost in Mr Penaluna's mind.

In addition to the food, Mr Penaluna had bought five hundred cases of red wine. He supervised the stowing of this himself because the weight was considerable and the outlay enormous. He had deliberately bought high quality claret, his thinking was that the costly timber he was carrying was intended for a firm who specialised in expensive ecclesiastical furniture – they would be used to the best and therefore he had taken a gamble that they would like and be prepared to buy good wine. This was how many Skippers made (or lost) their fortunes, if they were good entrepreneurs then there were good profits to be made.

Once he was happy that his wine was safe and his fresh food was aboard, Mr Penaluna went to the Harbour Master's office to arrange for a tow out. He was soon back.

"Half an hour" he shouted to Mr Baguly. "Make ready to sail in half an hour."

Some of the ladies had sobered up and were eager to come aboard again, and indeed they would have been made welcome by many of the crew but Mr Baguly would have none of it. "Be off with you, bunch of whores," he shouted to La Rochelle's beauties, they replied in similarly cultivated terms, but none got past him, and the half hour was soon over. A decidedly ancient wood-burning tug came alongside and the hawser was made fast. Two or three of 'Sails' light weight sails were ready to be loosened, Oliver and George were sixty feet up the main mast awaiting instruction, and they left La Rochelle in glorious sunshine. Some of the ladies were waving to their gallant lovers, but the men were under the watchful eye of Mr Baguly and the Bo'sun, so they were too busy to pay much attention to the farewells. A few miles out to sea and the little wood-burner cast off the hawser. The royals and t'gallants were ready to meet the challenge, Humpage was at the wheel and the west wind filled the sails with a crack, the 'Bulldog' went over, lee rails under water – the sea all over the decks and screaming through the scuppers.

"She's away" Humpage yelled.

"Ten knots already I'll be bound Skipper" Mr Baguly said.

Mr Penaluna looked about him, thought for a minute and said, "Nine – Mr Baguly, nine – not more." He looked up at the sails, put his hands behind his back – appearing to have his feet glued to the poop deck. He stood there in his plum coloured coat and his Lord Nelson hat, pride of ownership exuding from every pore. He knew they were waiting for his next word, but he kept them waiting. He looked over the side again and repeated, "Nine I think, Mr Baguly, just nine." He considered again for a moment and then said to Mr Baguly, almost as an afterthought, "Main sail – when you are ready please, Mr Baguly."

Mr Baguly roared the order and the main sail was carefully and gradually unreefed. The wind was going at a fair lick, so it was best to expose it to the wind slowly lest it ripped top to bottom and took half a dozen men with it. Once filled the main sail did its work. George was still sixty feet up the mast as she heeled over, cutting through the sea like a knife. The decks were under a foot of water, the jib and figurehead were in the sea as much as they were out of it. George looked at Oliver who, like him, was clinging to the rigging sixty feet up. George pointed to the top, Oliver nodded and they both scrambled to the very top, one hundred feet above the deck. It never occurred to them that a fall would almost certainly have been fatal. At that height with the ship rolling, the mastheads sweep across at great speed, and the likelihood of being catapulted into the sea, or worse still crashing on to the deck, is very pronounced unless you behave sensibly and take a good two handed grip. The two boys took off their caps and waved to the men on deck. Unfortunately one of them was Mr Baguly, he reckoned nothing of such sky-larking and roared at them to come down. Once on deck he brought out the holy stones (so called because they are the shape and size of a Bible).

"Scrub the decks, and make a good job of it," he said quietly but menacingly to the two culprits. This was a big job, the holy stones are heavy and take a lot of pushing, but gradually the slime was removed, and as Mr Baguly went off watch, other members of the crew joined in to finish off the work.

CHAPTER 7

Blue Sailing

Two days out of La Rochelle all was going well, the sea was gentle, the wind firm but steady. Mr Penaluna was going to disturb all this – he sent for Mr Baguly and told him he wanted the muskets taken on the deck and cleaned.

"Are you expecting trouble Sir?" Mr Baguly asked.

"No not exactly but if it comes I shall be ready for it – Morocco and Algeria will be just to the south of us for the next two weeks and their idea of how ships should behave is how Drake and Raleigh behaved four hundred years ago. Lay out some old tarpaulins on the deck and we'll oil the guns and make sure they are ready."

Mr Penaluna had two huge revolvers he had bought on one of his trips to America, and about twelve muskets, they were ex Crimean War specimens but well made and accurate. He showed the men how to clean the guns with oil and rag and emery papers. He then went through the drill of loading them, especially making sure George, Oliver and Matthew were adept at rodding out and reloading. He ordered an empty barrel to be thrown overboard for target practice, and told the men to fire at it, one or two scored a hit, but as they became more used to the kick, they began to enjoy it. Mr Penaluna told the boys that Nelson regarded one and a half minutes as adequate loading time for a cannon, so he expected better than that. He watched carefully who were the best shots and picked six men out and got them used to the idea of shooting and handing the used musket back for reloading, accepting a loaded weapon, taking aim, firing and so on. The three boys and three of the seamen were the loaders, all the others would be armed with twelve foot poles, suitably sharpened at the business end. Mr Penaluna went through the target practice routine on two more quiet sleepy afternoons and was happy that, should the need arise, his men could deal with unwelcome intruders.

The 'Bulldog' passed Gibraltar with the sun at its most fierce. Mr Baguly had the pumps going twice a day to moisten the decks – if they are too wet they become slimy and if too dry they crack or shrink. The wind was coming over from Africa and depositing sand on the deck, and bringing with it a distinctive odour from that great continent. The wind was gentle and coaxing with all sails out the 'Bulldog' was barely managing five knots. At this rate they had many days of leisurely sailing ahead of them, and there was not much to do. All jobs done and two hours of watch ahead of him, George crept out to the end of the jib; it protruded forty feet out in front of the ship and offered two or three safe resting places, also carried below the jib were of nets, placed there in case of anyone falling whilst attending to the jib sails, so even if George fell asleep he would tumble into a safety net.

George's vantage point was the kind which few could ever enjoy: he was looking back at a fully rigged ship, one hundred feet tall, with all the sails filled and pushing 'Bulldog' gently forward. The sea was the magical blue of the Mediterranean, creamy white spray was caressing the bows of the ship, and it was almost as if he were not on the ship at all, but a distant spectator and admiring its beauty. He thought about the letters he had received a few days before, of Clarissa's offers and entreaties for him to return to No 18, but he knew that this was the life for him, he would be a seafaring man all his life – he knew it.

Two days beyond Gibraltar and they had made barely one hundred and fifty miles, visibility was perfect, the wind was with them and some afternoons were spent sleeping – the four hours on and four hours off do not apply when there is so little to do, some men brought their mattresses on deck, found a shady spot and made up for some of the sleep that the watch on watch system denies them. Oliver spent his time right at the top of the main mast one hundred feet up, giving him a horizon many miles wider than for those on deck.

"Sail way," Oliver cried.

"Where sail?" replied Mr Baguly.

"Starboard" was as near as Oliver could describe it. Mr Baguly hauled his fifteen stone up the mast.

"Well spotted lad it's a xebec, faster than us and usually up to no good."

Mr Baguly and Oliver descended and found Mr Penaluna at his reckoning. He came on deck quickly and to the crews' astonishment was as quick up the rigging as any apprentice. He balanced carefully and trained his telescope on the approaching three master.

"She rigged with three lateens," he said, "and there's about six oars each side – she's coming after us – muskets Mr Baguly – muskets."

The xebec took about two hours to come really close. She came to about thirty yards distant when somewhat clumsily the three lateen sails were furled. The oarsmen kept her steady, and Mr Penaluna reckoned about forty men were on board. Their captain pointed to 'Bulldog's' flag and shouted, "English?"

"Yes English" replied Mr Penaluna and continued, "Do you need help or water or food?"

"No we need gold – you are in our waters and we always ask that you pay."

"We do not pay," said Mr Penaluna and gave a sign prearranged - all the studding sails he could muster were unfurled and 'Bulldog' responded with an extra knot immediately, building up to two, so she was doing seven knots as the captain of the xebec roared to his men to release the three lateens and get back to the oars. They were more pirates than sailors, and by the time they were underway 'Bulldog' had made two or three miles.

But the pursuer was the faster ship and an hour or so later the xebec was only one hundred yards distant from the stern of the 'Bulldog'. Mr Penaluna put his six marksmen on bales of straw, with the loaders in attendance, and issued spread shot. He also lined up his huge revolvers and said, "We are going to wait until they are fifty yards away and then, when I give the order aim at the foresail – if we can hole it enough, she'll lose way and we will escape. If that does not work we'll aim at their men, but I do not want to do that unless I have to – so when I shout "Foresail", all fire together, and you – the loaders – look lively, we have to get this right."

"Don't forget," Mr Baguly reminded the loaders – "load with spread shot until the Skipper says otherwise."

'Bulldog' was not one to give in easily and she fought for the last one hundred yards but slowly the xebec gained and at fifty yards Mr Penaluna shouted, "Foresail". Six shots rang out and hits were scored, the oars stopped, or at any rate lost their rhythm, the loaders did their work.

The xebec's captain regained control of his oarsmen and on she came – the foresail still intact – a huge blunderbuss was fired and a hail of scrap iron and rusty nails went into Mr Penaluna's saloon. Another volley was fired by the six musketeers, but no tears appeared, the xebec's sails must have been of fine leather rather than cloth, and they did not tear easily.

"Again and quickly," cried Mr Penaluna.

Volley after volley hit the sail and at last a hole four feet square was blasted through, a cheer went up from seventeen throats on the 'Bulldog'. The pirates lost way for a minute but then began to gain again, Mr Penaluna noticed fewer of the fiery faces were looking forward, the xebec's captain had put more men on the oars and they were closing fast.

"Aim for the rigging and we'll trust to luck," Mr Penaluna said.

By now the muskets were hot and difficult to handle. 'Sails' gave out rags to the loaders to help them, but it slowed up the procedure, and the xebec was almost alongside. Mr Penaluna could see the man who was handling the rudder, he laid one of his revolvers on the rail and taking careful aim, hit him in the shoulder, he overbalanced as the massive bullet went right through him. He fell into the sea and for a few seconds the xebec was out of control. Again 'Bulldog' drew away, the muskets were cooled with sea water, and the position was assessed by both sides. The captain of the xebec paid no attention to his helmsman – he was expendable – this message was not lost on the men aboard the 'Bulldog' – they were dealing with someone who did not turn back for an important member of his own crew, so there would be no mercy if he took their ship. The xebec came alongside again, this time about ten of their men threw grappling hooks on to the side of the 'Bulldog' and began to acrobat their way across, but the carpenter was there with an axe and he severed the ropes, sparing a second as he did so, to look at the terrible damage he was doing to the ship's rail. The pirates who ended up in the sea had to make their own arrangements, no one offered a hand and if they could not make it back on board by the rope they had hoped to board the Bulldog with, then they were left behind to drown.

"If we can keep this up for another fifteen minutes we've got 'em beat," Mr Penaluna said to his crew.

"How do you reckon that up Sir?" Cook asked.

"Because we are not rowing to keep up our speed and they are." The crew mumbled their acceptance of this logic.

"English – I want to speak with you," the pirate captain shouted.

"Don't get near the side Skipper," Mr Baguly shouted. "He'll have you with the blunderbuss."

"Thank you Mr Baguly – I am indebted to you – fix a hat on a broom handle and suddenly wave it" he said to Humpage. It had the anticipated effect, the hat was carried away, Mr Penaluna then stepped forward and shot the xebec captain dead. A groan came up from the smaller ship, no captain, no helmsman, shipmates lost – this was a bad day's work. A vicious looking member of the crew stepped forward and assumed command. He displayed his newly acquired authority by tipping the captain overboard without really ascertaining whether he was dead or not. He then addressed the crew, sword in hand, the words were in Arabic but left little opportunity for doubt. Mr Penaluna was tempted to shoot him as well, but Mr Baguly put a restraining hand on his shoulder and said, "Enough is enough Skipper."

"You are quite right Mr Baguly – I think we have them beat."

The new captain on the xebec shook his sword at the 'Bulldog', but that was all the belligerence he was capable of, and they turned away. He would have to prove at the next encounter that he could lead his crew to success or his reign would be short.

Mr Penaluna congratulated all his men, made sure no one was injured, took a rueful look in his saloon at the scrap iron and rusty nails lying everywhere, and the broken glass, he then announced that a double ration of rum would be issued all round, the boys received ginger pop. Then he added, "Double watch and no lights tonight Mr Baguly – they might decide to follow us in the dark." He then signalled to George to join him in his cabin.

"This £5 of yours – which I am keeping safe for you, might be of use to you in Taranto."

"I don't want to spend it Sir."

"No – you don't want to spend it foolishly but did I hear your sisters now run a shop?"

"Yes, they do Sir, – in Poole."

"Exactly, now if you decided to buy some nice trinkets in Taranto, you could let your sisters have them – via my Agents, and you could make a profit."

"How much, Sir?" George said, warming to the idea.

"Maybe double your money – how's that?"

"Yes, I think I would like that – and I have a little money of my own from when I," his sentence stopped there – he did not like to use the word 'stowaway'.

Mr Penaluna always sensitive, helped George out by finishing the sentence – "from when we became acquainted – that is how I think of it."

"Thank you, Sir, – is that all Sir?"

"Except to say thank you for your part in the work of the day – did you enjoy it?"

"Yes I did Sir – but I would not like to repeat it too often – we are merchant seaman Sir, not real Navy."

"Quite right Eefamy – quite right – by the way that is a most unusual name, Eefamy are you sure you have got it right?"

"Oh yes Sir – it is a name just known around the Poole area – it was my father's real name."

"Oh well, it must be so then, but it is a peculiar name."

George stepped outside the cabin and closed the door, wondered if he dared – decided to, opened the door again and said "Goodnight Mr Penaluna" and ran off. Mr Penaluna saw the funny side of it and from then on always called George, Mr Eefamy.

The 'Bulldog' docked safely in Taranto, and Mr Penaluna went in search of an Agent who spoke English. He soon found one, and all the arrangements were made to have the valuable timber unloaded. The recipients owned a family business making special furniture for churches and high class domestic tables, chairs, beds and wardrobes. It was a large family, with three generations all fully engaged in the business, the head of the organisation was a tall dignified man in his late sixties named Italo Baccaloni. He made Mr Penaluna welcome and invited him to his home for a meal. Mr Penaluna attended in his plum coloured coat, his Lord Nelson hat and with him came four cases of his expensive claret which he had bought in La Rochelle – these were a gift for his host, but more than that they, he hoped, would be a temptation. The meal was pasta and fruit, Mr Penaluna plied them with his wine. Signor Baccaloni deferred on most matters, including wine, to his beautiful wife. A lady of fifty or so, unlike most Italian ladies of this age she had not run to fat, she was like her husband, above average height with an hour-glass figure and blonde hair – a stunning sight. Her affection for wine was equalled by her capacity, and since there were about twenty of the Baccaloni family around the table Mr Penaluna's forty-eight bottles of best claret were soon emptied. The master of the house called for more, but his cellar had only local red wine which usually was well received by all his family and guests, but fared badly in comparison with the La Rochelle claret. Mr Penaluna wrote out a note and had sufficient command of Italian to indicate that he wanted this note delivered to his ship urgently. Signor Baccaloni arranged for a horse and trap to deliver the note which simply said, "Give the bearer of this note four cases of my claret." Mr Baguly saw that this was indeed Mr Penaluna's handwriting and the four cases were being 'attended to' within the hour. Mr Penaluna had a good head for wine but he and everyone around the table had consumed at least two bottles each. No doubt the precise mathematics of the drinking session would never be known because as the master of the house became merrier the servants of the house became more inquisitive as to why this particular wine was so well received. No doubt they satisfied their curiosity and their thirst and the best part of ninety-six bottles of choice claret were enjoyed.

The party ended at about three am. Signora Baccaloni still remembered her duties as hostess and found a young maid in the kitchen who was too young to drink. She instructed the girl to take Mr Penaluna to a bedroom, and to get him into bed. Next morning Mr Penaluna awoke at the crack of eleven to find himself almost naked in a large double bed – his clothes neatly laid at one side – what he did not have was the slightest recollection of how he came to be there. After fifteen minutes of lying there and tying to assemble his scattered thoughts, the scent of coffee drifted across his sleepy senses, and there standing at the foot of his bed was his attendant and valet smiling at him and offering a very large cup of hot, strong, fragrant coffee. She smiled at his confused attempts to cover up his near nudity, she placed his coffee on a bedside table and left him two large towels. Mr Penaluna drank the coffee which cleared his head, and he arose from his bed with some difficulty, his legs had no idea what the word 'obedience' meant, and picking up the towels he left his bedroom and went unsteadily in search of a bathroom. He had not far to go and there were no rivals, indeed the male Baccalonis arose as usual at 6.30 and after a coffee and a light breakfast went off to their factory. Signor Baccaloni was a great one for enjoying himself but that must not interfere with business, so the younger members of his family quickly acquired the iron will which is necessary to awake with a hangover and still be at work on time.

The bathroom was huge, the bath was about six feet square and the taps were of a Rococo design usually associated with candelabra or ecclesiastical ornaments. Mr Penaluma tried to focus upon the taps to ascertain which of the many ornaments would turn and produce water, he at last succeeded and stepped well back as near boiling water spat and bubbled out. He eventually got the mixture of hot and cold to his liking and persuaded his legs to take him into the bath. He lay soaking there for about fifteen minutes, much refreshed he climbed out, dried himself on the two enormous towels and felt he was ready to dress himself and go downstairs. As he descended, wonderful cooking smells greeted him, it was after all almost lunchtime! Signora Baccaloni greeted him and made light of his late arrival downstairs, she showed him out to the garden where comfortable easy chairs made of basket-work were spread about. The sun was not yet something Mr Penaluna was ready for, so he chose a chair in the shade and promptly fell asleep.

The family arrived home from their place of business, chattering loudly as Italians always do, this awakened Mr Penaluna who now felt quite recovered from his hangover. Signor Baccaloni came to him and greeted him expansively, he led Mr Penaluna into the dining room, already filled with dark shining faces, lunch was about to be served, and huge bowls of spaghetti were steaming in the middle of the table, meat and tomato sauces were brought in and the Signors Baccaloni made a grand, but quite unrehearsed entrance. Conviviality is a great contributor to appetite and this was indeed a room filled with happiness. Mr Penaluna looked at the formidable mountain of food in front, accepted the offer of Parmesan cheese topping and made a start. He had a lot to learn about the technique of handling intractable Italian food, but his partners around the table were too busy and too polite to notice his ineptitude. The meal was washed down with local red wine of a rough and ready quality. Mr Penaluna was rather sparing in his acceptance of this beverage – he used a similar liquid on board his ship for stripping off old paint. Signor Baccaloni had a little. English and he apologised for the wine, he also recalled the excellent quality of the claret Mr Penaluna had provided last evening. If only he could obtain more he would be very grateful. Wasn't it English wine? He wanted to know. No, it was French Mr Penaluna confided. "French"! The host was not aware that anything worthwhile came from that country. Still, he had to admit, even though it was French, it was special. Signor Baccolini said he would like to visit the docks that afternoon to start unloading the precious timber, he had made arrangements with local carters. They all met up at the docks: two of Signor Baccaloni's sons were there and they and their father expressed surprise and satisfaction at the quality of the wood, they stroked it and occasionally stood back to admire the lovely rich colours. The two sons were used to this work and combined well with Mr Penaluna's men on board the 'Bulldog'. Once it was all safely loaded onto the carts or laid on the docks ready for the next journey the two Baccaloni boys found the five hundred cases of claret, in the hold. They signalled to Pappa to come on board, he courteously looked to Mr Penaluna to see if he would mind. Mr Penaluna gestured his invitation and Pappa looked with astonishment at what remained in the hold of the ship. At this moment Mr Penaluna's agent arrived, he was English but with a good command of Italian. Signor Baccaloni was led by his sons below deck to fully take in just how many cases of the delicious claret were secreted there.

"I think they are very interested in your claret, Mr Penaluna."

"Well I hoped someone would be – it is high quality."
"Ask them, if you will please, just how many they would like."

The agent – Mr Willis, went below and held a conversation with Signor Baccaloni – the latter asked his sons not to interrupt but to listen and learn, this was business. Yes they did want the whole consignment but at their price not Mr Penaluna's. It called for a cool head and experience. In these circumstances no one was cooler that Mr Penaluna.

"Tell them," he said to Mr Willis, "I can spare twenty or thirty cases but I know someone in Malta who will pay a good price for the rest."

"Quanto. Il prezzo? Signor Baccaloni."

Mr Penaluna's knowledge of all the romantic languages was sufficient to give him a translation of that question. He knew he had them on the rack. He remained his usual affable self, but beneath this benign exterior Mr Penaluna was a business man and he loved to make money, he enjoyed playing his hunches and he obtained especial pleasure from winning. Some haggling ensued, finally Mr Penaluna conceded the point that the wine had travelled well so far, but a rough crossing might have a bad effect on the claret if he were to take it to Malta, and he was prepared to let them have all but twenty cases, which he had decided to keep for himself. A suitable price was arrived at, giving Mr Penaluna about 70% profit on his outlay and a great deal of satisfaction.

Signor Baccaloni's interest in the wine was not confined to the hedonic: in order to obtain the work in churches and cathedrals it was sometimes necessary to take a present along to the Monseigneur or the Bishop to lubricate the discussions. For the really big pieces of work, for instance a reredos, the Cardinal himself might decide to become involved, and Signor Baccaloni had discovered that three or four cases of good wine discreetly left behind after the negotiations, frequently brought forth a firm order. The wine he had just purchased should result in some excellent business, he knew of one church which was riddled with woodworm, so that the pews and confessionals were all in a distressed condition. Perhaps two cases as an opener to the negotiations might lead to a more protracted (and profitable) interview.

Mr Penaluna asked Mr Baguly to have George washed and dressed in his Sunday suit in an hour's time – he was going to take him into Taranto and introduce him to the delights of being a trader. He then resumed the polite conversations with his agent and with Signor Baccaloni and it was all proving to be very interesting: Mr Penaluna because of his overall knowledge of European languages was able to follow some of the conversation, when he became lost, a glance towards Mr Willis would produce enlightenment, and gradually it became clear that Madeira could well be Mr Penaluna's next destination. After twenty minutes or so of this conversation, Mr Willis thanked Signor Baccaloni, who by this time was ready to leave, he gathered up his sons, said a decorous 'Addio' to Mr Penaluna and drove off in his coach and pair.

"What was that really about, Willis, I only caught some of it?"

"Signor Baccaloni had a friend who is an expert in viniculture, he does have some vines which he allows to produce grapes but he is more interested in propagation of plants, and he sells these to vineyards who run into problems."

"Do you mean their plants are too old or have contracted some disease?" Mr Penaluna asked.

"Exactly. Now on Madeira they have had an attack of what Signor Baccaloni's friend calls phylloxera, and it has ravaged Madeira's vineyards. They are seeking to diversify and grow other fruits, but they are also trying to re-stock the vineyards with new plants, hoping that the new stock will thrive in their land – they have left it fallow for three years or more, so they are looking to plant with healthy stock and are hoping the disease has now died off."

"It would be a tricky affair taking hundreds of small plants – they would need watering regularly, so half of our cargo would have to be fresh water – well, I'll think about it – let me know if you hear anything – I am in the business of shipping items around the world, so if it can be done – I'll do it – Ah, there you are Mr Eefamy – we are going to Taranto now Mr Willis – this young man and I have some business to transact."

Mr Penaluna did not know his way around Taranto, but he had a 'nose' for direction, and was soon in a street with some very interesting shops, on either side.

"Ladies like brooches, you know, things they can pin to their dresses – like these." Mr Penaluna said indicating some cameos. George had seen similar objects at No 18, Mrs Collins had worn some expensive ones.

"I can't understand their money" George said. "How do I know what I am paying?"

"Leave that to me, I shall pay in gold – shopkeepers can never resist that – and I won't pay too much."

They went inside and began to examine the cameo brooches.

"Look carefully at the mouth, ears, and nose," Mr Penaluna pointed out. "You can see which are quality because they are delicately carved."

George picked out two or three which came up to Mr Penaluna's specification.

"We'll need more than that – you have seven sovereigns to spend. I am hoping you will have thirty or very nearly that, so choose away."

George picked out thirty – the shopkeeper was beginning to lose patience, so Mr Penaluna lined up six sovereigns on the counter. Affability abounded from then on and the word 'Grazie' was frequently in use. The jeweller thought twenty cameos was about right for the sum displayed. George was about to put some back, Mr Penaluna indicated that patience was required. He placed another sovereign along with the other six, and picked up a marquetry jewellery box, he held it in such a way as to indicate that he would need this to put the cameos in. The shop owner indicated acceptance of the deal and scooped up the seven sovereigns.

Once out of the shop Mr Penaluna said "If your sisters can't get a guinea each for those, I'll eat my hat – and at least a guinea for the box – you have a few shillings left, so you can buy me a nice lunch – do you like spaghetti Mr Eefamy?"

"I have never tried it Sir, but if you can recommend it, I am sure I shall enjoy it."

Mr Penaluna put him arm gently around George's shoulder and led him to a nearby trattoria – together they could wrestle with and enjoy Italian food. After the meal Mr Penaluna told George to return to the ship – he had other business to attend to: he went back to the jewellers and bought almost his complete stock of cameos and marquetry boxes, he told the jeweller to have them delivered to Mr Willis' office. He came out of the shop, buttoned up his fine plum coloured coat, adjusted his Lord Nelson hat and made for a little house at the end of the street, where, according to the jeweller there lived a lady who was fond of jewellery. Mr Penaluna kept one hand in his pocket and in his hand was an (almost) perfect emerald ring.

CHAPTER 8

Madeira and Home to Number 18

Mr Penaluna decided the journey to Madeira would be profitable, and arrangements were made for hundreds of small vines to be delivered to the quayside. They were in trays with forty plants to each tray. They had to be carefully handled and stowed so that the trays would not move about in heavy seas, but consideration had to be given to the duty of watering them, so gaps were left to enable a man to walk amongst them and keep the soil moist. It was time consuming and many barrels of fresh water had to be brought on board to ensure that the plants would arrive in Madeira in good condition. Indeed the deal was made on the understanding that the plants MUST be delivered alive and healthy. Once they were safely stowed and an adequate supply for water was aboard, Mr Penaluna contacted the Harbour Master and a creaky old tramp steamer acted as a tug.

The men had enjoyed a few days at Taranto, and had taken full advantage of all the different forms of hospitality, but now it was time for work and some of them were ill-equipped to meet the demands made by Mr Baguly. Some were skulking in the forecastle trying to snatch an hour's sleep. Mr Baguly told the Bo'sun, who certainly had a name but was always called Bo'sun, to bring them all on deck. Buckets of sea-water were lying handy, and the least energetic received the biggest dowsing, until they decided that work was preferable to buckets of water. There are no set watches on sailing day – everyone is needed – securing everything for sea, hauling in the towrope, setting the appropriate sails, stowing the anchors.

The hawser was passed to the tug, and slowly the 'Bulldog' was hauled away from the quay, so it was 'Sheet home'. 'Overhaul the gear'. 'Stamp and go'. 'Hoist away' and unwilling legs were dashing or stumbling in all directions as Mr Baguly rapped out the commands.

Mr Penaluna stood on the poop deck in his full regalia, smiling to himself as he saw his crew, far from 100% sober, being forced by Mr Baguly to behave like good seamen. "Get some sea air into 'em," he thought. "They'll be fine in two hours." None had gone missing that was the main thing, sailors could be lured by young 'ladies' into shady drinking dens, there they could be given drink with dope in it, and then sold on to a sea captain who was short of crew members. Shanghaied, it was known as, because in that town, so it is thought, this scheme was first invented. The people who adopted this profession were known as crimps, some were so unscrupulous as to pass on to unsuspecting skippers, at a good price, corpses, suitably daubed with liqueur. They would tell the skipper that he was extremely drunk. Twenty-four hours later the skipper would find himself involved in a burial at sea for the seaman he paid money for.

It was heavy work, this procedure of setting sail, and in Taranto it was about 90°F. The men wore only lightweight trousers, but they sweated themselves sober as they worked, heaved and pushed to obey Mr Baguly's commands. They began to overrun the tug, 'Check in the main yard', and as the tug released the tow rope, 'Haul in the tow rope' – more heavy work. Once the tug had released the rope the 'Bulldog' was on its own, with very little way, all sails were called for, so tired bleary seamen were up and down the rigging unfurling the tightly reefed sails. The men on deck were standing by to await Mr Baguly's further orders, all sails were set, but the 'Bulldog' was slow to respond. It was all a case of getting the angles right, the sails were coaxed round to gather what little wind there was. Mr Penaluna nodded his approval as Mr Baguly's orders resulted in full sails, and a slow but discernable increase in speed.

"Five knots I think Mr Baguly – put Humpage on the wheel, he will get the best results – tell Cook to prepare dinner for the men."

"Aye Aye Sir."

Mr Penaluna went below to consult his charts, he would need to go south of Sicily and turn west, go through the Strait of Sicily, keeping to the north of the tiny island of Pantelleria, trying to stay at least forty miles from Tunisia – he did not welcome the thought of another skirmish with pirates, who were very active in that area – he smiled as he thought of his cargo; should he be taken by a pirate – 5000 plants all in terracotta pots, what a disappointment! It was almost worth being taken, to witness the look of astonishment there would be on the pirate's face as he surveyed his prize. Once through the Strait of Sicily, it was approximately one thousand miles to Gibraltar and the Atlantic, and then a further eight hundred miles to Madeira. So a journey of two thousand miles lay ahead. If they were going to make five knots, because they were reliant upon the gentle breezes coming up on to their beam from Africa, it could take twenty four or twenty six days. Then there was the fresh water for the plants to think of, and the fact that keeping food for the crew fresh, in high temperatures, is difficult. So Mr Penaluna decided to make for Gibraltar and to take on fresh water and provisions there. The word 'provision' brought to mind that when he asked Mr Baguly to tell Cook to prepare dinner he had hoped that he would be included also. There was a make shift bell pull arrangement from his saloon to the Steward. Mr Penaluna gave it two or three hearty pulls, and two minutes later Steward appeared with Mr Baguly, both looked uneasy. Mr Penaluna looked from one to the other expecting some explanation.

"Well it's like this Skipper," Mr Baguly began falteringly.

"It's like what? "Come on let's have it – is Cook drunk or ill?"

"No Sir – he isn't"

"He isn't – what?"

"On board Sir – he isn't on board."

"Do you mean we left Taranto without Cook?"

"Yes Sir – he's definitely not on board."

By this time they were four hours out of Taranto, if they had gone about and tacked back to port, then obtained a tug it would be dark – the cost of the tug, in and out again would be £50 or £60 and a day lost. Mr Penaluna was thinking of all these things as he said to Mr Baguly, "If we went back would we be sure to find him?"

"No Sir, not sure – there were at least ten other ships, anyone of them could have lured him away."

"He was not the best cook in the world," Mr Penaluna said. "I wonder, if they have already regretted taking him."

There was a knock at the door. Mr Baguly opened it, and there was George bearing a tray, on the tray was a plate with a clean cloth over it. He laid it on the Captain's table and was making for the door when Mr Penaluna took the cloth away and revealed a large omelette surrounded by grilled plum tomatoes and a piece of Ciabatta bread.

"Who did this then, if we have no cook?"

"I gave him permission Sir." Mr Baguly said. "He said he could cook so I gave him the chance."

"Who's HE?" Mr Penaluna asked.

"He did it Sir – Eefamy."

"Well done Mr Eefamy. You can all leave me now, I'll ring in ten minutes and let you know what I think."

The three shuffled out of the saloon, leaving Mr Penaluna to his meal.

Mr Baguly and the Steward grabbed George as soon as they were out of earshot of Mr Penaluna.

"It'd better be good or we'll be in trouble and you'll be in even more trouble." Mr Baguly said. The Steward cuffed George's ear, just to show who held sway so far as food was concerned.

"And there's plenty more where that came from if your cookin's lousy – which it probably is."

"Ten minutes later the makeshift bell rang and Steward ran aft to Mr Penaluna's saloon.

"You rang Sir?"

"Yes of course I did – tell young Mr Eefamy that he shows an aptitude way beyond his years, and I look forward to his next offering."

"Is that the same as saying you liked it Sir?"

"Yes it is – don't you speak English?" "Has he made a meal for all the crew?"

""He's on with it now – he's cooking 'am, potatoes and onions all together, smells good but will they like it?"

"Do they have a choice – have we other cooks ready to step forward and volunteer – do you want to be cook?"

"No, I'm Steward." he said proudly.

"Right you are Steward – he is now Cook, encourage him, and help him, he is only fourteen – let him have good produce and I think he will prove to be an asset."

"Is that all Sir?"

"Yes thank you Steward, except perhaps you could rustle up some coffee as soon as you can."

Steward went back to the galley, saw that George was as busy as could be, so he shouted, "Skipper wants some coffee now."

"Right." said George. "Give me two minutes." And he meant it. He had been trained at No 18 by Rooney, so an extra coffee was no trouble. In the meantime the ham stew was coming along nicely, the ship was not rolling too much, so he left the huge pan of stew and laid out a tray for the Skipper's coffee, two minutes later he called out to the Steward, "Old man's coffee's ready." Mr Baguly came by to check on progress, and was handed a mug of coffee by George. "Thank you Eefamy – very civil of you." Mr Baguly said.

The meal was dished out to the men half an hour later, and George waited to hear what the response would be. It varied – some said "No peas – I likes peas." Others said "Never mind the peas – that was a good meal – well done George."

An hour or so later George was summoned to Mr Penaluna's saloon, there waiting for him were Mr Penaluna and Mr Baguly. He went along expecting the worst, but was in fact invited to take a seat. Mr Penaluna began by not beating about the bush. "Cook's gone missing, nobody knows where he is – did you know that?"

"It is gossip among the crew Sir."

"Do you think you could take over until we arrive at Gibraltar or maybe Madeira?"

"That means really for four or five weeks." Mr Baguly added.

"Yes I think so Sir – with a little help."

"What kind of help?"

"Please don't take this the wrong way Sir – I don't wish to undermine anyone, but Radford's not much use to anyone, is he?"

"It was very observant of you to notice, and very polite of you to couch it in those terms." Mr Penaluna looked across at Mr Baguly. "Do you agree Mr Baguly?"

"Every ship carries one passenger Mr Penaluna, and Radford is ours' – no doubt of that Sir."

"Well we seem to be in agreement that I have been paying Radford for doing nothing – what can be done about it?"

George decided to tread very lightly. "The stove burns a lot of wood and uses a lot of kindling, so if Mr Radford."

Mr Penaluna cut him short smilingly "Oh" It's Mister Radford now is it? Since he's been promoted to being your assistant."

George wriggled on his chair uneasily, then he saw Mr Penaluna and Mr Baguly were wreathed in smiles. "It's alright George," Mr Baguly said comfortingly. "We're only pulling your leg."

"Right, we want food and you are the only one on board clever enough and clean enough to do it – the job is yours. Radford will help – any problems in that direction see Mr Baguly and he'll sort him out."

George rose from his chair wondering what he had let himself in for, "May I go now Sir?"

"Yes you may go now, provided you promise to be back here in ten minutes with two cups of coffee."

"Yes of course Sir – I will be back."

"If I appear to be taking no notice of you when you return with the coffee, it will be because I am making a note in my ledgers to put you on to £3 per month."

"Thank you Sir – I will try to justify the confidence you have in me."

George's next few days were difficult: he was working a sixteen-hour day. Radford was a scrounger who objected to a fourteen year old telling him what to do. What made it worse, some of the crew started to taunt poor Radford about being apprenticed to a fourteen year old. George realised all this and with powers of diplomacy far above his years, he started to put it about that some of the improvement in the grub was due to Radford, and so gradually the crew grew tired of tormenting Radford and the worst was over.

The routine in the galley started each morning at 4.30 am. Someone who was on watch would rouse Radford, he chopped enough kindling to start the stove, then he would carefully add slightly thicker pieces of wood and a little coal. Once it was really going Radford would wake George and within ten minutes the two early risers would be enjoying their first cup of coffee. As they were positioned, when George took over, this was an idyllic way to begin the day: the 'Bulldog' looked wonderful carrying her full compliment of sail. They were in the Mediterranean, surrounded by a beautiful dark blue sea, it was warm, even at 5 am, and 'Bulldog's' bows were cutting though the sea at a steady five to six knots, making creamy waves and a sound that was music to George's ears. Sometimes they would take their coffee aft and watch the wake gradually spread wider. To George these were all very beautiful experiences. To Radford it was time wasted when they could be eating.

Mr Penaluna had bought twenty chickens and a cock whilst in Taranto and the ship's carpenter had knocked together a bigger hen cabin to accommodate these twenty one new members of the crew. He had also made an enclosure for them on deck, and because the passage they had enjoyed since leaving Italy was so gentle, this was where all the chickens lived. About six inches of straw was put down for them, and every week or so Radford would shovel it all over board as a present for Neptune and lay fresh straw down. Mr Penaluna had also bought two small Italian sheep. What he did not know was that they were both in lamb and seven days out they both produced. George was delighted. Chips the carpenter made another enclosure on deck for the sheep and lambs, which brought forward the comment from the Bo'sun that, "We are now running a bloody zoo."

But there were benefits all round: George learned how to steal a little milk from the sheep, and Mr Penaluna loved milk in his coffee, especially his first one upon wakening. The sheep quickly learned to trust George, because he used to give them little treats like cabbage leaves, or a couple of ship's biscuits, so they didn't object. The lambs were a source of delight to all the crew, and the extra chickens brought surplus eggs which, when added to the duff, made George's reputation as the prime maker of tasty duff. The cock did his part too and once settled on board, two of the hens became broody and three weeks later they had about twenty chicks. No one was quite sure just how many, because their alacrity made counting impossible.

Mr Penaluna had bacon and eggs for his breakfast, the crew had porridge with eggs stirred in to improve the flavour, and one weekend, the original sheep which had set out from England with them, was slaughtered and George's expertise in doing a roast was tested. He served a Sunday dinner to Mr Penaluna and the Mates complete with roast potatoes and onions. The Skipper was delighted and he told George just how good it was. This whetted George's appetite because he was about to enjoy exactly the same himself.

George found that he now occupied the status of a celebrity on board ship: everyone enjoyed his cooking, and he knew now that this was what he wanted to do, his nature, as far as work was concerned, was that of a loner. He had enjoyed the work on the masts with Oliver, but he never made any of the decisions. It was a case of 'reef up the t'gallant' or 'look lively with hauling in the tow rope'. Now he decided what to do and when to do it. Sometimes it was tea, sometimes coffee – George decided. True, it had to be good – or at any rate good enough to stop anyone saying, "I wish the proper cook was back with us." But George made sure that what he cooked was tasty and that the plates, dishes etc were clean. Radford could not understand George's insistence upon cleanliness, but George did insist and Radford knew which side his bread was buttered. He now fed better than at any time in his thirty years at sea, and it was because he was the Cook's assistant. George made Radford collect up all the plates and dishes after a meal, not just the Skipper's and the Mates'. All the plates had to be washed properly – it was unheard of, some of the plates had not been washed in years. If they were beyond washing because of years of encrustation, George broke the plate and replaced it with new. Humpage objected to this treatment of his plate. "Why I've had that plate for years."

"Yes I know" George said, "There was evidence of a thousand meals on that plate and it was all going green mouldy."

"Well it won't taste as good to me," Humpage replied.

"Perhaps not but you have less chance now of being poisoned."

Things had all worked in George's favour: the ship was steady – it is always difficult to cook on a rolling ship. Mr Penaluna had taken on good provisions at Taranto, the hens were laying two dozen eggs each day, he had help, but perhaps most of all, the previous cook was a slap dash fellow, who liked a drink, so George had nothing to beat. Of course at fourteen he was not a fully experienced Ship's Cook, but he was better than the previous one and that was what mattered.

Mr Penaluna decided to put in at Gibraltar, to obtain more water for his plants, and to take on more provisions. It was a coaling station for steamers now – indeed the Royal Navy had steam ships in the 1890's, so it would be a simple matter to buy a ton of coal for the galley, and a little for his saloon too, just in case there were chilly nights as they left the Mediterranean and made for Madeira. Mr Penaluna went ashore to gain all the information he needed and to generally put himself about and bring himself up to date with what was happening in England. He met up with some Naval Officers in a tavern and ordered a round of drinks for them. They were all feeling on top of the world – war was imminent.

"Who with?" asked Mr Penaluna.

"The Boers – in South Africa" replied a Naval Captain. "They have been asking for trouble for years and now we'll have to show them what's what."

"But they are all farmers aren't they?" Mr Penaluna said.

"Well yes, they are farmers but they are handy with rifles as well and they pay no respect to the British Government."

"They are mostly Dutch and German, so I've heard"

"Yes but South Africa is one of our Colonies – and a wealthy one too, so we are not likely to give it up."

"Are you a Skipper/owner?" one of the officers asked.

"Yes I am."

"If I were you, I'd buy a bigger ship – what tonnage is yours?"

"Three hundred and fifty" said Mr Penaluna proudly.

"You need a one thousand tonner, and you could make your fortune."

"How?"

"By getting a contract to take ammunition, food, stores."

"Don't forget horses," another officer butted tin. "They will need hundreds, even thousands of horses – have your seen how big South Africa is? Nobody could march across South Africa. Cape Town to Johannesburg is about eight hundred miles, so the distances are huge."

"Perhaps you don't know what it costs to buy a ship?" Mr Penaluna said. He then looked at the faces around the table – no, they didn't know. £25 per ton for a good ship, new. So your thousand tonner would be £25,000. Who has that kind of money?

"My father is a Director of Coutts. See him, he'll help," volunteered a young Lieutenant.

"Well I have learned a lot today gentlemen." Mr Penaluna said as he left them. "And I don't think any of it is good news, but I thank you for your company nevertheless."

The figures went round in Mr Penaluna's head. He would probably need to borrow £10,000 to find the ship he would need, at 4%, that's £400 per year interest to pay. To man a one thousand ton clipper, he would need thirty five men. Perhaps, if he could keep his present crew together, he could get away with thirty. If he sold 'Bulldog' he could hope for maybe £5,000. He thought he knew of a clipper that had been for sale in Southampton, she was about the size he would need. Would the ship have to be refitted to take horses? Yes it would – at considerable expense too. All these thoughts were buzzing around in his head as he went to the Harbour Master's office to enquire about who to go to for water, fresh provisions, coal etc.

George was still on board the 'Bulldog' he was now more knowledgeable about maritime flags, and he realised that most of the ships in dock at Gibraltar were British. Therefore it was safe to assume that at least one of them would be going to England soon – in those days 'soon' was anything up to a month – but it would mean that a letter written and delivered to a ship today <u>could</u> be delivered to No 18 in two weeks time, if the Bay of Biscay behaved itself. So George wrote – not individually – but to all the ladies at home.

Dear All

I am now the Ship's Cook – promoted because our Cook failed to turn up at Taranto, and we are now at Gibraltar, taking on supplies and water. The Skipper has put me on £3 per month which is good pay – same as an able-seaman.

We are on our way to Madeira, a small island, eight hundred miles off the coast of Africa, we are taking grape plants, because they lost all theirs' due to a disease. I think we are going to take on fruit at Madeira and try to make a really quick passage home (in case the fruit goes bad), so I might see you in two or three months time.

It is a good life being a sailor and I am never seasick.

Oh! I nearly forgot, we were attacked by pirates off the coast of Algeria, and Mr Penaluna shot their captain dead – it was very exciting and we got away from them quite safely. Skipper was pleased and gave the crew extra rum – I had ginger beer.

Love to all

George (Ship's Cook)

PS They all think my cooking is very good, so I am now very friendly with all the crew

G

The more Mr Penaluna went about his business in Gibraltar, the more he learned about the trouble in South Africa. It was on every one's lips. Many of the Royal Navy ships were making ready to sail back to England, and some of the merchant ships were even prepared to leave, in ballast, rather than wait for a cargo – the Skippers were so sure that Government contracts to sail to Cape Town would be handed out like confetti. Mr Penaluna was in no hurry, he had his cargo of small vines to deliver to Madeira. Once there he was hoping to buy some fruit and good quality wines, he would then return to Southampton and weigh up what to do next. He was not really a sentimental man, but he did love his ship the 'Bulldog' and he made a good living with her – so he would leave it at that for the time being.

Mr Penaluna arranged for large quantities of water to be delivered to his ship, one ton of coal, and provisions for the passage to Madeira, this all took three days, so George had time to deliver his letter to a ship which was about to leave for Southampton. Letters home were regarded as sacred by the Navy and by Merchant Ships alike, so there was no doubt that it would be delivered safely. There were many tugs to choose from, so Mr Penaluna did not have to wait, the crew was lined up on deck to make sure they didn't leave anyone behind this time. They were soon battling with the Atlantic, a different proposition altogether from the Mediterranean, the winds were fierce and not from the right direction, so they were constantly going about in order to tack and try to make headway – this was going to be a long eight hundred miles.

Navigation by dead reckoning, ie, purely by mathematics is made very difficult during this sort of passage, but Mr Baguly made sure that Oliver and Matthew pursued this method as part of their training.

Mr Penaluna had the advantage of two first class chronometers, of the type first made by Harrison, in the reign of George III. Mr Penaluna of course had full mastery of the dead reckoning system, but he knew that the modern method was by far the more accurate, and three weeks out from Gibraltar, he was safely in Funchal Harbour making enquiries about how to have the plants removed from his ship. They had in fact grown considerably, many were tangled together, but they had lost very few, and they were soon collected by the wine growers, and the 'Bulldog' was empty and waiting for her next cargo.

The crew was given time off once the ship was thoroughly cleaned, so they soon found Blandy's tavern and acquired a taste for the local brew of fortified wine. Mr Penaluna and Mr Baguly went to the market, to make enquiries about their next cargo – it would be a speculative one. Mr Penaluna had been approached by some merchants to take fruit back to England, but Mr Penaluna's thoughts were that if they could make money on fruit, so could he. The tricky part of this would be to buy fruit which would ripen during the trip back but not go off. With favourable winds, which he could virtually guarantee, he should be back in Southampton in fourteen or sixteen days. He finally decided upon bananas and nuts – the latter was a safe bet, and by the time he arrived in England, Christmas would not be far away, nuts would be in demand.

Mr Penaluna spent two weeks gaining information about bananas and nuts; he had to be sure that the price and the quality were right. He acquired the knowledge he needed by engaging the local suppliers of ships victuals in conversation, thus he slowly found out who could be trusted. Once he had made his mind up, he bought his ship's stores, and at the very last minute invested in bananas, oranges and nuts. He personally checked all he had bought, as they were delivered to the quay. What he did not like the look of he rejected, he was not the kind of man to part with his money unless he was sure he was buying top quality goods. Some of the fruit suppliers were angry but Mr Penaluna ignored their remonstrations. He needed fruit which would sell in England in three weeks' time. Finally the carpenter did his job and attended to the battens, a tug came alongside and the time honoured procedure of setting sail began. Ten miles out from Funchal, they had the sails ready. The tug cast off the tow rope. Sails were unfurled, Humpage was at the wheel, and 'Bulldog's' lee rails were under water.

"Main sail if you please, Mr Baguly."

The team was ready for the order and the main sail was unfurled into a really brisk breeze. The sail filled and 'Bulldog' gained speed perceptibly. Mr Baguly had men ready to release more sails, but Mr Penaluna was looking over the rail on the poop deck. He knew they were doing ten knots at least and gaining. His brain was working on a problem: he could order more sails to be unfurled, and rig up some back-stays to take the strain, but this was wear and tear on the masts and rigging. But by doing this he could get the 'Bulldog' up to thirteen – maybe fourteen knots, a quick passage home meant the fruit would not go off, but wear and tear cost money too.

"Royals please Mr Baguly." Mr Penaluna had decided he would make haste during daylight, and reef up some sails at dusk. It was safer that way: if a stronger wind did spring up at night it would not catch them with all sails down. Come dawn he would bring all the sails into play, and take her up to thirteen knots again. The winds were reliable, a good west wind was virtually guaranteed. Mr Penaluna retired to his saloon and pulled the bell for the Steward.

"Look lively with some coffee Steward and ask Mr Baguly to step this way." The ship's routine was back to normal now – this was Mr Penaluna's favourite part of being a Skipper/Owner, two weeks of sailing – maybe three, lay ahead of him, he had a good ship – a good crew, chance to make some money and the possibility of buying a bigger ship and making money by sailing to South Africa. His reverie was disturbed by what he saw on the horizon to the rear of the ship: a squall was rising, dark clouds were showing beneath the squall, and Mr Baguly had noticed it too.

"Starboard fore-brace!" roared Mr Baguly. "All hands on deck."

The second mate, Mr Sweeting, said that some of the men objected, having only just finished their watch of four hours.

"Mr Sweeting – listen carefully." Mr Baguly said menacingly. "When I says all hands on deck I mean it, and I mean now. You can't argue wi' me and I can't argue with that." He pointed to the approaching squall. "If that 'its us fully rigged we're pooped."

"Main sail next!" he roared as the disgruntled men filed out of the forecastle. Already the main sail was filled to capacity and the wind was screaming through the ropes. Mr Baguly moved to Mr Penaluna and said quietly. " It's always difficult to reef up the main sail, it's so dammed heavy."

"Don't worry Mr Baguly, they are trained to it, and it must be done."

Mr Penaluna surveyed the operation from the poop deck and saw that Mr Baguly and Bo'sun had matters well in hand. "Royals only!" Mr Baguly cried, and gradually all the sails but the Royals were reefed up. It was up to the 'Bulldog' now – it was a battle for survival. One hundred tons of water came crashing on the deck – Mr Baguly told the carpenter to hammer some of the bulwarks loose because the scuppers would not take off the water quickly enough. The water roared off through the gaps, and Mr Penaluna had life-lines rigged up, so he didn't loose half of his crew. Visibility was almost nil because of the amount of spray, four men were on the wheel and they could hardly hold her. Mr Penaluna stood on the poop, in at least three foot of swirling water. He didn't mind this – he was being carried in the right direction at high speed, and the battens were tight, so his cargo was safe.

"Lee fore-brace!" Mr Penaluna called out, the yards swung round, the 'Bulldog' heeled over, her lee deck filled with water. The black cloud was overhead now and lashing rain added to the men's discomfort, but the ship was off at a good nine or ten knots and Mr Baguly went to the poop deck to stand with Mr Penaluna. Once the ship gained speed, the scuppers were not asked to work to capacity, and the two men stood on a drying deck.

"She has a fat rear end Mr Baguly, but I like that in a ship and in a woman." Mr Penaluna said. "You see, when the sea comes from behind as it does now, the sea has something to get hold of and lift – do you follow me Mr Baguly?"

"I think so Sir."

"Whereas with a slim schooner or clipper, the sea from behind divides and comes over from both sides and we would be standing in six feet of water now."

"I'll get Chips to repair the bulwarks Sir, but I had to tell him to knock 'em out."

"Quick thinking that was Mr Baguly – leave the bulwarks as they are and the life lines in place – this squall isn't finished yet."

The gale continued to howl through the rigging, sometimes so much sea crashed against the ship, that it shook from stem to stern. The four men on the wheel, wrestled to keep her steady, sometimes they were waist deep in water, even with the bulwarks knocked away, there was still tons of water on the deck. The ship was now at thirteen knots and going forward into inky blackness. The look-out stood at the forecastle rail, straining his eyes anxiously forward.

The Captain took his turn halfway up the mizzen rigging, peering forward, but seeing nothing but the upheaval and turmoil of an angry sea. The lights were spread all over the ship, to make it as prominent as possible, they didn't want a crash at this speed. They couldn't heave the log with the seas around as unruly as this, but Mr Penaluna knew, that with just the Royals unfurled she was doing at least thirteen knots. He ordered the halyards to be led up to the poop, so if there did happen to be an extra fierce gust of wind, the sails could be lowered without men having to go aloft. Mr Penaluna was well aware that the men on the wheel would need a rest, they had fought the wheel for over an hour, and that was enough. But in such mountainous seas, even a split second mishap during the change over could cause the ship to broach to, and all would be lost.

Suddenly the ship was sliding down a fearful incline. The men at the wheel do not look aft – had they done so they would have seen a black mountain of sea seventy feet high. The crew saw what was approaching and locked their arms through the rigging, but it was, as Mr Penaluna said: she had a full broad bottom and the sea got underneath her and lifted her clear. A hundred tons of water crashed on to the deck and filled the waist, but the vast majority went under, and though it frightened all the crew to death, it did no damage, and the gallant little 'Bulldog' continued to ride out the storm. The noise was increased by the chickens and the cockerel, all of whom raised strenuous but amusing objections to being subjected to all this turbulence. How can a well brought up Italian chicken be expected to lay eggs if she is catapulted from one end of her cabin to the other? And how can a vigorous cockerel ply his trade, if his harem is airborne? He left no one in doubt as to his opinion about this state of affairs. Mr Penaluna and Mr Baguly smiled at each other, together with the 'Bulldog' they had this storm beaten. Another massive wave curled over them. "Steady" snapped Humpage to his mates on the wheel, and they eased her amidships, so the ship was still on course in spite of the weight thrown against her.

Half an hour later there is a slight decrease in the wind. "Clew up mizzen topsail!" cried the Skipper, and the crew hauled it close up in the gear and then went aloft to furl it. The men clutched the rigging to prevent going overboard. Some of the massive waves reached a speed of sixty miles an hour, but the 'Bulldog' battled on at fifteen knots, taking Mr Penaluna and his expensive cargo ever nearer to the safety of Southampton harbour. The storm had not finished yet though, some skippers in this weather would heave to, and hope to ride out the storm. Mr Penaluna's preferred method was to take advantage of the gale and try to go through the storm and hope for a calmer passage in an hour or two. He believed it better to drive his ship forward, he knew her every move, and he refused to lower all sails. Mr Penaluna checked the barometer – it was beginning to rise – the storm was not finished yet.

The men battled with the storm and new emergencies occurred every few minutes, one of the seamen was thrown down steps and broke his arm. Some of his mates carried him to Mr Penaluna's cabin, when, having plied him with half a bottle of rum, Mr Penaluna felt the fracture and set it to the accompaniment of the man's screams. Mr Penaluna and the Steward then lifted the injured man into Mr Penaluna's cot, and the Skipper went back on deck to see what the situation was. Mr Penaluna looked uneasily up at the Royals just as one tore across like paper, the loose pieces of cloth streaming forward. Mr Penaluna felt the back-stays, they were taut fit to break.

"There's two feet of water in the hold Sir." Chips reported.

"Right, tell the Bo'sun to put six men on the pumps and to relieve them every twenty minutes."

They continued to race forward, it offended Mr Penaluna to see a torn sail flapping about, but he had other things to attend to. He personally supervised the change over on the wheel, just one man at a time changing places. Humpage wouldn't be moved. Mr Penaluna tried to persuade him, but no, he was the helmsman, and no storm would beat him. Just at that moment a freak wave enveloped the wheel, the men, the Skipper and all, and tons of water ran down into the waist. More water to be pumped out thought Mr Penaluna as he made his way to the poop deck to see how Mr Baguly thought things were going.

"There's two in the sick bay – knocked themselves out they did, but I think another hour or two and we'll be through it."

"I hope you are right Mr Baguly." Mr Penaluna said, but actually ten or twelve hours would have been more accurate.

"Any chance of coffee Mr Baguly?"

"I'll see what young George is doing Sir – it is easing a little."

"Ask about food as well – the men must be famished."

"Aye, Aye Sir."

George told Radford to go to the hen cabin and pick up all the eggs.

"There won't be no eggs." Radford said.

"There might be," George said, "sometimes this sort of weather frightens the eggs out of 'em."

The hens' boxes were all over the place, but eggs were to be found. Radford picked up about fifteen. Then he noticed one chicken lying over sideways – it's leg broken and out of shape. He picked it up by its one good leg and carried it and the eggs back to the galley.

"Look what I got," he announced as he entered. "Skipper can have 'er for his dinner."

"No, he cannot," George said. "That's Bessie – she is one of our originals."

"Look at 'er leg then."

"I'll bind it up with bandage – it'll mend."

Radford did not give up easily – he especially liked George's chicken soup.

"Let me neck 'er – she aint no good with a leg like that."

"Supposing you fell over and broke your leg – would you like me to make soup out of you?"

Radford knew he had lost the argument. "I'll get some bandage off the Steward, and I'll bind it up."

"Right. Give me the eggs and I'll make some pancakes."

George broke all the eggs into a large basin, and grated in about one pound of cheese, he melted some pork fat on top of the flat stove and poured out a cup full of the mixture – keeping it more or less circular with a fish slice, after fifteen seconds he turned it over – part way through the job he noticed the mixture was disappearing quickly, so he added about one pound of flour, some more grated cheese and a pint of milk. He consoled himself with the thought that some of the crew would receive a cheese omelette and some a cheesy pancake, but it would be the first food they had tasted for sixteen hours. He got the coffee pot boiling and Radford and the Steward began to take the meal around the ship. Skipper and Mr Baguly got theirs' first and were agreeably surprised.

"Radford and Eefamy works together well Sir."

"Mr Radford if you please," answered Mr Penaluna with a wink. "Yes they do and have you noticed Mr Radford is a different colour now he works with Mr Eefamy – is it magic?"

"No Sir, I think it's soap."

"Pity they don't all work with Mr Eefamy, there is so much water around and yet they rarely wash."

Mr Baguly rapidly changed the subject, he was not too keen himself on matters ablutionary. "Do you think we are through the storm Sir?"

"I'll let you know when I've finished this pancake – ring for the Steward Mr Baguly, and we'll have another cup of coffee."

Mr Penaluna went on deck to have a good look around and to check his position. The storm had abated but the wind could still fairly be described as fresh. "Heave the log" Mr Penaluna shouted. "Fourteen knots and a bit." the second mate shouted. Mr Penaluna consulted his chronometers and a watery sun allowed him to take a reading. "In the last sixteen hours we have travelled over two hundred and fifty miles," he announced. "Relieve Humpage at the wheel and he is to miss a watch – double rum all round lads and beer for the boys – you have done me proud." "Chips – put the bulwarks to rights, and let's have the decks clean – clean decks are safe decks – Bo'sun – I look to you to see to it."

Bo'sun – a man of few words, touched his forelock and turned to the men with one or two well chosen expletives, to indicate that it was time to get to work with holy stones.

George found a wooden box about two feet square, he put straw in it, and this was Bessie's orthopaedic ward. He looked after her by giving her all the bits he could find in the galley. After about ten days she was walking about, and looking quite perky. George knew she could not go back with the rest, because the cock, christened Cromwell by the crew, would wish to claim his conjugal rights, and Bessie's leg would be as bad as ever. So Bessie was separated and remained so, she found her way onto the various decks and though she had a pronounced limp, she was soon laying regularly and had the run of the ship. Mr Penaluna's sense of humour led him to ask George if he thought she was malingering in order to gain favours. She certainly became the ship's pet and continued her days as a spinster well away from the libidinous Cromwell.

Once the storm was abated Mr Penaluna's thoughts returned to a little rest, he looked over the rail, and guessed the speed at around eight knots – fast enough. He looked up at the sails and rigging, the torn sail was still flapping about untidily, but the men had had a hard sixteen or eighteen hours – it would do until the watches changed. He went to the helmsman – not Humpage now, he was fast asleep. Mr Penaluna checked the compass, saw the man had 'Bulldog' right on course, thanked him for that and allowed his thoughts to turn to a large glass of Madeira, a pipe of tobacco, and a few hours of peaceful sleep in his cot. He entered his cabin, it was dark and evil smelling – then he remembered about Treleaven, a fellow Cornishman, he was the person whose arm he had set. He had helped to put the injured man to sleep in his own cot, and he was now paying the price for his act of generosity. Treleaven's acquaintance with soap and water was infrequent and cursory and the malodorous state of his cabin was entirely due to this fellow's personal habits. Mr Penaluna thought of ringing for the Steward, decided against it, went into his saloon and flopped onto a chair, he was asleep in seconds. Treleaven's efforts, during the night were restricted to giving off a miasma and to snoring. Next morning Mr Penaluna asked the Steward to remove the unwashed patient and to tub all the bedclothes. Mr Penaluna called Mr Baguly into the cabin and gave him some of his best tobacco.

"Help me please Mr Baguly – puff away I must be rid of this smell."

Mr Baguly was glad of the tobacco, but in truth failed to notice anything untoward.

Progress was good until they were about two hundred and fifty miles from Southampton. Mr Penaluna beat to windward for three days because a north-east wind prevented any gain in their quest from home. The Skipper ordered tack upon tack to try to find a favourable wind, other homeward bound ships were trying the same tactics but none succeeded. One ship sent a rowing boat out to the 'Bulldog' with the message that they were ninety days out of New Zealand and running short of grub and water. Mr Penaluna sent the boat back with a cask of beef, two bags of potatoes and twenty gallons of water. Twenty minutes later he received a hearty wave from the Skipper of the ship, and his men looked forward to the first good meal for days. Day after day, but no chance of making headway, Mr Penaluna became concerned about his bananas, and one calm day he told Chips to take off the battens and let him have a look at his cargo. Most were alright and would survive, but he brought some hands of bananas on deck and told George to sort out the good bananas and throw overboard the overripe ones. The men helped themselves, some with disastrous results, really ripe fruit can be a fierce purgative. George threw overboard the really soft fruit, but kept the good ones and chopped them into the porridge for the next few days. A week went by and no progress, there were now about a dozen ships, schooners, clippers, barques, ketches all waiting, tacking, cursing. Sometimes a steamer, outward bound would stop and offer help to one of the waiting sailing ships and pass some food across on a bo'suns chair. A thoughtful skipper on one of the steamers telegraphed back to Southampton about the plight of the sailing ships and two days later three tugs arrived offering a tow back to Southampton for £100. Mr Penaluna signalled to a tugboat Skipper that he was interested – they finally settled on £80, and they were off on the last stage of the journey. The weather was calm and the men had nothing to do so Mr Penaluna ordered tar to be melted and paint and brushes to be made ready. 'Bulldog' would have to suffer the indignity of being towed all the way up the English Channel but as she entered Southampton she would be the smartest little ship to be seen.

Ships were all around them now: stately clippers, snowy towers of canvas, with their cargoes of tallow, copra, nitrates, hides from Africa, timber from Canada, rum, molasses, and sugar from the West Indies, fruit from the Azores, and going outward, were just as many carrying flags of all nations, bound for destinations as far apart as Hamburg and New Zealand, Antwerp and South America. George was on deck enjoying the thrill of seeing all the beautiful vessels, some possibly on their last trips, because by this time, steam was inexorably replacing the sailing ship as the main bulk carrier. George hardly saw the steamers, he concentrated on the sailing ships, he was not old enough to be aware of the passage of time which cruelly leaves behind something which is beautiful merely because it no longer pays enough.

The tug slowed down and the river Pilot came on board with the Customs men. They went along at five knots, the Pilot decided not to bring the ship into dock with a fast running tide. The traffic was crowded now, there were steamers everywhere, and all kinds of barges, even sailing barges with their distinctive tan sails. Little tugs puffed by, hauling a string of barges loaded with coal, some barges were worked by hand, with brawny men operating the oars known as sweeps. They passed miles of funnels and masts, and barges. The Pilot knew exactly where the 'Bulldog' was going, and he put her into a lock. The lock gates closed and she was lifted so all the crew could see the dock beyond crowded with three and four masters, and a few steamers. A little tug came along and berthed the 'Bulldog'.

"Coil up all the ropes and get the brushes out – let's have 'er tidy." Mr Baguly shouted. When this was done to Mr Baguly's satisfaction he said, "That's fine men." The voyage was finished.

Mr Penaluna emerged from his saloon looking splendid: he had had the Steward sponge and press his plum coloured coat, his boots were polished and his Lord Nelson hat finished off the picture. He had shaved with more than his usual care, and Steward had made some attempt to trim his unruly hair. Mr Fothergill, his Agent, was waiting for 'Bulldog' to dock, and he was soon aboard and in Mr Penaluna's saloon enjoying a glass of Madeira. There was much to talk about and both were keen men of business. There was not a moment to lose so far as Mr Penaluna's cargo was concerned, and Mr Penaluna rang for the Steward.

"Ask Mr Baguly to step this way please."

"Aye Aye Sir."

"Now what were you saying about the fruit I have – you have a buyer?"

Mr Fothergill replied, "Yes I can move the lot, oranges, nuts and all, and they can be on a train to London by tomorrow, can you have your men unload them?"

"Well it's true the job isn't finished until we are unloaded and this is the kind of cargo which needs careful handling – a clumsy docker could cost us a fortune. I'll pay the men when the ship is unloaded, if I pay them now they'll be off to the Inns and harlots."

"Ah there you are Mr Baguly – we were just saying it would not be wise to pay the men off today because we will need them tomorrow to unload. Tell young Eefamy to go ashore and to buy fresh beef to make a really good English meal for the men, and to bring a dozen prime lamb chops for Mr Fothergill and me. Tell him to take Mr Radford with him and to buy fresh vegetables as well. But the men are to stay by the ship, preferably ON the ship until all our business with the cargo is finished."

"The men won't like it Sir – they likes to be paid up and be off about the town."

"Tell 'em it's ten bob extra per man, see if that works, but I do need them – bananas need careful hands."

"Aye Aye Sir."

George and Radford had not far to go to find a good butcher, and there he bought two fifteen pound rolls of brisket and a dozen lamb chops.

"What do you fancy Radford?" George asked. Radford was speechless – in his whole life, and he was about fifty, no one had EVER asked him that.

"Well I don't really know – what do you think?" he asked the butcher. The butcher examined Radford's gums where the occupancy by teeth was scattered to say the least – "I think lamb's liver perhaps would suit you."

"Very good George, I'll have a pound of that please."

Radford's face was lit up with pleasure and anticipation. The butcher pointed out a good vegetable shop and there George bought two sacks of new potatoes, a sack of onions, some carrots, cauliflowers, and cabbage, and a sprig of mint. The Greengrocers employed a boy for doing deliveries such as this and George's purchases were wheeled back to the ship on a little handcart.

Humpage was leaning over the rail as the little procession approached. "What you got there George?"

"The best meal you have had in weeks." George said.

"We chose it all." Radford added, determined not be left out of it. "Only the best for us."

"I'll give you a hand." Humpage volunteered, and soon all George's selections were in the galley. George had thought it all through – timing is everything in cooking and he explained all this to Radford who was anxious to sink his few multi-coloured teeth into the liver.

"Liver takes five minutes to cook, whereas these rolls of brisket with take four hours."

"Do I have to wait four hours too?" came the pathos laden query.

"Just let me put the brisket in the oven and then I'll do something specially for you – bring some more wood and two buckets of coal – there's a good chap."

Radford had heard the words "specially for you" before from George and he knew he was in for something very tasty. One of George's purchases had been twenty barm cakes or muffins, as they are sometimes known, and from the butcher ten pounds of smoked bacon. He laid the bacon out on the flat top of the oven and soon the magical scent of smoked bacon was drifting all over the ship. The Bo'sun came to enquire, as did Mr Baguly, the Second Mate was soon in attendance, as was Steward. Radford came back with the fuel but couldn't get near the galley.

"Make way, make way – we can't cook if you lot are in the way all the time." The queue jostled Radford good humouredly and some of the coal was spilt on the deck, and the noise became louder. So much so, that Mr Penaluna having rung for the Steward in vain, came to see what all the racket was about. His anger subsided as the aroma of smoked bacon invaded his senses. The queue divided to let Mr Penaluna through to where George was presiding over the bacon sandwich ceremony.

"Have you enough there?" he enquired

"Yes Sir, would you like one?"

"Serve the men first, then send Steward in with one for Mr Fothergill and one for me, and two cups of coffee – but serve the men first."

George put two handsome rashers on each sandwich, having just opened up the muffins and wiped up some bacon dip. Mr Baguly supervised the distribution to ensure it was only one each, and soon the whole crew was nodding approval of George's special treat. George did the last two for the saloon put them on a tray with two cups of coffee, covered it with a clean cloth and presented it to the Steward. He then turned his attention to his own bacon sandwich – there was no hurry now - the brisket would take four hours, so there was plenty of time to prepare the vegetables. He took his sandwich and his coffee to the rail and looked out at all the other ships, they were from Morocco with its distinctive tapered flag complete with a golden new moon, Sardinia, largely navy blue but showing a white cross in the left hand corner, three different flags from Persia, a yellow and white striped flag from Smyrna, red and white chequers from Brabant. The red flag with a star and new moon from Arabia. The wonderfully decorated blue flag from the Empire of Brazil. There was one from Chile, one from Peru and the gold circle topped with a crown to show it was from Naples. George had taken the trouble to learn all the different flags, and every time he thought of the flag from Persia he longed to go there. He did spare time to think about No 18 Wellington Terrace, but he knew that he was going to travel the seas and see the World.

His cooking ability would ensure that he was welcome aboard any ship, just as he had nothing to beat when compared with the previous cook. So it was on most ships: the cook was usually an able seaman who was too old to go up aloft or an ex Navy man who had lost a leg but not his desire to go to sea. George loved cooking and he loved the sea, the combination made any further discussion about what he intended to do with the rest of his life irrelevant.

The two large rolls of brisket were beginning to give off information as to the delights in store for the crew later in the day. This was a busy Dockland area, with porters, carters and people selling their wares walking by the ship all day. George left the galley doors open, and the scent was blowing about causing quite a lot of interest, especially among the crew of the 'Bulldog' because they knew it was for them. Meanwhile Mr Penaluna and Mr Fothergill had papers all spread out over Mr Penaluna's dining table. This was the time of the 'reckoning'. Mr Penaluna needed to be sure that he was paid for everything: twenty cases of the best claret from La Rochelle, the bananas, oranges and nuts, not forgetting the cameos he had caused to be forwarded from Italy. He rang for the Steward. "Take this tray away please and ask Mr Eefamy about scones and tea – he could send Mr Radford in search of clotted cream too – Oh! Steward before Mr Radford goes off for the cream make sure he has a wash."

George went back to his galley, lifted out the two briskets, thus allowing even more wonderful smells to escape, he basted them with beef dripping and put them back. He attended to the fire and then went to see where Bessie had laid today's egg, he would need it for Mr Penaluna's scones.

Later in the day, Mr Penaluna and Mr Fothergill returned from the Agent's offices. Steward had laid out Mr Penaluna's dining table in fine style, with a damask tablecloth, two ornate candlesticks, heavy solid silver cutlery and cranberry ware glasses. He had been ashore and obtained ten pounds of ice, so the sherry could be chilled, and he had opened four bottles of the La Rochelle claret, so that it could warm gently. George's handwriting was good and together with Steward he prepared menu cards as follows:

Beef and Onion Soup

Lamb chops with roast potatoes, roast onions, cauliflower & carrots,

Served with mint sauce

Apple dumplings with cream

Fruit and nuts

Cheese

Coffee

Mr Penaluna and Mr Fothergill came into the saloon and picked up the menu cards. Mr Penaluna rang for the Steward. He held up the card.

"Whose idea is this?" Mr Penaluna enquired.

"Young Eefamy's Sir, don't you like it?"

"I like it of course, but can he do it – that's the question?"

"The soup's ready now Sir, I'll just help you to the chilled sherry, and then I'll bring it in."

"Don't let Radford bring anything Steward, one whiff of him and I'm off my food for a week."

Steward brought in the soup, it was a rich brown colour, and an even richer flavour. Mr Penaluna and Mr Fothergill exchanged glances, and fell to with a will.

Next came the chops, four on each plate and four in a dish, in reserve. The vegetables were served in separate tureens with close fitting lids, the gravy was in an elegant silver gravy boat and the mint sauce in a small Chelsea bowl. The Steward had his smart navy blue jacket on and a dazzlingly clean serviette over one arm, he served with great panâche, and it all added to the occasion.

"You do yourself proud, Mr Penaluna," said Mr Fothergill, as he cast admiring glances at the table.

"It's my young cook you know – he's only fourteen, he was a stowaway, been very harshly handled by his step mother – or some such relative – By God these chops are delicious."

"And the gravy too – how does he make such flavours as this?" asked Mr Fothergill.

"As I was saying," continued Mr Penaluna. "He was a stowaway, and by some mischance we left our cook in Italy – this lad took over and this is the result."

"Are there more chops?" Mr Fothergill asked.

"Yes help yourself and I'll fill up your glass, I bought this claret in La Rochelle, never had better anywhere."

Steward was hovering and trying to be of help when Mr Penaluna said "We can manage now Steward, you have yours and we'll ring when we want you again. What has young Eefamy cooked for the crew?"

"Brisket Sir – two large rolls."

"Brisket Eh? How do you like brisket Mr Fothergill – have you the appetite?"

Mr Fothergill surveyed the tables, took a good swig of the claret. "Not too much mind – but I could manage a slice or two."

"There is apple dumplings and then cheese to follow." Steward said, seeking to protect the brisket from their ravenous predations.

"Dumplings and cheese are all very well but meat is the thing." Mr Penaluna averred. "Not too much mind, we don't want to deprive the crew of a well earned meal."

"Just four slices then?" suggested Steward.

"Aye well, for now anyway," Mr Penaluna said. "Away with you now and bring some beef gravy too – this lad does make good gravy."

Steward went to the galley mouthing a few oaths which contained the words greedy, and swine, as well as a few less acceptable expressions.

"Now they wants brisket," he said to George.

"Not after twelve lamb chops surely?"

"They just wants to sample it – so give me four slices, cut thin, and a splash of gravy – they are taking the food out of the men's mouths."

Steward returned to the saloon, and dumped the plate on Mr Penaluna's dining table and left without so much as by your leave. The decorous behaviour was gone. Mr Penaluna cottoned on and said to Mr Fothergill – "I don't think Steward wanted us to share in the brisket – but it's here now so we'll try it."

The two gourmets made appreciative noises as they dispatched their thin slices of beef.

"Will he stay with you, this lad, or will he go back home now?"

"I think he will stay, he loves the sea, and I intend to treat him like a son."

"Few people can cook as well as he can, he could have a job in any hotel in Southampton,." Mr Fothergill said.

"I think the sea is a big attraction and as Cook he is his own boss."

Back in the galley the rolls of brisket were out of the oven 'resting'. Lovely rich juices were oozing out, and George carefully collected these up, to add to the gravy. Each plate received a slice about an inch thick, on top were piled potatoes and cabbage, and a cupful of gravy was poured over. Radford had his pound of liver which offered little in the way of a challenge to his teeth, so they were able to maintain their tenuous position in his shrivelled gums.

Mr Baguly was the first to finish and the first to come forward, plate in hand, to offer George his thanks for a hearty meal at the same time cherishing a hope that there was just a little left for 'seconds'. George was busy with his own meal and he indicated that half of one roll remained – an invitation to cut another slice. Mr Baguly said, "Thankee George – I'll just take a small slice." True enough the slice started only a quarter of an inch thick, but it was nearer two inches thick when the knife reached its ultimate destination. Mr Baguly somehow managed to look guilty and pleased at the same time, and he was followed in by others with vigorous appetites and suppliant plates. George cut the slices himself, and there was enough for a slice each. Radford had one too, at grave risk lest his teeth forego their uneasy tenancy, but he managed. It said much for his capacity because his pound of liver was a generous pound, but like the rest of the crew he drank at least two pints of ale with his meal and was really ready for apple duff. "Where does it all go?" George thought.

Steward carried in apple dumplings and cream for Mr Penaluna and Mr Fothergill.

"Ah, dumplings splendid – thank you Steward – give Mr Eefamy my congratulations – a fine meal."

"What was that name?" Mr Fothergill asked.

"Name – what name?" Mr Penaluna said – eager to make acquaintance with the dumplings.

"Eefamy – is that the stowaway's name?"

"Yes it is – do you know him?"

"I think I knew his father, he owned a pottery company in Poole, died young and it was taken over by his widow – she runs it now, and very efficiently too from all I hear."

"He came to us in a very poor condition, he had been thrashed until his back was raw and bleeding, but he has never spoken of how it all happened. He writes letters home and receives letters too, so I suppose that now we are here for a week or two, he'll go back to Poole – but I want to make sure that he comes back here when I send for him."

Mr Fothergill then said, "Now, about the Boer War, how does that affect us, what can we do to increase our business?" The discussion carried on for the four full bottles of claret and became increasingly incoherent as the fourth offered its last drops.

George had finished in the galley, Radford had rounded up all the plates, often this was an enjoyable occupation, because there were usually scraps left, welcome bits so far as Radford was concerned, but today – nothing but cleared plates. Mr Baguly and George were leaning over the rail looking at all the other ships in the docks.

"Will we be long before we set off again Mr Baguly?" George asked.

"A week at least, the Skipper is lookin' for a bigger ship, so he might sell the 'Bulldog', then if he does buy a ship, ten to one it'll need a refit to suit his Lordship."

"So we will be here a week at least – do you think I can go home and see my sisters?"

"Course you can, once we're in dock you're a free man like any of us – leave me your address and I'll send word, when we needs you back here."

George wrote out his name and address and gave the piece of paper to Mr Baguly.

"Well if it's alright with you Sir, I'll see Mr Penaluna tomorrow, draw my money and take a train back to Poole."

The next morning George went to see Mr Penaluna who was busy doing his reckoning. He confirmed what

Mr Baguly had said, and he too made a note of George's address. The meal of the day before confirmed that George was indeed a very fine cook, and Mr Penaluna did not want to lose him. But apart from that Mr Penaluna had a real affection and respect for the boy, as if George were the son he had never had. Mr Penaluna carefully reckoned up what he owed George. Most owners would have deducted the expenses incurred whilst George was recuperating in Denmark but in many ways Mr Penaluna was not as other skippers/owners and the thought never crossed his mind.

"Have your packed the trinkets for your sisters' shop?" asked Mr Penaluna, ever alert as to how to make money.

"Yes I have Sir – what should I charge do you think?"

"Leave that to the ladies – they will know the selling price, and then let them deduct twenty per cent commission – it will be your first financial adventure, but not I hope your last."

"May I go home in the uniform you provided Sir?"

"Why, of course, you will want to look at your best. Now when you come back, do you want to work with Radford – I was thinking of paying him off."

"Oh, No, Sir please don't do that – he has nowhere to go, he has no home and no relatives and I know it seems odd since I am fourteen and he is fifty, but somehow he relies upon me and I know he enjoys his work now, which he never did before."

"Very well then – but do try to encourage him to take a bath now and again and to tub his clothes every week."

"I will Sir – may I tell him that he is retained – I think he had a suspicion that he was for the chop?"

"You're a good lad Mr Eefamy – yes you can tell him – just add that it is conditional upon a bath occasionally and encourage him to spend some of his wages on decent clothes."

"I will Sir, I'll tell him."

George went on deck and found a very disconsolate figure looking out into the Dock. The crew had convinced Radford that his job, helping the Cook, was a sure sign that he was 'out' and that he had had his last trip. George brought the news to Radford who had just received his pay.

"I'll go now and get drunk,." Radford said.

"Let me look after some of your money." George pleaded. "Even if it's only ten shillings – otherwise you will waste it all."

Radford dutifully but regretfully handed over ten bob, and then went off in search of Hazel a particularly repulsive harlot who somehow continued to ply her trade. Radford found her quite attractive once his powers of discernment had been dulled by five or six pints of strong cider. The rest of the crew dispersed to various addresses: Mr Baguly went to stay with his sister, Humpage to his young wife and two children, Sweeting down to Falmouth, Bo'sun stayed on board ship as he had no relatives in the World. Chips the carpenter who was a real bore, said he could not be spared off the ship and anyway, someone had to feed the chickens and look after the sheep. 'Sails' who was extremely mean, sought work at a local chandlers repairing sails and doing any menial work to earn a little extra money, Mr Penaluna would continue to sleep on the ship but would eat in the local Inns, and keep his ears open for opportunities.

George gathered his possessions into a haversack, made by 'Sails' (at a price), put on his best clothes, and went off to Southampton Station to enquire about a train to Poole. The trains were at regular intervals. George chose an express, at nine pence more than a stopping train, and was soon in Poole. He emerged from the station and there was Tom, with his horse and cart, he had just been delivering some crates to the Goods Depot.

"Hello Tom." cried George.

"Who are you?" Tom asked aggressively – used to people who wanted to beg a lift.

"George – I'm George. Don't you remember me?"

"Bloody Hell! I would never have believed it – you've grown up in a few months – and look at your uniform! Are you in the Navy?"

"Merchant Navy – I'm a cook – three pounds a month paid in cash."

"Jump up here, and I'll take you home, this is my regular job now, I have my own horse and cart, and I deliver all over the County."

They went past Wilkinson Butcher's Shop, then the Chemist's, past Mr Hemsley's Church, second on the right was Wellington Terrace, and there was No 18, the door a rich blue and the brass work all shiny. Tom jumped off the cart with George and picked up his haversack. He rattled the door knocker loudly. Polly came to the door.

"Look what I've brought," Tom shouted. George rushed into Polly's arms, Marie and Rose joined in the scrummage. Tears flowed in all directions, they were still on the doorstep, passers by were looking and tutt-tutting. Tom pushed the whole lot into No 18, and closed the front door. He left them in the hallway, crying laughing, asking questions and grappling with dishevelled, tearful happy George. Tom went into the kitchen and swivelled the big kettle round on to the fire. He looked into the tin boxes which he knew contained cakes, syrup tarts, scones etc, and laid some out on plates. He knew his way around the kitchen, and why not – he was engaged to Rose.

A big pot of tea was brewed and the cakes were laid out on the table. Excitement, emotion, coupled with mouthfuls of cake, preventing coherent conversation, but the moment was there to be enjoyed, and George could not have had a more enthusiastic and indeed loving welcome. He gradually learned how Mrs Collins and Rooney had gone, how Rooney had disappeared with all Mrs Collins' money – upon hearing this he said, "Serves her right," and everybody laughed. George told them of his travels across Denmark to loud "Oos and Aahs" from the girls and looks of envy from Tom, who had never been anywhere. He recounted his trip right round Scotland, the Irish Sea and down to France. "France – just fancy" said the girls.

"And on to Italy via the Mediterranean where we were attacked by pirates."

"Not real pirates," they all shouted.

"Yes real pirates – honest! I was loading the muskets and Mr Penaluna – he's my Skipper, shot their Skipper dead."

More "Oos and Aahs" were followed by offers of tea and cakes. Laughter, jollity and whoops concealed the fact that the front door had just opened to let Clarissa, Anne and Caroline in – home from their business affairs. Clarissa opened the kitchen door and stood there framed by the architraves, a picture of dignity. With Thurza just behind her this was the new confident Clarissa, but when she saw George she came forward with her arms spread wide to gather him in. George was not one to look back, he craved affection and if offered he was quick to accept. Anne and Caroline came forward and George was again engulfed in soft feminine arms and rustling silk gowns. Polly refilled the kettle and brought out some more cakes and tarts. George would have to recount his travels all over again, and this would take some time – a large pot of tea was urgently required, and everybody gathered round the table to enjoy George's stories, servants and Mistress together, this was unlike most Victorian households, they were all equals here. Mrs Collins' reign had shown Clarissa enough of the harsh discipline of a typical Victorian regime, she had now gone in completely the opposite direction and it worked. They were all friends, who respected each other's work, but they knew who paid the wages. The discussions went on for about an hour and then Clarissa resumed command.

"What would you like for tea?" she asked George.

"Mr Wilkinson's sausage, mashed potatoes and onion gravy – please."

This was greeted with great acclaim by all present. Tom volunteered to go to the shop and insisted upon taking Rose with him. Clarissa agreed, "Let's go into the parlour now. Polly and Marie will need time to tidy up the kitchen and peel the potatoes."

George stopped for a minute to untie his haversack and retrieve the marquetry box he had bought in Taranto. He laid out the cameos on the kitchen table and invited all the ladies present to choose one as a gift. When all were satisfied he returned the remaining ones to the box, and carried it into the parlour.

Clarissa made it clear from the start that so far as she was concerned his sailing days were over. "You are welcome to join me at my Works, or you could go to a private school for two or three years and then go on to Oxford or Cambridge."

"No, they are not for me" George said quietly but firmly. "I love the life at sea – I have a responsible job, and I am sailing with people I like – my Skipper Mr Penaluna is like a father to me, and when he is ready to leave on his next journey he will send for me."

"But you don't have to go – you are home now, and we would like you to stay wouldn't we?" said Clarissa, trying to recruit the help of Anne and Caroline.

"Yes, we would – it would be nice if we could all be together again," Anne said, Caroline smiled in agreement.

"No I won't be able to do that, I am a seaman not a landsman, I can't explain why, I just know I would never settle ashore. When you have sat on the jib of a sailing ship in the middle of the Mediterranean with warm breezes and dark blue sea all around you, and you have looked back at the white canvas tower which is coaxing you along, and heard the gentle ripple of the water as the bow cuts through and makes a creamy spray each side of the ship – there is nothing like it."

Clarissa was by this time in her life not one to give up easily but she had acquired man-management skills by running her Company, and she knew that this was one argument she was not going to win.

"Right – what are we going to do with the rest of the cameos you have brought back with you?" and the conversation carried on the way Clarissa preferred: it was all about business. The two girls agreed that they were items that would easily sell in their shop, and George left the pricing to them.

George spent the next few days at home, some of the time was spent in his bedroom, but now the room was quite different for him: he had grown away from all his toys and his collection of boy's books. He was actually happier in the kitchen watching and sometimes helping to prepare the meals. He exchanged ideas with Polly and Rose who were the two most involved with cooking, Marie spent half of her week in the shop with Anne and Caroline, sewing little roses on to hats and making alterations to dresses which didn't quite fit the would be purchaser. Polly and Rose knew that George had changed, it was not the beating which had changed him, it was George's positive grasp of how he saw his life developing, it was almost tunnel vision: he wanted to become a really skilled cook so that he could be sure of being needed aboard a ship, because he wanted to see the World but most of all he wanted to be at sea, on a sailing ship where the men around him were intent upon harnessing the winds and defeating the storms and doing what George perceived as a man's job.

George went out for walks, usually down to Poole Harbour to look at the ships, on three of the days he went out to help Tom doing deliveries and pick-ups around the area, with Tom's horse and cart.

"Don't you fancy breaking away from Poole and travelling all over the World – I expect Mr Penaluna would take you on and train you to be a seaman?"

"No, no not for me, I fancy settling down in a nice cottage with little Rosy and just doing my job here, I might get promoted – I do know about horses and I understand the paperwork to do with the haulage business, and that will do for me."

"I can't describe what it is like to be in the middle of an ocean, late at night with millions of stars overhead, with the sails nicely filled and you are scudding along at a nice ten knots, a cup of coffee in one hand and bacon pancake in the other – my ideal of heaven."

Tom was not impressed "I'll stick to Dorset and Rose – come on giddy up, let's do some deliveries or Mrs Eefamy will want to know why."

George had been at No 18 for ten days when, at about six o'clock one evening there was a knock on the door – Polly went to answer it – there stood a man of less than average height, but made taller by his Lord Nelson hat, wearing a plum coloured coat and carrying a large basket of fruit.

"Good evening" said the owner of the Lord Nelson hat. "Does George Eefamy live here?"

"He does Sir and what may your business be with Master George?" Polly asked.

"I have the honour to be Skipper of the 'Bulldog' upon which Master George is the Cook."

George heard the familiar voice from his chair in the kitchen and he rushed along the hall to greet Mr Penaluna. He drew him into the kitchen and proudly introduced him to everyone gathered there.

"Do you take tea Sir?" Clarissa asked.

"Thank you Ma'am, yes I would like tea, with milk and sugar please – this young man (he placed his arm gently around George's shoulders) makes a bonny cup of tea and coffee usually with a little sheep's milk in it."

"It's true." George said. "We have two sheep aboard, two lambs and a good few chickens too."

It was indeed a very different life than that at No 18 but it was obvious to all that George was delighted to see Mr Penaluna, and that his arrival heightened George's anticipation of a new voyage.

"What brings you to Poole Sir?" asked Clarissa – fearing George's instant removal from home.

"I am here to look at a large ship which is for sale, I have brought Mr Baguly with me, he is inspecting all the sails and riggings. If she is what I want I shall buy her because the Government needs big ships."

"Why is that pray?" asked Clarissa.

"For the War in South Africa – the Boers have risen against their rightful Queen, and many ships will be needed to take men, guns, horses."

"Horses – will they take horses all that way?" Tom asked.

"You will not be going Tom, horses or no horses." Rose clung on to Tom's arm.

"No, I don't want to go, but fancy horses in a ship's hold. For how long Captain?"

"Could be six or seven weeks."

"Cruel I call it – horses don't like to be cooped up like that."

"No – I'll have no part of that, don't worry. I am not going to turn my ship into a giant stables."

"So what will our part be Sir?" George asked.

"Provisions, food, blankets, straw and hay, tents – that sort of thing – I shall avoid ammunition too, if possible."

"Will it be dangerous – do you think?" Clarissa asked.

"No, they have no Navy, so they can't come after us, we will land the stores at the Naval Base, under protection, hope for a cargo back to England, and so on until the War is over."

"What's the galley like on the new ship Sir?" George asked.

"You had better come and look – tell me and Mr Baguly what you think – I'll be looking round her tomorrow morning at nine o'clock – she is in Poole Harbour." And at that point he made to leave.

"What's she called Sir – the new ship?"

"The North Star."

"I'll find it Sir – and I'll see you tomorrow – nine o'clock Sir."

If any of the ladies present or Tom ever doubted where George's future life lay, it was dispelled when Mr Penaluna had gone: George – his voice filled with anticipation, emotion, wonderment and sheer joy – said "Just think – me and the North Star."

CHAPTER 9

Mr Penaluna & Mr Strange

Mr Penaluna was up early this particular morning and he had warned his first officer Mr Baguly to be likewise "up betimes". They were visiting Poole Harbour to view a selection of sailing ships which were for sale. Steam had largely succeeded in supplanting sail as the main method of transporting bulk materials by sea and Mr Penaluna knew this, but he drew comfort from the fact that few people would be in the market for a sailing ship and he would dictate the price – he liked to be in charge. He was very much in charge of his other ship the 'Bulldog', he knew every timber, every sail, every rope and he loved them all. Now he was looking for a bigger ship, possibly 800 or even 1,000 tons, more than twice the size of the 'Bulldog'. He knew of contracts being handed out by the Government to take supplies to the troops in South Africa. What later became known as the Boer War was just beginning and he knew that with a slightly bigger crew than he usually had on the 'Bulldog', he could take possibly three times the load. He had heard prices like three pounds ten shillings, even four pounds per fifty cubic feet – rich picking indeed, and Government money was sure – slow but sure – and he could wait. It was a fine morning as these two gentlemen began to look over the four ships on offer. The Agent in charge of the sale was too effusive and attentive for Mr Penaluna's liking.

"Please leave us to our discussions and deliberations Mr Strange," a frustrated Mr Penaluna said. "No decision will be made today nor tomorrow," he continued, "buying a ship is a lengthy affair but we will keep you advised." Mr Strange bowed obsequiously and backed away, as if from Royalty, and smiled an oleaginous smile.

"I'll call in the office when we have finished for the day," Mr Penaluna said with an air of finality. Mr Strange nodded and said "But if I can be of any help, do let me know."

"We will Mr Strange – we will."

Once they were really alone Mr Baguly offered his opinion "Can't say as I like the schooner Sir. She looks to me as though she's been converted."

"She has – she was a clipper – look at the bows and the stern as well – Suez Canal put her out of work thirty years ago."

"How's that Skipper?"

"The clippers used to do the run from China with their precious cargoes, right round Cape of Good Hope, but steam ships nearly halved the trip by coming through the Suez Canal, and she is one of the casualties."

"How about this next one then?" Mr Baguly said as they approached a huge iron hulled ship.

"I don't want an iron ship – you can't get warm on 'em and they don't "live" like a wooden ship – I don't mind an iron frame – they creak less, let's look at the next one, she's wood alright, oak and elm I'd say and about the right size."

They went on board and expressed dismay at the way she had been left. This was the 'North Star.' The bankruptcy of its previous owner meant the ship had completed its last trip, been emptied of cargo and just left, and that was over a year ago. Rotting food was in the galley and the cabins. The captain's quarters had been the location of some form of farewell party and the remains of food, empty bottles and squalor were everywhere. Rats scuttled about, their privacy interfered with for the first time in months. As the two would-be purchasers opened up the hatches the stench rose from below: the bilge water was stale and foetid. The previous crew had dumped all their surplus food down there and the smell was overpowering.

To Mr Baguly's surprise Mr Penaluna suddenly said "I like her."

"Do you really Sir?"

"Yes I think she has possibilities. Look at the deck – teak, Mr Baguly – teak – this has been a quality ship. And the brass work – filthy of course but high quality. The bitts too – hard wood with brass coach bolts holding 'em in place. The ropes are Manila ropes – but quality, some will be stretched, some rotten, but quality Mr Baguly is everywhere."

George arrived as instructed by Mr Penaluna and soon found Mr Penaluna and Mr Baguly in earnest conversation. He was not sure if he had been invited because his opinion was wanted or just out of politeness, so George made no attempt to distract these two experienced gentlemen during their deliberations. Mr Penaluna however caught sight of George and called him over. "Have a look at the galleys on all four of these ships and let me know what you think would suit you."

"Yes Sir – I will." "Good morning Mr Baguly, it is very nice to see you again." Then George went about his duties.

"A real little gentleman isn't he Sir? Mr Baguly said to Mr Penaluna.

"Yes he is – I have never had any children of my own Mr Baguly." Mr Baguly looked at his skipper a bit quizzically. "Well none I need own to anyway – but I do feel a fatherly affection for young George – I do regard him now as my son."

They moved off to the fourth ship but Mr Penaluna's mind was more or less made up. The important part of the game, and to Mr Penaluna, the most enjoyable was yet to come – the bargaining. He loved it. The last of the four was a brigantine, according to the information sheets provide by Mr Strange, it was of Danish origin, built in 1870.

"Should never have been built, not one as big as this – the Suez Cancel opened in 1869 and this ship like the other one was built originally to bring tea from China – it was obvious that steamers would take all the trade in tea." Mr Penaluna continued to look through the sheaf of paper the Agent had provided.

"She's plenty big enough for what we want Sir," Mr Baguly offered.

"Too big I'd say, and the ropes are all differently rigged, it would take forty men to run this ship and probably a month of trials to get 'em used to it." "We'll concentrate on this one, and ask a lot of questions, avoid talking about the 'North Star' altogether, but I am going to say that I need them pumped out and cleaned up – then I'll get a man from London who is in the Insurance Business to come and take a look. We'll tell Mr Strange we are interested but we need to have them more presentable for our Ship's Surveyor."

Mr Strange was not happy about cleaning up all four. "Let me know which one you prefer and I'll clean that one up ready for inspection," he said.

"If you really want to sell 'em you will have to clean them, so make them ready for say next week and I'll get a Surveyor down from London to have a look. I am a buyer Mr Strange and I am serious."

"But can't you tell me which one or two perhaps – it will cost a fortune to clean all four."

"Are you married Mr Strange?"

"Yes – why do ask?"

"Would you take your wife to look at houses in that condition – of course not – you wouldn't get her over the doorstep. My men and I have to live in our ship – weeks at a time – think about it Mr Strange – think about it – I'll be back next week."

Mr Penaluna and Mr Baguly then took a slow walk along the docks and looked again at the four sailing ships. Pathetic, unwanted veterans, each with thousands of miles of adventurous and dangerous sailing behind it. A wind came and it caused some of the loose rigging to flap, as if in a vain attempt to attract attention to its owner's plight and to beg for rescue. Mr Penaluna was not unaware of this, he regretted the ascendancy of steam, and he hated the bullying tactics of some of the new skippers who paid little attention to the time honoured courtesy of giving way to sail. He had noticed, especially in the English Channel (one of the busiest stretches of water in the World) how some steamers hooted and held their line. But he knew he would have to spend £6,000 at the very least and he could not allow sentiment to hold sway. He only wanted one and he had made up his mind.

Back at No 18 Wellington Terrace George was really enjoying life: the only male in a household of seven – he was being spoilt and he loved it. He spent some of his time in the kitchen, keeping his hand in and learning too. Now that Clarissa's income was assured, the menu at No 18 had moved up a notch or two, and George liked the idea of surprising Mr Penaluna with roast turkey or goose one of these days. He also saw how Marie and Polly had learned from their days at the Embassy Hotel in Bournemouth, that there are a lot of ways to present the humble potato at the table besides just roast and boiled. George loved food as well as the sea, and he was happy to learn everything about cooking.

When he had been at home for about a week Clarissa suggested that perhaps he would like to come down to the factory and spend a day with her. She was still hoping that he would find some aspect of life ashore sufficiently attractive to give up the sea. He went along with the plan and spent the morning with Tom tidying out the stables. In the afternoon Tom had deliveries to do all around Poole and he took George with him. As they neared the docks, George could glance down some streets and see the masts and funnels of ships in dock. When the deliveries were finished he persuaded Tom to go back to the factory via the dock road. They went past the four derelict sailing ships and on board one of them was a familiar figure in a Lord Nelson hat and a plum coloured coat. George leapt off the cart without so much as a wave to Tom, and he hurtled up the gangplank. "Is this ours Sir?" he breathlessly asked Mr Penaluna.

"Shush lad, shush, we have our plans."

Mr Baguly took George on one side and said "Skipper's trying to do a deal of bargaining – it is not this one, but the next one he's set his heart on – this one is very expensive, and he's going to make it look – oh – don't ask me. I can't follow his plans. Anyway let's look over this one and keep out their way."

Tom was quite forgotten, after ten minutes or so he realised this, and drove back to the factory, where Clarissa met him.

"Where's George? – I thought he was with you."

"He was Ma'am, we did some deliveries near the docks and he met some people he knew, and that was it – never saw him again."

Clarissa did not give in easily but she had a feeling that she was beaten this time.

An hour later Mr Penaluna and Mr Strange were still on board the Danish brigantine. George and Mr Baguly were going over the whole ship. George was especially interested in the galley – it was coal fired, twice as big as the one he was used to on the 'Bulldog' and had working surfaces, chopping boards, and a full set of pans, kettles, knives, ladles etc and two ovens. He looked at the fire bars and saw they were good and that there were even spares to replace burnt out ones.

"Do you think Mr Penaluna will buy this one?" George asked Mr Baguly.

"No. I think he'll go for the 'North Star'."

"Let's go and have a look at her then."

"Best to wait and see which way the cat jumps – I don't want to defeat the plan – whatever that is – but we'll keep off the 'North Star' until the skipper says to go on."

George couldn't follow the logic of it, but he didn't have Mr Penaluna's labyrinthine mind. They came back on deck just as Mr Penaluna was saying to Mr Strange "Well it's not my first choice, but I'll agree to your putting the 'North Star' into a dry dock and I'll have it surveyed."

With that Mr Strange went back to his office, while Mr Penaluna gathered up Mr Baguly and George and took them into a nearby chop house for some lunch. They had to discuss tactics or rather listen to a lecture in deception from Mr Penaluna. "We'll play up the big Danish ship next time we meet – you be here as well George – make a lot of the galley on the ship. I'll bring you into the conversation so you can make your point, draw attention Mr Baguly to the wheel and the compass, both are first class. Then I'll agree to buy the 'North Star' provided he pays to have the galley moved out of the big 'un and onto ours."

"And the compass and wheel?" Mr Baguly reminded Mr Penaluna.

"Exactly – we'll get what we want off the other two as well – I want complete freedom to remove tackle, blocks, rope – I want no wire rope at all, and we'll refit the 'North Star' at their expense."

"Do you think he'll stand for it Sir?" Mr Baguly asked plaintively – he was no business man.

"Can you see any queue forming of prospective buyers – no, the ships are out of date."

"And we are out of date too," George volunteered.

"Yes you're right lad – yes we are out of date, and happy to be so, I want no steam driven ship. Now where are these chops – will they be as good as yours George? - that is what I want to know."

"Yes they will Sir."

"Why? How do you know that?"

"Because mine are all eaten and these are still before us."

"Yes there's logic in that and optimism too – I like optimism – but not as much as I like lamb chops – look out there they come."

George spent some of the next seven days helping all his lady friends in the kitchen. He spent half a day at his sister's shop. They had sold the cameos which he had bought in Italy, and he was now the proud possessor of £15 cash. He went out with Tom a few times on his rounds but finally, the call he had been waiting for arrived, and he went back to the docks with Mr Penaluna and Mr Baguly to look over the ships. Mr Penaluna was in his best coat and wearing his Lord Nelson hat. Mr Baguly was wearing his ill-fitting suit. George was in the uniform originally provided by Mr Penaluna: his navy blue coat, white trousers, a bow tie, and his sisters had treated him to a nice velvet hat – he looked very neat and prosperous. This all suited Mr Penaluna's plans: they were not a bunch of dockers and loafers and time wasters, they were people of ample means, well able to buy a ship – any ship.

Mr Strange was there to greet them, and the surveyor from the Insurance Company was also in attendance. The 'North Star' had been scrubbed, and it was revealed that she was actually cream coloured and the rails, cabins, companion ways and decks were of teak – just as Mr Penaluna had anticipated. The contrast of the cream and dark brown appealed to Mr Penaluna, he went forward, greeting the Surveyor and took him on one side. "We'll look at the 'North Star' first, but I might ask you to look at another later." The Surveyor looked concerned – who was going to pay him? It takes two days to look over a ship properly. Mr Strange was brought into the conversation and pronounced the idea that HE should pay the Surveyor as preposterous – unheard of. Mr Penaluna conceded the point, and they all walked towards the dry dock where the 'North Star' awaited their inspection and as it turned out it required all Mr Penaluna's guile, and indeed duplicity, to conceal his approbation. The ship looked fine. She had powerful clean lines, a good bow and a broad stern. Timbers were loosened from the hull –

she was doubled skinned, each layer of planks being three inches thick – they were oak and elm. The Surveyor tried to plunge his knife into the masts – expecting rot, but found none. He forced Mr Strange to unship the rudder, so that he could examine the fixings. He insisted that ALL the bilges must be pumped out dry, so that he could see the iron frames and check for rust, and so it went on for two days.

The only serious criticism he made was that the copper plates nailed to the hull to keep away worm, had been shed, and possibly a zinc sheath would now be regarded as preferable. He said some of the tackle was faulty, some blocks cracked and some missing and about half of the ropes were rotten. This is a major item; there are about twenty miles of rope required to run a three masted ship.

The Surveyor wrote out a list of the faults and Mr Penaluna presented it to Mr Strange. "It's not a ship if it will not sail – and with all the faults it certainly is not seaworthy." Mr Strange trembled – was this dreadful man in his Lord Nelson hat going to make him put another ship into dry dock?

"Well, come into the office – we'll have some coffee and discuss what to do next," Mr Strange said. Mr Penaluna made a sign to Mr Baguly and George to indicate that they should wait around for awhile, and in he went for the coffee and to further pulverize poor Mr Strange.

An hour later Mr Penaluna emerged looking triumphant. "She's ours," he said.

"Which one? asked Mr Baguly.

"'North Star' of course. Now I want 'Chips', 'Sails', Humpage, Sweeting, Bo'sun and the rest of the crew rounded up and here by the day after tomorrow – I want that ship refitted, and with us supervising – by that I mean you and me Mr Baguly. I want her ready in four weeks.

"Have you told him we'll be taking tackle off the Danish ship, Skipper?"

"No – he's had enough shocks for one day – have mercy Mr Baguly – have mercy."

Mr Strange came out from his office, dressed for going home – he had a sale but Mr Penaluna's terms were so rigorous that he was wilting under the strain.

"Good day, gentlemen" he hesitated before using the word 'gentlemen', because Mr Strange was sure that he was sacrificing accuracy in the interests of etiquette. He looked bent and tired as he walked towards the nearest Inn, there to ponder on how he came to be so completely out manoeuvred.

CHAPTER 10

The Refit Begins

Two days later and a very different Mr Penaluna was assembling his men. He was dressed exactly as they were, in working clothes, the men gathered round and he took them onto the 'North Star'.

"This is it men – this is our new ship and I want her out of here in three weeks." Mr Baguly winced when he heard 'three'. He had reckoned four, if they were lucky.

"Now 'Sails' look at what there is, put into the sails locker what are good. Chuck out what's bad, and feel free to wander over to the other three ships and take whatever you like, until we have two good sets – is that clear?" Even the miserable 'Sails' had to agree that it was.

"Humpage – please go with 'Chips' and take the whole wheel housing and compass off that Danish ship, and fix it on ours."

"Bo'sun – please go with young Mr Eefamy and see about transferring the galley off that Danish ship onto ours – the quicker we do that, the quicker Mr Eefamy gets back to doing what he does best – cooking. He can then feed us while we are doing the refitting."

"Mr Sweeting – use our best mast head men, and check all the ropes, any which are fraying, throw down to the deck – also any cracked blocks. Splice ropes where you can, and cut away any wire ropes – I'll use them as back–stays but not as tackle or riggings. Is that clear? If in doubt, ask Mr Baguly, he knows my methods of working."

"Mr Eefamy – where is Mr Radford your honoured assistant?"

"I did leave a note for him, I don't know why he's not here Sir."

"Cos he can't read – that's why" Humpage volunteered.

"Do you know where he lives Mr Eefamy?"

"Yes Sir."

"Right go and fetch him – he can clean out all the cabins – it's not fo'c'sle sleeping on this ship, it is cabins and I want all the rats, mice and bugs swept overboard."

George ran off to knock up Radford (and Hazel) and the rest of the crew severally dispersed to their different duties. The refit was underway.

George returned half an hour later with Radford and the formidable Hazel in tow.

"What is she going to do?" Mr Penluna asked, somewhat rudely for him.

Hazel spoke up for herself. "I can't cook but I can clean and polish and I'll make your cabin like new." Mr Penaluna did like his cabin just so, and the 'North Star' afforded him a lovely saloon as well as a good dining area and two roomy cots in his cabin.

"Very well" agreed Mr Penaluna. "Ask Steward for scrubbing brushes, cloths and polish and you are welcome to join us – until we sail – let me make that clear – just until we sail." Hazel bobbed Mr Penaluna a slightly sarcastic curtsy and went off to find Steward.

"Now what are you going to do?" Mr Penaluna said to George and Radford – the latter looked to George to speak on their behalf.

"If it is in order Sir – we are going to dismantle this galley and then help to fix the new one, so perhaps by tomorrow, we will be in business and feeding everybody."

"Including Hazel?" Radford added.

"Especially Hazel" said the mischievous Mr Penaluna who had not failed to notice Hazel's considerable tonnage.

Unwanted rope and cracked blocks (pulleys) soon began to come down from aloft. Radford saved all the broken blocks. "Good firewood" he announced. Sails were spread over the decks and carefully checked over by 'Sails'. 'Chips' was measuring all the yardarms so that only suitably sized sails would be filched from the adjoining ships. Mr Baguly's choice was, where possible, to have flat sails rather than full bellied ones. He reckoned, and Humpage agreed, that they responded more quickly when they were going about, so this was all borne in mind.

The galley on the 'North Star' was quite small so it was soon dismantled, and by mid afternoon George and Radford were ready to go onto the Danish brigantine and to start bringing the pots, pans, ladles etc on board. Bo'sun was well on with taking the twin-ovened galley apart, but decided that the proffered help of Radford was not just what he needed, and he told Radford he would not avail himself of the kind offer. Radford never minded being told he wasn't wanted, indeed most of his life he had found that his inefficiency had secured him a very cushy existence. But Bo'sun was exactly the opposite; he knew what he was doing, drove his men hard and ahead of what was expected, had rigged up the necessary pulleys and ropes to swing the very heavy cast iron ovens over to the 'North Star', where 'Chips' was ready to secure them and then build the galley around them. George was going to have a splendid galley about eight feet square and six feet high to work in and he was already considering what the inaugural meal would be.

Mr Strange was not very happy: true he had sold a ship, but he had not expected Mr Penaluna's men to treat his other ships as a free source of supply for tackle. He did try to impress this point upon his client but Mr Penaluna just wasn't listening. Hazel was working hard to make Mr Penaluna's quarters as presentable as possible. Her weight and strength were equalled by her zeal and since all the rest of the team were working on the deck or on the rigging, no one knew exactly what she was doing. In fact she was revealing treasure. When Mr Penaluna was talking to Mr Baguly about the prospect of buying this ship he had spoken of quality and Hazel, by accident was revealing just that. The more she scrubbed at the painted panels of Mr. Penaluna's saloon the more timber panelling was revealed. She was not an insensitive woman, and though, at first, when the paint began to flake off, she was apprehensive, as the work proceeded she realised that some Philistine had used cheap distemper paint, and they had concealed beautiful panelling of a type quite unknown to her. The cabinets, desk and table in the saloon were also covered in cheap paint and a brief attack of elbow grease showed Hazel that they were all made of the same wood.

As the day's work drew to a close, Hazel locked up Mr Penaluna' private area and put the key in her pocket. She was sure that if anyone saw it in its present state she would be in trouble for ruining the paint but if she could keep it concealed until she had finished completely: eh presto – a miraculous transformation would be revealed. When she went up on deck to collect Radford and go home for a meal, Mr Penaluna stopped Hazel and asked if his cabin was ready.

"No not yet. It'll take two or three days, whoever used it last was a disgrace, but in a few days it will be ready and I'm sure you'll love it – I have the key here – I don't want anybody going in yet."

Mr Penaluna for once was quite non-plussed he wasn't used to anyone saying quite categorically what would happen on HIS ship, but he was very happy with the day's progress, so he let it pass.

The next day was beautiful, and all the crew arrived on time – 8 am. The riggers were up the masts, they had put all sails and yardarms on the deck and starting right at the top – 120 feet up, they began painting the masts. The yardarms were checked over by Mr Baguly and a team of men; they made sure the clewlines and burntlines were all in good order and then painted the yardarms white. Bo'sun and his team were helping 'Chips' put the galley into shape, erecting the two chimneys, one for each fire, and putting the ovens in place with huge coach bolts. Two teams of painters were over the side on platforms – the first team scraping off the flaked paint and the second team slapping on a new coat of cream. Beneath the Plimsoll line, four men were nailing on zinc strips each about two feet wide and one eighth of an inch thick. This would make entry by worms impossible and meant that instead of the ship having to be careened and scraped every three or four months, two years or so would be the interval. George was in the team of painters, together with his young mates from the 'Bulldog' Matthew and Oliver. Hazel was hard at it in Mr Penaluna's quarters, the panels were now finished and she had started on the furniture. Mr Penaluna could not understand why he was being kept out of his cabin, it was HIS cabin after all, nor could he comprehend why pounds of beeswax polish were demanded by this Amazon who was ruling his life. But he was happy, he knew he had bought a beautiful ship, it was coming to life, and so he was feeling indulgent. He decided to ask a nearby innkeeper to bring food and beer over to the 'North Star' at 12 o'clock. The landlord arrived with his two barmaids and they had brought piles of sandwiches, beer, ginger pop and huge fruit cakes. George and his mates didn't bother to clean themselves up and probably swallowed more paint then was good for them, but it was a wonderful lunchtime and it certainly fortified them all for the rest of the day.

At six o'clock Mr Penaluna rang the ship's bell and told Mr Baguly to get everyone on deck.

"Now lads – everything is going well, and tomorrow the galley will be working, so get here early and our Mr Eefamy will surprise us all – won't you George?"

"I will Sir – it's roast leg of pork with plenty of crackling – it is all ordered."

"One each I hope" Humpage shouted, to merry acclaim. The team broke up and went off in all directions to their evening meal. Hazel was the last to leave, she gave Mr Penaluna a coy look and said "Not quite ready yet Sir, give me another day and you will not be disappointed, I promise." Then with a naughty look she held up the key and popped it into her pocket. "Goodnight Hazel" Mr Penaluna called as she left the ship. Then he went to look at his quarters, but cloths had been put up at all the windows, so in fact he could see nothing of the inside at all. He was not worried but he was intrigued.

Next morning George was up really early, Rose, Marie and Polly were already in the kitchen and the business of getting No 18 going was underway. Clarissa, Anne, Caroline and Thurza would be down soon and, as usual they would all breakfast together. This system suited Clarissa especially, because once she had everyone round the table with their porridge, bacon and eggs, toast etc she could ensure that they had a full day's work ahead of them. She did this in the nicest possible way, but her way of life now depended upon work and the way she did it, it was not just work, it must be work with positive results. Anne and Caroline knew that the success of the shop was largely due to Clarissa's ideas. Everyone in Poole knew that her pottery and haulage business was thriving, she now employed twice as many people as two years ago and she owed nothing. At first she was aggressive and obtained results by bullying but her management skills had developed and her edginess had receded in direct proportion to the way her overdraft reduced. Her financial stability was important to her because she knew it was due to her own efforts and though for her first twenty five years she had been dependant for everything upon her mother, Mrs Collins – still, to Clarissa's great relief residing in Dunoon, Clarissa was now a person in her own right. She made her own decisions. Success makes some people arrogant and difficult, it didn't do that to Clarissa, she became radiant, she put on a little weight and positively bloomed. She conducted all her management meetings with charm and persuasion, and because, over the previous years, she had made so many correct decisions for her managers and foremen, far from arguing, usually left the meetings with the feeling that the firm was in good hands. Once or twice a week she and Bert Tremlett had a good tumble, sometimes in the office, sometimes in the stables. No one seemed to suspect and if they did, they knew better than to mention it to anyone. Perhaps it was part of the recipe for success, all employees were enjoying the success so why rock the boat?

Clarissa turned to George and asked "What are your plans for today George?"

"I think my ovens will already be warming up. Radford – he's my helper – said he would be there at six o'clock to make the fires, so I am going to cook for everybody."

"How many are there?" Polly asked.

"About twenty" George replied.

"Twenty?" Polly said. "I wouldn't like to cook for twenty and I've years of experience."

"You get used to it – it is the same as cooking for six, but you need bigger pans, which I have, and bigger joints of meat, so you leave 'em in the oven longer."

Clarissa looked at George admiringly. "I don't think it is just as simple as that," she said.

"Don't forget I have Radford to help me, and the new galley is very well equipped – it should be, we've pinched all the best stuff off three other ships." He then added "Mr Penaluna said we could help ourselves – this is the arrangement." George glanced at the clock, "I must be off now – I have to call in to see Mr Wilkinson to order the meat."

Mid morning, Mr Wilkinson's little pony and trap drew up at the docks, close to the 'North Star', and he began bringing George's selections on board – three legs of pork, fifteen pounds of sausages, ten pounds of smoked bacon, two pounds of dripping and six dozen eggs. Mr Baguly spotted Mr Wilkinson's predicament and told two of the men to bear a hand. Mr Penaluna came forward and greeted Mr Wilkinson. "Where's the bill? – let's keep straight". The bill was slightly stained with blood as butcher's bills usually are but it was paid on the nail.

"Can I see where George works?" Mr Wilkinson asked.

"Of course" said Mr Penaluna expansively. "Follow me." "Visitor for you Mr Eefamy," Mr Penaluna called as he approached the galley. George emerged in an immaculate white cook's outfit. "Let me see in" Mr Wilkinson asked.

George took him inside, where Radford was tending the fires, he too was in white. "I wish I had these ovens George, at the back of my shops – I would go into the pie job in a big way." He then turned to Mr Penaluna "Look after him – I've known 'im since he was a toddler – always been a nice lad – from a nice family."

"Don't worry" said Mr Penaluna gently putting an arm around George's shoulder. "I'll treat 'im like me own son – so I will."

Steward came forward to help stow the meat away. "Are you going to do the legs today?" he asked.

"No – I'll give the ovens a good test today with baked potatoes – if they spoil, it's nothing lost."

Mr Penaluna heard this attention to detail and approved of George's planning – he knew his galley was in good hands, and went to ensure the rest of his new ship was being equally well cared for. Mr Penaluna was becoming used to walking the length of his ship, she was 210 feet from stem to stern and 36 feet wide, she weighted 930 tons and the height of the main mast was 160 feet. She promised to be a 'dry ship' because the poop was over 3 feet higher than the fore deck and the main deck only 1 foot lower than the poop. This was an unusual but welcome feature of the 'North Star's' construction and would almost certainly lead to a greater degree of comfort during rough seas; no one enjoyed working in two feet of water all day and night.

Mr Baguly and 'Sails' were now working together very well and though initially they did not have a system, one had at last been thought out and from now on, until the ship was fully rigged, they intended to deal with just one sail at a time, and to make sure that they had a heavy weight sail and a lighter one for every position. For the first few days, there had been sails and rigging everywhere and there was confusion. Now the system was working. They started with the main sail, moved to the main lower topsail, then the main upper topsail, the main top gallant and the main royal. Once they had the two sets (heavy and light) sorted out, the men fitted the heavy set and stowed the lighter ones in the sails locker. 'Sails' marked each sail with coloured string embroidery in a way which allowed him to positively identify which sail was which. The sails locker had been completely emptied and repainted white, and it was now being filled up, slowly and meticulously with spare sails. Mr Penaluna noted all this and was pleased with the general progress.

'Sails' – though an employee, like everyone else aboard the 'North Star', was a grumpy man. "How long before all the sails are checked and ready?" Mr Penaluna asked.

"As long as it takes." 'Sails' answered.

Mr Penaluna, a patient man, persisted. "Should we say one a day?"

"Guessing gets us nowhere – we've fifteen sails and four on the jib – then double that for heavy and light."

"And a few spares – I hope" Mr Penaluna said.

"Exactly – and a few spares – so that's over forty, and each one, averaged out, is forty feet by twelve feet and every square foot needs checking – if one blows apart, I'll get it in the neck."

Mr Penaluna looked at Mr Baguly for assistance, the latter shrugged his shoulders – he had no solution as to how to speed things up.

"Supposing I ask the Chandler to lend me a man for a week – just to look to the spanker and the jibs and the studding sails?"

"It's your ship not mine – but I'll have to mark them, so we knows what's what."

Mr Penaluna went in search of a mug of coffee wondering how he had managed to choose a person as rude as 'Sails'. The coffee mollified him as did the gentle aroma of smoked bacon which was beginning to waft from George's galley. Mr Penaluna wandered slowly in that direction and said to George," Mr Eefamy – it appears that 'Sails' is incapable of a polite word this morning, could you please take him and Mr Baguly a bacon sandwich and we will all hope that it will sweeten his acid tongue."

"Certainly Sir – in five minutes at the most. Would you like one yourself? – have you had any breakfast?"

"Yes I have had breakfast but a bacon sandwich might bring me some comfort – 'Sails' never will – you can be sure of that." He added as an after thought – "I'll be in my cabin." Then he remembered that his cabin was occupied by Hazel, and he was being kept out. He leaned over the taffrail, stopping for a moment to examine the wood. 'Chips' was just passing with his bag of tools. "'Chips' – is this teak?" Mr Penaluna asked tapping the taffrail. "Mahogany – this is – from Brazil."

"How can you be so sure?"

"Mahogany is brown with just a hint of red, but teak is solid brown and you can see the grain clearly, now with rosewood". Mr Penaluna stopped him there and said "And oak, elm, beech etc, you would know them as well?"

"Course I would – if you are a proper carpenter you has to, because they work differently, some you has to be gentle with, cos they splits, some don't take kindly to sawing – some you can't carve at all because it breaks off. Walnut is a lovely wood but difficult."

"Thank you 'Chips' – thank you."

"I was thinkin' about them 'ens' 'Chips' said, apropos of nothing.

"Hens? What hens?"

"Yours o'course – what we had on the 'Bulldog'"

"Yes – I must admit I had quite forgotten the white Leghorns. I have got someone looking after them until I decide what to do with the 'Bulldog'"

"If you wants 'em over 'ere – I'll have to knock up a cabin for 'em."

"If they do have a cabin it is more than I'll have – I can't get into mine."

"Why is that?"

"Radford's lady friend is cleaning it out and I'm barred until it is finished."

"Let's have a look then, and see if it's ready." As they walked towards the captain's quarters, George hove into view bearing a bacon sandwich and a mug of coffee for the skipper.

"Come with me Mr Eefamy, and we'll see if we can gain admittance to my quarters."

They arrived at the door and found it locked. Mr Penaluna knocked and Hazel shouted "Who's there?"

"It is I, the owner of this ship and with your permission, the future resident in that cabin."

"Very good Sir" Hazel answered and then she opened the door.

"Goodness gracious me" exclaimed Mr Penaluna. "How have you done this?"

"I just cleaned it" Hazel said.

"It is from Finland" 'Chips' said. "From Karelia, only seen it once before, but I'd know it anywhere."

Mr Penaluna's quarters were panelled and furnished with Karelia Birch, a rare timber grown only in Finland and North Baltic countries. Mahogany looks warm and welcoming, oak gives the impression of reliability and strength, teak exudes quiet, calm and good taste, but this was exuberance and though, at first glance, the various shades of colour seem to dance, they gave off at the same time, the gentleness of Autumn. Every colour was there from yellow to gold, orange, beige, light brown, all beautifully mingled, never clashing but always delighting the eye.

"It was worth the price of the ship just to see this – and I will be living in it – with your permission of course," Mr Penaluna said to Hazel. Hazel smiled and bowed.

'Chips' started to examine the table, the cabinets and the panels. "Good job none of it is damaged" he said. "You'd 'ave an awful job trying to locate even a small amount of this timber, it is so rare."

"How did they come to use it?" Mr Penaluna asked.

"They had to, because of the American Civil War and trouble in various counties in South America, timber was in short supply so someone came up with this."

"Thank goodness they did – I love it – may I move in now?"

"Yes it is all ready for you now Sir – is there any other work for me? – I don't really want to." At that point in her sentence, Hazel tailed off. Mr Penaluna always a sensitive man, knew why.

"Yes, the men's Mess Room wants tidying, now young Mr Eefamy is going to feed us we need somewhere decent for the men to eat – so ask Mr Baguly to show you what is wanted and leave me now to enjoy your handiwork and before you go Hazel." Hazel stopped and looked back at Mr Penaluna, who just said "Thank you, your work will give me a lot of pleasure."

George placed Mr Penaluna's coffee and sandwich, which were on a tray, carefully onto a Karelia Birch table and left Mr Penaluna to commune with his autumnal cabin.

Two weeks on, and the transformation of the 'North Star' from an unloved wreck to a thing of grace and beauty was almost complete. 'Chips' had made suitable areas for the chickens and for the sheep, by now the two lambs were half grown and Bo'sun was beginning to cherish the idea of reducing their number. George had arranged transport with Clarissa, and he and Tom had fetched them over to Poole from Southampton by horse and cart. Mr Penaluna had sold 'Bulldog' to a firm of ship owners in Charlestown who did a lot of journeys across to France for fruit and vegetables and they needed a small fast ship. Mr Penaluna was happy to see his ship happily engaged in useful work and not rotting in a yard awaiting the breakers axe. He honestly believed that 'Bulldog' was going to be happy and that made him feel as though he had not betrayed her. He had dreaded the thought of the breakers yard, as a man who loves horses abhors the knackers man.

"Ballast next, it is?" Mr Baguly said to Mr Penaluna.

"Yes. It's one thing clearing out old stale stinking ballast, but putting a fresh lot in it will be quite a job."

"That big iron ship has a lot of pig-iron in her, we could swing some of that across, and get the men in the hold laying it out."

"Yes we'll do that Mr Baguly, you go down with 'em, and see we don't have too much right on top of the keel – that way she would be too stiffly ballasted, and she'd roll like hell. We want the weight well spread, some on the keel, but placed out towards the sides, as well. Once we are ready, we'll take her out as far as Plymouth and see how she goes."

Over 300 tons would be the minimum required to ballast a ship of this size, the projected test run as far as Plymouth would be without cargo, and ships do handle better when fully loaded. Three days later the 'North Star' was ballasted, but she was riding high above the Plimsol Line and Mr Penaluna was not sure that even a short trip would be comfortable but he was certain that they would learn a lot about his new and beautiful ship, as they undertook the hundred mile trip to Plymouth.

Mr Penaluna called Mr Baguly and Steward into his cabin and told them to provision the ship for a seven day trip.

"I thought we was just goin' to Plymouth" Mr Baguly said.

"Yes, that is the plan, but who knows what might happen, contrary winds, on a ship we don't know: could be difficult."

"Are we going to dock at Plymouth?" Steward asked.

"Yes we will dock, Fothergill and Jones have an office there, and I have informed them that from next week we are ready to go to South Africa. They are looking into that for me, and also looking for return loads. So tell the men that once we cast off from here we may not be back for sometime, if we do good business, it will be months – I reckon each trip to and from Cape Town will be about 6,000 miles, say two and a half months, ten weeks there and back. Let the men know and then you and I Mr Baguly will go over the ship and check everything.

Humpage asked Mr Baguly when they would actually be leaving, he had small children and his wife was pregnant. "We don't really know, I would say tomorrow or the day after at the latest."

"I've got to make arrangements because of my missis."

"That's understood, you go and do what you have to, but be back here tomorrow – just in case."

"Ah! There you are Mr Baguly, we'll go over the ship now, we'll start at the bows," Mr Penaluna said.

"I was just tellin' Humpage 'ere that he'd better go and see to his missis, cos we might be off tomorrow."

"Is she alright Humpage?" Mr Penaluna asked with genuine concern in his voice.

"Yes she'll be alright Sir. She didn't have no trouble with the first two."

"Wonderful creatures women – braver than men too, childbirth must be torture. Ah well. Give her our best wishes, but be back here early tomorrow. If all goes well we'll be away on the noon tide and you will be at the wheel as the Channel winds come to her."

Mr Penaluna and Mr Baguly began their tour of inspection, looking carefully at every detail.

"Look at that bowsprit Mr Baguly. 70 feet long if it's an inch."

"She'll help with steering though, we can put four sails on her, and she should come round nice and easy."

"It is one of many things we shall have to watch Mr Baguly. Going about in a ship this size can take a couple of miles – we will all be learning."

"At least the front of the ship will be clean now that the men has proper lavatories. I'll have to 'ave a word with Bo'sun to make sure the men empties 'em out everyday."

"I'll bet on sunny mornings you see some perched there relieving themselves – it's a long tradition and tradition dies hard with naval men."

"Well so long as they cleans up after I don't mind," Mr Baguly said.

"It'll give her ladyship something to look at," Mr Penaluna said referring to the splendidly proportioned figurehead. She had been lovingly restored by one of the men who was very skilled with a paint brush. She now had blue eyes, rosy cheeks, brown hair and a beautiful green gown. The lips had been painted to indicate a permanent smile – George had suggested a moustache but Dredge, the painter, decided against that, without realising that it was actually meant to be a joke.

The inspection continued with Mr Penaluna affectionately fondling the ship's rails as he progressed. He was keeping an eye on everything but he was enjoying himself too: he knew he had bought a thing of beauty the likes of which would not be seen again and the ownership gave him a lot of pleasure. They looked at the rigging, made sure the belaying pins were correctly looped with rope – the odd one wasn't and Mr Penaluna adjusted it. They passed under the two very large boats, they were lifeboats and were each thirty feet long. "I reckon 'Chips' could put a mesh top to these boats and we could keep the chickens in 'em," Mr Penaluna said. "Let's find room on the main deck instead of 'aving 'em slung up" Mr

Baguly added "Good idea that Sir – I'll get Bo'sun to get 'em down."

And so the inspection continued and at one point they were met by Mr Strange. "Good morning Mr Strange," Mr Penaluna called in a welcoming fashion. "Now what do you think of her – do you regret selling her?"

"No not at all Mr Penaluna – I am happy that she is in good hands." "When do you think you will be sailing?"

"Tomorrow or the day after, why do you ask?"

"I would be grateful for a few words in private, if I make take up a little of your time."

"Certainly Mr Strange – ask Mr Eefamy to bring coffee to my saloon Mr Baguly if you would be so kind." "Come this way." Mr Penaluna was going to enjoy this because he was sure Mr Strange had no idea about the quality of Mr Penaluna's quarters. As they entered Mr Penaluna's quarters Mr Strange did register mild surprise but he had more weighty matters on his mind. "Do you have a ship's clerk or a purser?" he asked suddenly.

"No. I do most of the reckoning and Steward helps me out with the rest of it. Why do you ask?"

"I am looking for a position."

"Have you been to sea before?"

"Yes many times, I was at sea on the big Danish ship as ship's clerk for four years." Mr Strange said.

"Well then I am sure Mr Baguly could use an extra able bodied man, have a word with him."

At this point Mr Strange allowed the cuff of his right sleeve to slide back and revel his hand. It was terribly small, like the hand of a five year old.

"That's why I am a clerk," he said quietly.

"But aren't you married and part owner of the dry dock and those other ships?"

"Yes, and both are reasons why I would like to be part of your crew."

"Ah come in Mr Baguly, please put the coffee on there, and take a seat. Mr Strange was just explaining to me why he wants to join us."

Mr Strange continued his sorry story: he had been duped into marrying his boss's daughter, a lady of forty or more, and of less than attractive manner and appearance. The father died shortly afterwards, leaving the ship repair business and four sailing ship to his daughter. But the onset of steam meant that a business solely repairing and selling sailing ships was doomed. Unfortunately Mr Strange's new wife could not see this, and she attributed its perilous financial position to Mr Strange's inadequacy. So Mr Strange was in a very unhappy situation and with nothing to lose but a stone cold marriage and a failed business. The prospect of being a ship's clerk looked quite rosy.

"You'll have the wages to attend to."

Mr Strange said "I could do that, Bills of Lading, manifests, visas and entry forms. If you do work for the Government, they insist upon no end of forms and red-tape."

"Yes, you have a point there Mr Strange. Give me twenty four hours to think about it – in the past I have always done my own reckoning, but this is a big ship, with a big crew and it might need a full time skipper."

Mr Baguly joined in at that point. "We all needs to get used to 'er Sir, and two 'eads is better than one."

"Yes I think you are right Mr Baguly. But see me tomorrow Mr Strange and I will give you a firm answer." "Come on now Mr Baguly we must continue our inspection – let's look at the cabins next."

Mr Strange left the ship looking downcast, but he was cherishing just a slight hope that tomorrow would bring good news for him.

Mr Penaluna led Mr Baguly down the companion-way towards the cabins, allowing himself the luxury of stroking the teak hand rails as they descended. The brass fixtures shone like gold. "Who cleaned all the brass?" Mr Penaluna asked.

"That woman of Radford's – she looks a mess but she can work."

"Come, come Mr Baguly, where is your charity?" Mr Penaluna said, laughing.

"Well it's true Sir, she is ugly, but wait till you see these cabins – fit for royalty they are." And they were: quite immaculate, and what's more they smelt sweet – a most unusual state of affairs for seamen's cabins.

"She's polished the wood, it's lavender polish she uses. Steward goes mad, he says she's used buckets full of it already."

"And it shows Mr Baguly it shows." Then he continued "Where do Matthew and Oliver sleep Mr Baguly?"

"In this next one here Sir – it's a three bunk cabin and I thought young George could 'ave the third one."

"Yes, good idea – that will do nicely – let's continue and look at the rest."

"I've told the men that the lavatories 'as to be sorted out properly everyday Sir. They said they wanted Radford to do it ……..

"No, I'm not having that Mr Baguly, Radford works in the galley and so far as I am concerned the two jobs do not make a good pair – make out a roster once we are at sea, and tell Bo'sun to see to it."

"He'll say to me "I'm not the shit-house orderly.""

"If he doesn't do it properly – and I'm looking to you to see that he does, they will all have to hang their arses over the bows, like they have always done."

They reached the next cabin – the door was bolted from the inside. Mr Baguly knocked. "This is Radford's cabin Sir," Mr Baguly confided. Mr Baguly knocked again. "Just a minute" cried a distant voice from inside. "'Ang on, can't you?"

"It is the Skipper 'ere." Mr Baguly shouted. The door opened slightly to reveal a naked Radford. Mr Baguly pushed the door open to reveal the Rubenesque figure of Hazel. Mr Penaluna grabbed the door handle and shut Mr Baguly and himself out in the corridor.

"If he can tackle that he deserves privacy," Mr Penaluna said.

"If you ask me, he deserves a medal," Mr Baguly retorted. Skippers even in the Royal Navy were very tolerant of 'goings on', when a ship was in dock and Mr Penaluna himself – though he did not invite ladies on board his ship, he did look forward, after a long sea journey, to shedding the burden of celibacy. So he did not pay too much attention to Radford's inventive method of spending his mid-morning break.

They inspected all the cabins, including Mr Baguly's and they were all at least presentable, most of them were positively tidy and clean. "So who has wrought this change in the men's behaviour? Mr Penaluna asked.

"They 'asn't changed – it's 'er – she tidies up after 'em, like they was kids, and she does their washin' as well."

"Is she on the books Mr Baguly, am I actually paying her?"

"Payin' 'er. No." "Feedin'er – yes, and that takes some doin' – I've seen some appetites! 'Er stomach must be like a ship's 'old Sir."

"Well it is worth our consideration – I mean keeping her – full time. She could keep everything clean – she could do the lavatories. Having just one woman on board could lead to problems but I can't think that we would have two members of the crew who would be so indiscriminating as to take a fancy to her. So rivalry should not be a problem."

"I don't know Sir. They all looks lovely if you 'avn't seen one for ten weeks."

"True, Mr Baguly, quite true, but there are limits."

"We will go right below now Mr Baguly and just satisfy ourselves that the ballast is as well placed as it can be." They continued their inspection and found everything was ship-shape and Mr Penaluna's next instruction ensured that Mr Baguly's attention was drawn to Mr Penaluna's desire to have this state of affairs continue.

"The bilges on a ship of this size can stink, the French, in Nelson's time, used to bury their dead under the gravel in the bilges. I want the lower decks caulked tight, so no water gets down there, no lavatories emptied down and no slops and slush either from the kitchen – it all goes overboard from now on – tell Bo'sun and young Mr Eefamy." "Aye Aye Sir" Mr Baguly said, hurriedly making notes of all the various instructions.

"Slush' was the grease that rose to the top of the pan when salt meat was cooked. It was not sought by epicureans but after two weeks or so at sea, the butter was rancid and some men would use it as butter, if only to camouflage the maggots which often took up residence in the ships biscuits. If allowed to get into the bilges the smell would have pervaded the whole ship, and Mr Penaluna was determined that the high standard already reached on his beautiful vessel, would be maintained, even if he had to employ Hazel. In fact he was beginning to look upon the prospect favourably and Mr Strange also was in for a pleasant surprise. Mr Penaluna was in expansive mood, and he was sure good times lay ahead.

CHAPTER 11

The Open Sea

The time of year was September, and a beautiful sunrise got the day off to a good start. Mr Penaluna had slept on board the 'North Star' and rose early. At about six o'clock he roused out his irascible Steward and asked for coffee and toast. Radford was already in the galley and the fire for one of the stoves was well away. Mr Penaluna stood at the portside rail munching his toast, slurping his coffee and watching his crew arrive which they did with varying degrees of enthusiasm. Mr Baguly was always alert and jaunty. "Good morning Mr Baguly" Mr Penaluna called out.

"It is a fine morning Sir."

"Have a word with Steward, he's just made some coffee."

Humpage came into view with his wife and two children. The children were skipping along but Mrs Humpage was obviously sorry to see her man about to start off for goodness knows where and be back goodness knows when. It was hard being a sailor's wife. Humpage himself was torn into two directions; he was sorry to leave his lovely wife and his two children, but was dying to lay his hands on the magnificent wheel of this beautiful ship, and to feel her respond to his touch.

Sweeting arrived with his younger brother, he was going to be one of the 'extras' needed to cope with this ship, so much bigger than the 'Bulldog'. Bo'sun arrived looking grumpy as usual with barely a word or a grunt for anyone. 'Sails' and 'Chips' arrived together. Mr Penaluna was counting them aboard and he was always relieved to see these two; both very skilled men, awkward, rude sometimes, but very trustworthy and proud of their abilities.

George arrived having said 'goodbye' to all the lovely ladies at No 18. Tom brought him by horse and cart. This time George did remember to turn and wave to Tom, and to shout "Thank you," as he ran up the gangplank.

Mr Strange arrived by horse and cart also, Mr Penaluna had managed to get a message to him the night before, so that Mr Strange was prepared for a very early start. His wife usually 'slept in'. So he was able to rise early, pack his box and arrange for a carter to transport him to the docks. He left his wife a note to say that it was part of sales agreement when he sold the 'North Star', that he would spend time on board looking to the paperwork. Mrs Strange knew little of business matters so she would accept this, and if the seafaring life did not suit Mr Strange, this ploy left the door open, not exactly to a loving return, but at least to a bolthole until something better turned up.

The ship's complement was complete, and Mr Penaluna awaiting the arrival of the tug. He had planned it so they would go out with the tide, there was a lively wind blowing from the East and it would take him down the English Channel towards Plymouth and if they had clear horizons, with no other vessels around, he could make a few turns and get the crew used to going about, and he, Mr Baguly and Humpage would get the 'feel' of her. Mr Penaluna was really excited and had difficulty maintaining his usual quiet demeanour. In order to assist him in his quest for dignity, he dispatched Steward for his plum coloured coat and his Lord Nelson hat.

The tug arrived. Mrs Humpage shivered, and pushed the two children into their father's arms, then she joined them. To everyone's surprise a very prosperous looking lady was waving in a spectacular fashion to, and being acknowledged by Bo'sun. Clarissa, Ann and Caroline had made a late arrival – George was brought out of the galley, resplendent in snow white overalls and cap. It was too late for propinquity – the gang plank had been withdrawn. The hawser was connected. Mr Penaluna signalled to the tug to draw the ship away from the wharf. As the rope tightened Mr Baguly roared "Let go forrard'. The last ropes were hauled in. Mr Penaluna's hands were clasped behind him, giving the impression that he was quite relaxed, in fact he was anything but. Handkerchiefs were dabbing eyes and noses, as well as waving. Mrs Humpage could not bear to look. Mr Humpage was grasping his beloved wheel, his feet a yard apart, ready to follow the tug. He gave the wheel a full turn each way just to make sure the chains were not caught up on anything and he heard the re-assuring clatter as the massive rudder moved on its pintles.

She was being towed out but she still looked beautiful. The 'North Star' was cream coloured, her masts black and the spars white. Her rails were all of teak and they contrasted satisfyingly with the cream coloured hull. Mr Penaluna had bought a new large red ensign and three pennants flew from the main mast 160 feet up. They were red white and blue. Mr Penaluna was staunchly English, and somewhat eccentric: pennants were usually flown on Royal Navy ships if an Admiral was aboard, but Mr Penaluna liked to be a little flamboyant: hence the plum coloured coat and the Lord Nelson hat.

As the 'North Star' met the swell of the English Channel, she curtsied politely. Mr Penaluna and Mr Baguly looked at each other – now came the real test. The tug cast off the hawser. Mr Penaluna looked aloft, men were along the yards awaiting instructions to release the royals and the top gallants.

"Royal first – watch the bunts," Mr Baguly roared.

The bunt is the middle of the sail and if it goes out too quickly it can blow upwards and take men off the yards, and the deck is over 100 feet below.

"Sheet home Royals."

"T' gallants now."

"Belay weather sheets."

This was answered from above.

"Sheet home." "T'gallants."

"Belay weather sheets."

"Sheet home mizzen topsail."

Commands rang out and were echoed from above to indicate compliance. Other men were shouting rhythmically as they united to pull in the massive hawser. This was all music to George, who had bobbed his head out of the galley to witness the 'North Star's' initiation.

The commands came one after another, a constant delight to George. Humpage edged the 'North Star' into wind, and tug came alongside to collect the fee. "Safe passage – she looks wonderful!" the tug skipper shouted. Mr Penaluna waved.

"Keep her full and by" Mr Baguly called.

"Mizzen top halyards" he then roared – followed by "Port watch fish anchor."

"Inner jib and spanker."

All hands set the mainsail, and tightened it.

"Slack away the weather clew-garnet."

"Belay the sheet!" "Hook on chain fore tack."

The men started to sing 'Sally Brown, I love your daughter'.

George came to the rail, with a coffee in his hand, enjoying the magical sound of the commands, and luxuriating in the moment when the sails filled and the rails went under as the 'North Star' gained speed. To him the words he heard gave him assurance that this was how he was going to spend the rest of his life. Just in the same way that Verdi knew, when he saw the words to the Hebrew Chorus in the libretto 'Nabucco', that he was going to be a composer for the rest of his life.

About two thirds of the sails were set. Mr Baguly looked at Mr Penaluna. They understood each other – this was enough for now. "Eight knots I'd say" Mr Baguly hazarded.

"I think you are right Mr Baguly – I think you are right," Mr Penaluna said.

"It's enough for now – Humpage – how does she feel?"

"She goes like a bird Sir." Humpage had always loved the 'Bulldog', but this was something different. The 'North Star' was a huge white cloud, and he was steering it. He was a happy man. Two or three hours later he would be relieved of the wheel, reluctantly. Only then would his thoughts turn to home, his lovely wife and his two children.

Mr Penaluna and Mr Baguly stood on the poop deck, George had given Steward coffee for them, laced with rum. Both men looked aloft. Men were still up there waiting to be told to release more sail. Mr Baguly looked at Mr Penaluna who shook his head. "No, eight knots is enough – let's treat her gently." Mr Baguly signalled for the masthead men to come down, which they all did with grace and agility. Matthew and Oliver came back to the deck, by what is regarded by experienced older hands as the tom-fool method of descending like trapeze artists at the circus. Just for once Mr Baguly let it pass. Mr Penaluna pretended not to notice, though he knew that Mr Baguly would later have a word with Bo'sun, who in turn would correct matters.

The Bill of Portland was soon in sight, and beyond that Lyme Bay. "We'll go about in Lyme Bay Mr Baguly – stay with Humpage on the wheel."

"All hands on deck – stand by to go about." Bo'sun was among the men, making sure they all had hold of the correct ropes. The sails flapped idly for two or three seconds – the ropes tightened then into their new positions and the 'North Star' leaned over, her masts describing a huge and glorious arc of 40 or 50 degrees, as she turned. The sails re-filled and she was off.

"She's like a sheep dog – does as she's told, nice as nine pence," Mr Baguly said.

"We'll try again" Mr Penaluna said, and then he said to Humpage "Would all the jib sails help?"

"Might do, but we won't get a much tighter turn than that Sir."

"Mr Baguly" Mr Penaluna called. "Kindly set the fore topmast sail and the fore staysail, as well as the two jibs."

"Aye Aye Sir."

Mr Penaluna was determined to play with his new toy, but he did want to know exactly how she behaved in all circumstances, and Lyme Bay was a wonderful place to have chosen, little used by shipping and covering two or three hundred square miles. They completed two or three more manoeuvres and Mr Penaluna saw that the crew had benefited from these experiences, the extra hands were working in well with the old 'Bulldogs' – Mr Penaluna was at ease. All the more so when the smell of roast lamb began to be carried away from the galley towards the poop. Mr Penaluna had arranged with Steward to have a special meal, he had also asked Mr Baguly to have Matthew and Oliver scrubbed up and to invite Mr Sweeting (the 2nd Mate) and Mr Strange who was now the Ship's Clerk – although he readily took to calling himself the Purser.

Mr Penaluna's saloon looked quite splendid for the first dinner on the 'North Star'. Hazel had put the finishing touches to the polishing and the Karelia Birch gave off a warm glow. A snow white cloth was on the table and Mr Penaluna's best cutlery was carefully arranged. The guests came trooping in, all in their best clothes, and Mr Penaluna was at his most benign. Steward enjoyed these occasions and did know how to serve at table, so with Mr Penaluna carving the meal was soon underway.

The messing facilities for the men were very commodious and quite different from those on the 'Bulldog' – this was a proper dining room, not just some empty barrels with a disused door on top. The men's favourite was beef stew with plenty of bread to mop up the gravy. Duff was on the menu for both groups of eaters, tho' Mr Penaluna's saloon was offered fresh fruit as an alternative. George's first really big meal at sea on the 'North Star' was a huge success. Once it was over he went to the taffrail with a plate of beef sandwiches and a pint mug of coffee. He needed the fresh air and he wanted to look at the gentle countryside that was just five or six miles away to the North. The first day at sea in the 'North Star' had gone well for George – in fact for the whole crew. After the evening meal Mr Penaluna came on deck and ordered Mr Baguly to make for Plymouth, but to shorten sail. "No point in arriving in the middle of the night, Eddystone rocks are best approached in daylight – we will aim to arrive just after dawn."

Mr Penaluna said 'goodnight' to his men, raised his hat to George by way of thanks for the meal and went off to his cabin. He had two beds to choose from: a cot which swung from the ceiling and a standard one. He decided he would try the one which hung from the ceiling, but first he walked round his saloon and then his cabin, enjoying the wonderful colours in the wood, and feeling the smoothness of the pieces of furniture. He loved this ship, and he settled down for a good nights sleep, confident that he had bought a really beautiful and seaworthy vessel.

They were towed into Plymouth early next morning. Mr Penaluna soon located the local agent who worked with Fothergill and Jones. No Government contracts were ready yet, but there were kerbstones and flags to be taken to the Azores and oranges to come back. Just what Mr Penaluna wanted to hear. They would have to wait four days for the full 500 tons of stone to arrive, that was quite acceptable, but what Mr Baguly had to report was not: bugs were on board – bed-bugs and rats.

"Can't understand it Sir – I was sure this ship was clean – but some of the new members of crew brought their own mattresses on board – and now we has 'em."

"Burn all the mattresses and get new – I'll stop it out of their pay – bugs indeed!! And they can sleep on deck till we get the cabins fumigated. Now as to rats, I'll enquire if there is a local ratter, who can come on board – some of 'em have little terriers, we don't want any rats on board. Tell young George to be careful about scraps of food and leftovers."

A ratter was found and he came aboard with swagger, quite disproportionate to his lowly calling. Mr Tregorran, was how he introduced himself to the Bo'sun. He had a small handcart, piled up with traps and empty sacks, but no terriers.

"No I don't kill 'em," he said. "I catch 'em and sell 'em."

"Sell 'em?" queried Bo'sun. "Who buys rats?"

"Local sportin' gentlemen – they keep terriers and they have competitions to see whose terrier can kill the most – 'eavy bettin' goes on, though the Police would stop 'em if they got to know."

"So you trap 'em and tie 'em up in sacks."

"Zackly – zackly" Mr Tregorran said. "You got it in one – so you pays me for catchin' 'em, and they pays me two bob for a sack of ten." "Now show me where they are and I'll get started."

The ratter called back next morning and by lunchtime he had removed thirty rats from the 'North Star', and he had found out exactly, or as he would have said 'zackly', where the galley was. Mr Penaluna viewed his fellow Cornishman with some amusement, but he had to agree thirty was a good catch for one day. Three sacks of writhing bodies were on his handcart, half a crown was already in his pocket as he said goodbye to Mr Penaluna.

"I'll be back tomorror – I've set the traps again, don't let anybody touch 'em."

Mr Penaluna assured him that no plebeian hands would desecrate his traps and waved him off.

Clydesdales and Shire horses began to arrive at the docks, two to each cart, and three tons of kerbs and stone flags was their burden. Bo'sun and Mr Baguly supervised the handling, and soon their knowledge of pulleys, ropes, levers and cranes enabled the 'North Star' men to be safely stowing their cargo below. Mr Penaluna himself was below, he was ensuring that the weight was evenly distributed, and he had 'Chips' nail strong ropes to the frame of the ship. This cargo would have to be tightly secured or in rough seas it would be like a loose cannon, and it would go through the hull like paper.

Four days later and 500 tons heavier, they were ready. Ratter was paid up, new mattresses installed – all the cabins had been fumigated and scrubbed out by Hazel. Supplies were laid in for the trip to the Azores, and 1000 miles of the Atlantic lay ahead. They were towed out in to the English Channel, keeping well clear of the Eddystone rocks, the breeze was from the east, precisely what was needed. Mr Baguly under Mr Penaluna's supervision set all sails apart from the main courses, and the 'North Star' soon cut into the sea at a good seven knots.

"Heave the log if you please Mr Baguly," Mr Penaluna requested politely.

"Heave the log" Mr Baguly roared to the second mate.

"Seven and a bit," the second mate said.

"Main courses please Mr Baguly," Mr Penaluna said.

"Main sails now – look lively," Mr Baguly shouted.

The main sail, all of 400 square yards of it, made a loud cracking noise as it filled out. 'Sails' looked anxiously on as it took the strain for the first time, he had repaired this sail and expended a lot of time and energy on it. The great sail did its job and pushed the ship forward with a noticeable increase in speed.

"Heave the log," Mr Baguly boomed.

"Just over eleven knots" came the reply.

"That'll do," Mr Penaluna said, "but take the main courses out of it at dusk – we can then all sleep in peace."

Like all experienced sailors Mr Penaluna took his sleep when he could and he fancied that as they left the busy narrows of the English Channel and sped into the vastness of the North Atlantic, now would be a good time. He conveyed his intention to Mr Baguly, who gave the usual "aye aye Sir." Mr Penaluna lay in his cabin and listened to the murmur of the water all around his lovely ship. He relished the constant hum which rope under stress generated, to Mr Penaluna this was music – he was soon asleep. George lay in his bunk, he too enjoyed the same sensations and the same pride of ownership – to George, this was HIS ship. He too fell asleep knowing that Radford would be up at 5 am and by the time he (George) arose, the stoves would be well lit and the first cup of coffee would not be far away.

They arrived in the Azores seven days later, it was now Autumn, but the seasons treat this area gently and their stay in port was blessed by wonderful weather; each day it was 70° or even 80° Fahrenheit. The men worked stripped to the waist and George kept them supplied with orange juice. Initially this beverage was not welcomed, because it argued against their manhood, but they acquired a taste for it and began to enjoy it. Very slowly and carefully the kerbs and flagstones were taken out of the hold and laid on the dockside. There, ponies and carts, they had no Shire horses, moved the weighty stones one or two at a time. But the leisurely ways of these islands, as with Madeira, relieved the workmen of any sense of strain or urgency. Indeed the pace of life was such as to make the word 'urgent' fall out of the dictionary.

Mr Penaluna found Mr Strange very useful once they started to unload: he kept records, attended to Bills of Lading, ran errands to the British Consul's office and helped with the paperwork when the oranges began to arrive for the return load. Mr Penaluna was grateful because he felt he had still a lot to learn about the 'North Star', and Mr Strange's help left him free to have discussions with Mr Baguly about correct use of the sails, rigging etc. Hazel, another new member of the crew was proving to be a treasure: she insisted upon the crew changing their clothes every week. She tubbed all the weeks washing and hung it out to dry and she kept Mr Penaluna's quarters quite spik and span. Other new members of the crew were working well, so Mr Penaluna had an efficient and happy ship.

Five days after docking they were ready to leave Azores with a full load of oranges. They were towed out five miles or so, and then released, by nightfall they had covered 80 or 90 miles and Mr Penaluna was ready to turn in for four or five hours sleep. He spoke to Mr Baguly. "It's a fine following wind, so keep the Royals and the t'gallants only. We'll make full sail at dawn, and then try to crack on."

"Goodnight Sir – I'll wake you if anything happens Sir."

Mr Penaluna strolled round the deck and found George at the taffrail, looking at the rudder and at the wake.

"Is the rudder to your liking Mr Eefamy?"

"Yes indeed it is Sir – I was just thinking that it looks very small when you consider that it has to turn the ship."

"And it has to make the ship hold its course when hundreds of tons of waves at trying to make it deviate."

"Do we carry a spare one Sir?"

"Yes we do – a makeshift one to be sure, but good enough in an emergency."

"Would you like ham and eggs for breakfast Sir?"

"Yes please Mr Eefamy; three eggs are enough, you sometimes send five or six."

"It's the hens, you see Sir – they lay like Billyo."

"Well let the crew have some as well, but I shall look forward to my breakfast. Good night Mr Eefamy."

"Goodnight Sir."

Mr Penaluna lingered over his return to his quarters: torn between the beautiful night he was leaving and the unprecedented luxury which awaited him.

CHAPTER 12

The North Star and The Storm

At 3 o'clock in the morning a storm struck the Atlantic and Mr Penaluna was roused not by Mr Baguly but by sheet lightening and thunder. Mr Baguly arrived at the cabin door seconds later. Mr Penaluna was struggling into his sea boots and wet weather suit. The 'North Star' was in the epicentre of an electric storm, gales, crashing rain and hailstones. Mr Penaluna went to the rail and saw the sea, clearly illuminated by sheet lightening: as far as the eye could see it was white – it was in fact boiling and tumbling. Waves forty and fifty feet high composed entirely of tossed foam were on every side. Even though this was a ship which stood out of the water three or four feet higher than most, she was flooded from the sides and this was added to from above, hailstones as big as walnuts crashed down, making useful work dangerous and nearly impossible.

"There's only two Royals out Sir – I got the rest reefed up."

"Maybe two's too many, but we'll see – get Bo'sun to rig up life lines and nets at the bows. Tell 'Chips' to check the hatches and perhaps knock in some more wedges."

Humpage was at the wheel with three other men, it took all four to hold the rudder steady – they were standing more or less permanently in two feet of water, sometimes they were waist deep in it. The shrouds, and halyards were screaming their defiance as seventy miles an hour winds hurled their malevolence at the ship. Wave after wave, each one weighing many tons crashed into and onto the ship, sometimes the ship was sloping up at 45°, at other times going down a similar gradient. Humpage and his helpers kept her rear straight, so the storm was chasing them, they knew a succession of high waves at her side and she would be pooped.

The lightening lit up the ship so that Mr Penaluna could witness Bo'sun's progress, as his men battled to put up lifelines. The main yard was wrenched loose and came crashing down onto the deck. Mr Penaluna was tempted to have it cut away and tossed overboard, but 'Sails' and 'Chips' and four other men, man handled it and seized it to the ship's rail. Mr Penaluna saw this expert handling of the situation and make a mental note.

Mr Penaluna looked up at the masts and saw that they were describing crazy arcs in the sky, sometimes they were lit up by lightening and he could see his pennants gamely flying in the wind. The particular kind of light accentuated the colour of the teak rails and every few seconds the similar colour of the decks would be revealed only to be covered again and again with tons of water and spray. The only consolation was that storms of this ferocity exhaust themselves, blow themselves out. Just a few more hours and they would be through it or more likely, it would meekly fade away. Mr Penaluna warmed himself with that small glimmer of optimism and went to look at the barometer – the glass was falling – worse to come or at any rate more of the same.

Suddenly the wind veered and the first monstrous wave from the new direction almost caught the wheel men unawares, but they pulled her round in time and most of the wave passed underneath – lifting up 1000 tons as if it were a child's toy, as she sank into the trough, she shipped hundreds of tons of water, companion ways were crushed, rails went overboard, a lifeboat, complete with chickens, broke loose and was carried over the side where the rails had just gone. Bo'sun rushed his men, all securely tied around the waist, to where the rail had disappeared and he fixed up a double lifeline to make sure that anyone washed that way would find something to grab hold of.

George could do nothing. Mr Baguly had told him to douse his fires, which when the storm bursted upon the 'North Star' were just embers. But a fire, as innocuous as they were, could still add to the confusion if the embers were thrown about. Radford was furious because all his carefully trimmed kindling was floating in the companion way and most of his supply of firewood had gone overboard. George tried to go on deck but he was ordered below by Mr Baguly.

"Get below and bar your cabin door." He was told in a voice that left little room for discussion.

Mr Baguly joined Mr Penaluna on the poop deck they had done all they could . The storm had done its utmost but it had not defeated them. They were evenly matched.

Mr Penaluna was confident that another four or six hours and the storm would have to give them best. The intervals between the flash of the lightening and the clap of thunder were lengthening, this was a good sign – the precipitation was now limited to the purely liquid variety – the storm had run out of his glacial missiles.

The lightening stopped as suddenly as it had begun. They had almost grown used to the light and now by contrast the darkness was complete. Men groped around afraid to move in case a false step took them overboard or down a flooded companion way. The wind moved up a notch or two and was now a genuine force 10 gale. Suddenly sheet lightening flashed across the sky. Mr Penaluna looked up and saw twenty or thirty broken ropes held horizontal in the wind and his three pennants were at 90° to the mast like painted sticks, just the last six inches of each pennant twitching. The curious light and the unnatural angles of the broken ropes turned the 'North Star' into a ghost ship. Then came the clap of thunder, reassuringly a few seconds late.

"Eight or nine miles away I'd say," ventured Mr Baguly.

"Still too close for comfort Mr Baguly – it's not finished with us yet."

Daylight came at last, a watery sun showed itself slowly at the horizon, as if ashamed to have been no help in the contest and then, scared of the light, the furtive invisible wind scuttled away and left Mr Penaluna, his ship and his crew in peace.

"Clap on some sail Mr Baguly." "We have too little on now to give us steering way. Rouse out the men – make sail Bo'sun, find Steward for me – now."

"Ah! There you are Steward – tell young Eefamy to light his fires and make coffee for the men – lace it with rum – not too much – their bellies are empty."

"How about food Sir?" Steward implored.

"Leave that to Mr Eefamy – he'll know what to do."

This was Mr Penaluna at his best, he was the man to have around in an emergency – his orders came out like machine gun bullets.

"Mr Baguly assemble all the injured in the seamen's mess. When they are all there – tell me and I'll come and have a look." "What's this rope doing here right across the deck?" He told Sweeting to tidy it up.

"It's fastened Sir, and it goes overboard."

They looked back over the stern, and there was the lifeboat – still by some miracle attached to the 'North Star' forty yards astern.

"Fasten the tope to a winch Sweeting and get the boat to the side – and ask the hens how they managed it."

Sweeting was dumbfounded, he had never heard Mr Penaluna make a joke before.

Coffee was going round the ship and the crew were congratulating each other, and indirectly, themselves, for having got through the ordeal.

"Coffee to the mess room Mr Eefamy and make theirs' extra sweet – now how many have we Mr Baguly? – seven eh? Right let's have a look."

Cuts there were – these Mr Penaluna stitched up, with the recipient sat holding a cup of rum in his lap. Just one fracture – it was young Oliver who had broken his arm. Bo'sun came into the mess to ask the Skipper to come up and assess the damage.

"Men first Bo'sun – ship second – them's my priorities – now go and rig up davits and pull the lifeboat back on board – it's worth £30 if it's worth a penny."

"Now Mr Baguly give young Oliver a good swig of rum – and another. Hold him tight Mr Baguly. Let me have a feel – ah yes I have it."

Oliver screamed.

"Steward, bind up his arm and make a sling." "Are you alright Oliver?"

Oliver nodded.

"Good lad. Put him to bed Steward – find a warm dry one for him." "Is that the lot Mr Baguly?" "Right on deck now – tell 'Chips' I want the hatches opened."

Mr Baguly looked at him in dismay.

"I want to see if we took on water – we'll start from the keel upwards."

Water had got into the cabins via the companion ways but the decks have proved water tight and the bilges were virtually devoid of water and the cargo was safe. Men were rigging up pumps to dry out the cabins, Hazel was busy carrying soaking wet blankets out into the fresh air. George, Radford and Steward were scuttling in all directions bearing sandwiches and hot coffee, Bo'sun was hovering like an old mother hen.

Mr Penaluna said "Bo'sun – I want you, Mr Baguly, 'Sails', 'Chips' and Sweeting in my saloon in ten minutes, and rouse out young Eefamy – I want him now."

Bo'sun went to the galley where George and Radford were tucking in to their first bite of the day.

"Skipper wants you now."

George, put down his coffee and his sandwich, looked at his 'whites' – saw they were respectable, and went to Mr Penaluna's cabin. He knocked gently. Mr Penaluna was sat at his desk – "Come in Mr Eefamy, come in. Quite a night we had – were you alright? Not hurt? Not seasick?"

"No Sir I'm fine – I'm never seasick."

Mr Penaluna smiled benignly at his youngest crew member and made an announcement. "The men have done extra well this last twelve or fifteen hours and now I want you to do a special meal for all of us." "What is it to be?"

"Mutton – saddle of mutton with potatoes, cabbage and carrots and freshly baked bread."

"Followed by?" said the insatiable Mr Penaluna.

"Duff Sir – make with eggs and honey poured over it."

"Regal, Mr Eefamy – I call that regal."

There was a knock at the door. Mr Baguly was there with his helpers.

"Come in gentlemen – Mr Eefamy was just leaving – oh, Mr Eefamy tell Steward it's dinner in my saloon for seven people, and you inform Steward when our feast will be ready."

"Now gentlemen take a seat, there is a glass for everyone, and Madeira to warm us." "As you will see Mr Strange is with us, and if you would be so kind Mr Strange, will you please write down all the faults and breakages, then during the ten or twelve days it will take us to return to Plymouth, we can, in an orderly fashion, put our ship to rights." "Tell me your news – how does the 'North Star' look after last night's little breezes."

They all began at once and then stopped. The ever courteous Mr Penaluna said "Bo'sun – you first." And so the meeting continued – the lists got longer and the bottles got emptier. But they were used to tougher stuff than Madeira and a thoroughly accurate account of the damage was completed.

"Thank you gentlemen – we have all survived that is the main thing. I suggest that you return to your cabins to make sure your beds are warm and dry. Mr Sweeting leave enough sail on her to give us four or five knots. We will eat well in two or three hours time – then sleep well. And tomorrow we will start on the lists and gentlemen – thank you for all your hard and skilful work."

In the galley there was firewood a plenty. Radford had checked with 'Chips' and the smashed up rails, ladders, doors etc were all at Radford's disposal. The saddles of mutton, bought fresh in the Azores, were in the mighty ovens, and the whole crew was going about its duty with a will. Some of the men were singing – why not? They were alive, and when the storm was at its worst they must have allowed a few doubts to creep into their normally sanguine thoughts.

When the meal was ready Mr Penaluna sent for Steward and told him the names of the six guests he proposed to entertain in his saloon. They were the six who had rescued the main yard and sail when it crashed on to the deck; 'Sails', 'Chips', Tregorran, Smith, Yardley and Barnes.

"You can't have them lot in 'ere Sir, 'ave you seen 'em eatin?" Steward spluttered.

"No, I must confess I haven't had that pleasure Steward."

"Pleasure? T'aint no pleasure, they can't use a knife and fork at all – the food'll end up on the floor and I'll have to clean it up."

"Well they did save me twenty or thirty pounds, and I would like to thank them."

"Only did their job – same as I done."

Mr Penaluna couldn't think of anything that Steward had done during the storm, but he let it pass. "Right then Steward, I'll take your advice, we'll have Mr Baguly, Mr Sweeting, young Oliver, if he feels up to it, Matthew." Steward was waiting expectantly for his own name to be mentioned. Mr Penaluna continued " Mr Strange and Bo'sun." Steward's face told the story, but Mr Penaluna's list was finished. Steward turned on his heel, slammed the beautiful Karelia Birch door as he left, and went to the galley to have a good shout at George and Radford, whom he imagined were part of his staff.

Two hours later the Captain's saloon was host to the mutton dinner. Enough wine was put on the table, ie a bottle per person, and beer for the boys. George took the trouble to cut Oliver's meat up into bite sized pieces so he could manage – he still looked a little pale, but the meal brought the natural colour back to his checks. The men all had the same, saddle of mutton, as much beer as they could drink and a huge pile of duff with honey poured over it. George took his plate to the taffrail, and balanced it there, he looked back at the new calm and tranquil view, and was filled with wonder as to how such a beautiful place could within minutes became as tempestuous and just a few hours later revert to this idyllic situation. George looked up, at the masts, they were in disarray with 'Irish pennants' as sailors call loose ropes, dangling from every mast and yardarm. Just the Royals were out, and they gave the ship enough speed to have steering way. The 'North Star' leaned just slightly leeward, they were doing four knots at the most. There was a gentle murmur as the bows cut through the water and an occasional slap as a loose rope came in contact with the mast. Apart from three or four of the men, the whole crew would be asleep in an hour or so, and tomorrow the repairs, the tidying, the renovations, would begin.

In the saloon, the guests were just saying their 'thank you' to the Skipper. Mr Penaluna followed them out and took a walk round the decks – he found George just finishing his duff.

"Carry on Mr Eefamy – don't let me disturb you. The mutton was excellent, an admirable choice."

"Glad you liked it Sir – that's how Rose used to do it when I was at home – very slowly and baste it with wine."

"Rose taught you well – I am grateful to her – do you still write home regularly?"

"Yes Sir I do – there was a fruit ship leaving the Azores the day we docked, and I was just in time to put a letter on board her."

"It might be there now – what was it? No 18 Waterloo Terrace?"

"No Sir, Wellington Terrace."

"Ah yes – Wellington – same thing really I suppose," Mr Penaluna said dreamily and slowly sauntered off to his cot. "Goodnight Mr Eefamy."

"Goodnight Mr Penaluna."

Next morning the work began to put the 'North Star' back in order: the mast men were up there cutting away the broken ropes, men on the deck were sat in twos and threes splicing them. 'Chips' was repairing the rails and companion ways. 'Sails' had three large sails to repair and he was not in a good mood, despite the mugs of coffee George distributed at regular intervals. The less skilled members of the crew holy-stoned the decks and the ship began to look presentable. Mr Penaluna was especially keen to make if not a grand entrance, at least portray an image of efficiency and neatness: Government officials might be out and about looking for vessels to go to South Africa and Mr Penaluna wanted to be considered for this kind of work. Six days later the 'North Star' arrived at Plymouth, she looked wonderful: 'Chips' had replaced the rails so badly smashed in the storm and had matched up the teak with paint, which he had carefully mixed to arrive at the right colour. The rigging was now complete and trim, and she made a fine sight as she was towed into harbour.

George stayed with the ship for two days, so that he could feed the crew and some of the dock workers too, whilst the oranges were unloaded, then, at last, he was released with his pay in his pocket and was lucky enough to find a small coaster that was due to sail to Poole the next day, and he was promised a free passage provided that he helped out in the galley. She was a wooden two masted schooner 'Adelaide' built in Falmouth thirty years before and of about 180 tons. She was a neat, and to George, a very small ship with a tiny galley, but the skipper, Mr Woods, reckoned they would be in Poole 'sharpish', but he would not be drawn as to how long that would be, but twenty four – thirty six hours seemed a reasonable guess, and George just loved sailors, sailing and sailing ships. They arrived at Poole the next day and George ran most of the way to No 18, there to be greeted and welcomed by all the lady occupants, it was just time for the evening meal and what is intended for six, can easily be made to accommodate seven, and after the usual and by no means unwelcome hugs, George's feet were under the table and Polly's hotpot was before him.

The conversation was really varied, as indeed it should be around a civilised dining table; Ann and Caroline discussed their shop. This they now did with enthusiasm, Clarissa's energy and keenness had spread to the two girls and they now actually enjoyed their work, and the independence that financial success brings with it. Polly liked to discuss new recipes, this was welcomed too, because everyone tasted the benefits. Marie was partly employed at No 18 and for three days was at the shop, her ideas about decorating hats were relished and laughed at by all around the table, including herself, but the hats did sell. Rose, by far the quietest diner really wanted to talk about Tom, her wonderful husband to be, but she was usually, (good humouredly), shouted down. Thurza spoke for as long as she was allowed about her bookkeeping, but even she couldn't make that topic very interesting. Clarissa talked about horses, she loved the haulage part of her business, and had been to look at a steam driven wagon, but she was still hesitant about moving into the new century, although it was only weeks away. George, though a quiet modest speaker always had the greatest news to impart, and the latest was that his beloved Mr Penaluna was seeking contracts from the Government to haul hundreds of tons of materials thousands of miles to South Africa. In fact Mr Penaluna was on a train, going to London with Mr Fothergill for precisely that purpose.

If you have enjoyed this book, the sequel is now in stock at Linghams (0151 342 7290), Smiths of Wigan (01942 242810) or you can borrow the sequels from any library in WIGAN, or on WIRRAL.